John Temple Leader

Life of Sir Robert Dudley, Earl of Warwick and Duke of

Northumberland

Illustrated with letters and documents from original sources

John Temple Leader

Life of Sir Robert Dudley, Earl of Warwick and Duke of Northumberland
Illustrated with letters and documents from original sources

ISBN/EAN: 9783744715331

Printed in Europe, USA, Canada, Australia, Japan

Cover: Foto ©Raphael Reischuk / pixelio.de

More available books at **www.hansebooks.com**

LIFE

OF

SIR ROBERT DUDLEY,

EARL OF WARWICK AND DUKE OF NORTHUMBERLAND.

BY

JOHN TEMPLE LEADER,

M. P. FOR BRIDGWATER FROM 1835 TO 1837, AND FOR WESTMINSTER FROM 1837 TO 1847,
KNIGHT COMMANDER OF THE ORDER OF THE CROWN OF ITALY.

Illustrated with Letters and Documents from original sources,
collected by the Author, and hitherto inedited.

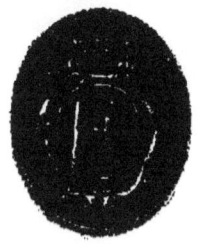

Florence,
PRINTED BY G. BARBÈRA.

1895.

AUTHOR'S NOTE.

——

I feel in duty bound to offer my best thanks to Mrs. Baxter, who is well known in the world of letters as Leader Scott, for her able supervision of this work, also to the distinguished printers and publishers Barbèra of Florence, and to those employed by them, for the admirable manner in which they have executed the difficult task of so correctly printing an English book in Italy.

J. T. L.

PREFACE.

ONE day, more than forty years ago, on examining the plan of a little farm just bought by me, and situated in the parish of Saint Martin at Maiano near Florence, I found that an adjoining farm belonged, or had belonged, to a *Duca di Berlicke.* The title puzzled me. I thought at first it was an Italian corruption of Duke of Berwick, who possessed estates in many countries; but on careful examination of the documents relating to the former possessors of the farm, it appeared clearly that *Berlicke* meant Warwick, and that the farm had belonged to a Dudley who was styled Earl of Warwick, and Duke of Northumberland; and who was a son of Robert Dudley, created Duke of Northumberland in 1620 by the Emperor Ferdinand II.

This Emperor was a brother of Maria Maddalena, Grand-Duchess of Tuscany, married in 1608 to Cosimo II, who died in 1621, aged about 31 years. Maria Maddalena was joint Regent of Tuscany during the minority of her son Ferdinand II, (who died in 1670),[1] an office she held conjointly with Christina of Lorraine, widow of Ferdinand Ist.

---

[1] Maria Maddalena d'Austria, Grand-Duchess of Tuscany, died in 1631; Christina of Lorraine, Grand-Duchess of Tuscany, died in 1636.

Robert Dudley was Grand Chamberlain to Maria Maddalena, as he was afterwards to Christina of Lorraine, and to Vittoria della Rovere, Princess of Urbino and Grand-Duchess of
Tuscany, having thus been Grand Chamberlain to three successive Grand-Duchesses of Tuscany.

The corruption of a name, from Warwick to *Berlicke*, may
appear incredible, but in the course of my enquiries concerning
the Dudley family, I have found many such strange Italian cor-
ruptions of English names.

A neighbouring farm, now my property, belonged to the same
Dudleys, and their descendants, the Paleotti of Bologna.

In the farm house I found, among other things, a little carved
wood sideboard or buffet, of the 17th century, in a very dilapi-
dated condition, past repair. An exact copy of it was made
for me, and is now in the entrance hall of my Villa at Maiano.
The little farm had evidently been made to serve also as plea-
saunce or wilderness. Green alleys had been traced, and oaks,
ilex and pine-trees planted, to the great detriment of the crops,
the olive trees and the vines, and probably to the despair of
the *contadino* (the peasant farmer). Many of the trees had
been cut down before it became my property, and the little
farm had been partly restored to its original agricultural state.
But enough still remains to show that it had once been in the
hands of a landscape gardener.

Continuing my researches relating to the Dudleys, in various
places, more especially in the public libraries of Florence, in
the offices for registering marriages, deaths and births, in the
Archives of State, at the Specola or Museum of Natural History,
and in buying and consulting all the old books I could find
on the subject, I collected, in the course of many years, a large
mass of documents and letters concerning the Dudley family,
which I examined and read attentively and scrupulously, copying

exactly what I thought interesting in them. The result of this study I now lay before the reader.

The principal documentary evidence that I have gleaned has been from the following sources :

1st A large collection of MSS. notes and copies of letters relating to Robert Earl of Leicester, given to me by the late lamented Earl of Crawford and Balcarres ;

2nd Family Documents, many of them original, some written by the hand of Robert Dudley himself;

3rd Pedigrees of the Dudley and Southwell families ;

4th The original MS. by Dudley of his *Direttorio Marittimo*, preceded by a short autobiography, as far as concerned his naval career ;

5th Copies of Letters in the Medicean Archives, and the Archives of State in Florence. The originals of many of these are in the writing of Robert Dudley and his sons, some from the Grand-Dukes Cosimo III, and Ferdinand II. The greater part however are official letters referring to Dudley and his affairs, which passed between the *Signori Cioli* and *Picchena,* secretaries of state for Tuscany ; and the foreign ministers of the Tuscan Court, in London, who were successively the *Signori Lotti* and *Salvetti.* These letters, many of which I have reproduced in the original tongue in the Appendix, proved a mine of information, giving facts and dates, where before all certainty was wanting, and adding many a graphic touch of life to the events so long past.

Notices of Robert Dudley are to be found in many publications, but in all of those seen by me there are inaccuracies and omissions.

I will give here a list of the books referring to him :

Regum Pariumque Magnæ Britanniæ Historia genealogica, etc. Studio ac opera JACOBI WILHEMI IMHOFF, Norimberga, Sumptibus Johannis Andreæ Endteri Filiorum. Ann. MDCXC.

The *Athenæ* by ANTHONY WOOD, who wrote from information received from Don Carlo, son of Robert Dudley.

DUGDALE, *Warwickshire* and *Baronage*.

COLLINS, *Peerage*, 1727.

Biographia Britannica.

Dr. SAMUEL JEBB, *Life of Robert, Earl of Leicester*.

CRAIK, *Romance of the Peerage*, 1849.

NICOLAS, *Report on the Barony of Lisle*.

Rev. Dr. VAUGHAN THOMAS, Vicar of Stoneleigh, Warwickshire, *The Italian Biography of Sir Robert Dudley;* privately printed for presentation, 1849.

MICHAUD, *Biographie Universelle*. Paris, 1855.

Life of Lord Herbert of Cherbury.

EDMUND LODGE, *Portraits of Illustrious Personages of Great Britain*, a grand illustrated book.

NICHOLS, *Pedigree of the Dudleys*.

The Newgate Calender : 18th century.

GALLUZZI, *Storia del Granducato di Toscana*.

Le Nozze degli Dei, Court revels in Florence.

LITTA, *Famiglie Illustri*.

PAOLO VERZONI, MSS.

RICHA, *Delle Chiese*.

Dottore MARCO CORNACCHINI'S *Medical treatise on the Warwick powder*.

GEORGE ALLARD, *Amye Robsart*.

ROSSI, *Osservatore Fiorentino*.

GIUSEPPE PIOMBANTI, *Guida della città di Livorno*, 1873.

SUSAN and JOANNA HORNER, *Walks in Florence*.

Now most of these, as I have remarked, contain inaccuracies. I will here mention a few. Imhoff in his *Regum* etc. *Britanniæ* gives the " schema Familiæ Suttonico Dudlejanæ " as follows:

" Robertus Dudley B. de Denbigh. C. Leicestriæ, Eq. Per. ✠ 4 Sept. 1588 ux. 1. Anna Joh. Robsart f: 2, Duglassia Howard, Wilhelmi B. D'Effingham f. Joh. B. Sheffield vid: 3. Lætitia Francisci Knolles f. Walteri d'Evereux C. Essex vid, 1576."

And of his son by his second wife thus: " Robertus Dudley n. 1574. Dux a Cesare Ferdinando II. a. 1620 creatus, ✠ Florentiæ a. 1650. I. N. Cavendish Thomæ soror: 2. Alicia, Ducissa Dudley, Thomæ Leigh de Stonelay f. ✠ 22 Jann. 1670. 3. Elizabetha Roberti Southwell f."

Now Dudley died in 1649 not 1650, and his first wife was Frances Vavassour not Cavendish. As to his children and their descendants, Imhoff makes many mis-statements. He gives Dudley five daughters in England, where he had but four; and his list of Florentine children is very mixed indeed, and faulty. Of the son Carlo he says: " Carolus Dudley dictus Dux Northumbriæ ✠ Florentiæ circa n. 1687, married Maria Magdalena Gouffier," and by her had issue " Robertus Dux Northumbriæ dictus — Gufferius Dudley Florentiæ — Antonius Dudley Canonicus ad S. Petri Romæ — Catharina nupta Marchioni Paliotti in Bononia — Carola."

Returning to Robert Dudley, he says: " De Roberto Dudleo, quem parens Leicestriæ Comes unicum tantæ familiæ ac fortunarum hæredem in gratiam Lætitiæ Knolliæ illegitimam declarasse dictus est, refert Dugdalius." There follows a short narrative of his life and death, neither complete nor accurate.

In many notices of Robert Dudley it is stated that he was buried in the Church of St. Pancras in Florence. This is certainly a mistake. There may have been some funeral service in that Church soon after his death, but he was not buried there. He died on the 6th of September 1649, at the Villa Rinieri now Corsini, near Quarto, about four miles or less from Florence. His body was conveyed to the neighbouring monastery of Boldrone, where his daughter Teresa had passed several years for education, *in conserva* as her father expressed it in a letter, till her marriage in 1645 with *Fulvio della Corgna, Duca di Castiglion del Lago*. In that monastery the corpse of Dudley still remained in 1673, twenty four years after his death, according to a letter of that date from his eldest surviving son Carlo, the second Duke of Northumberland.

The author of the " Italian Biography of Sir Robert Dudley " observes: " Suffice it to say, that the Duke of Northumberland was entitled not only to an honourable grave, but an ample record of all the important services he had rendered to the Grand-Duke of Tuscany. His celebrity as a philosopher and statesman, civil and military engineer, naval architect, hydrographer and geographer, mathematician and physician, demanded of the gratitude of the Tuscans and the admiration of Italy, the honour of a public funeral as well as the memorial of a public monument. But if Etruria had chosen to forget its debt of gratitude, it must be remembered that the deceased left five surviving sons ; and that Carlo il Duca di Nortumbria, and Enrico il Conte di Warwick, could not have failed to bestow sepulchral honours suitable to so eminent a man and so affectionate a father. For it appears by an entry made in the *Arrolo* or roll, in the Registration office at Florence, that they entered into possession of their father's property at Florence on September 2nd 1652 ; that their sisters had formed honourable alliances with the nobility of the land; and that their brothers, Ambrose, Anthony, Ferdinand and Enrico, were alive to remind them all of their duty to their father,[1] if the two who were successors to his property in Florence had omitted to do so. We are compelled by this residence of his children upon the scene of their

---

[1] Here the author is wrong. All the brothers, except Enrico the youngest, died before their father. Carlo the heir was always at variance with him, and would not have been likely to do much for his memory.

father's services, and some living under the very eye and observation of the Tuscan Prince, to acknowledge their obligation to pay some last tribute, and that of an enduring nature, to the memory of such a father. As children they must have felt obliged, by the recollection of his Florentine reputation, his devotion to the fame and interest of Tuscany, and specially by their natural love and affection to rescue from oblivion the existence of such a man, and an exile in the Grand-Duke's dominions. Summing up these various considerations, it may be concluded, though without such auxiliary evidences as would be necessary to prove it, that some *arca di marmo* was at some unknown point of time erected in St. Pancras, either by the country's gratitude, or domestic reverence, worthy of the splendour of his abilities, and the greatness of his achievements; and worthy too of that spirit, which had been so often attested as a statesman by the boldness and wisdom of his counsels; as an author by the extent, variety and greatness of his knowledge; as a master of the national works of Tuscany by the greatness of his undertakings, by the *costruzioni et miglioramenti* which he executed for the improvement of commerce and agriculture.

" The foregoing considerations, when combined, direct the memorialist to the belief, that this distinguished man was not left without a monument in the Church of St. Pancras. But the discovery, made by the writer's able and accomplished friend the Reverend William Falconer, Rector of Bushey,[1] of a fragmentary stone in what was once the cloister of the Church, and representing what was intended for a Ducal coronet surmounting the never failing accompaniment of the Dudleys, alive or dead, on tomb or tower, fabric or fitting up, has greater weight and

---

[1] Also my own esteemed and lamented friend.

value in the writer's estimate of it as visible and tangible evidence, to prove the existence of some former *arca di marmo*
in honour of the Florentine, or rather Imperial Duke, than all
the sayings and unsayings, all the *gratis dicta* and hearsay state-
ments of all the Duke's biographers put together."

Notwithstanding this reasoning, these declarations, and this
impassioned pleading of the author of the Italian Biography
of Robert Dudley, it is almost an absolute certainty, that no
private or public monument was ever erected to Robert Dudley,
either in the now desecrated Church of St. Pancras in Florence,
or at Boldrone, which is now private property, or anywhere
else. It must be borne in mind that Carlo, his eldest son, was
in his youth riotous, extravagant and unruly, at variance with
his father, whom he once encountered pistol in hand, near
Quarto. One evening he was violent and made a disturbance at
a great reception in Palazzo Strozzi. He was for some time in
disgrace at Court and confined by the Grand-Duke's order in
the Fortezza at Florence.

The other children, probably, had not the means to have a
monument erected. Their father left but little real property
and most probably very little money. As for public gratitude,
if felt, it left no visible memorial.

In August 1852, my old friend William Falconer, mentioned
in the preceding quotation, thus describes the cognizance of the
Dudleys — the Bear and Ragged Staff — in a letter to the Author
of the Italian Biography of Robert Dudley:

" I remembered very well the monument you mention, and
I went immediately to find it out; it is but a small stone, about
two or three feet long. There is no inscription, but simply the
arms in the most common Italian style, without supporters,
crest, or motto. The coronet is as above drawn, and that of
a sort of Marquis instead of a Duke's, owing most likely to the

ignorance of heraldry, so general in Italy, then and always. The stone has not even a name upon it, and is known only by tradition. It is fixed with many others on the wall of a little cloister, and most likely was originally in the Church[1] in which was the epitaph on the *arca di marmo* of Anna Southwell (Dudley?). Perhaps the accompanying shield may have belonged to the Dudley's monument, for no heraldic distinctions are to be relied on in this country. However that may be, it is called the husband's at the present day.[2]"

The following is an inscription quoted by Richa, but now lost, on Elizabeth Dudley, born Southwell; composed, it is said, by Baccio Bandinelli: not the famous sculptor, but another and later Baccio Bandinelli of the same family, who possessed a house and property in Florence, and had a branch of the family at Cracow in Poland.

In S. Pancrazio ne' sotterranei. — Cassa di marmo.

DIVÆ MEMORIÆ.

QUID SPECIEI? QUID GLORIÆ? QUID COLITUR QUICQUID
EXTOLLITUR SI QUID · IGITUR HOSPES ADVOLA

ECCE ELIZABETH SOVTUBEL DUX INCLITA NORTUMBRIÆ
ROBERTI ADMIRAGLI FILIA PATRIÆ DOMUS

NOVELLI REGIÆ NORTFOLCIÆ, NOTINGAMIÆQUE SPLENDOR
HIC . CUM ALMÆ PIETATIS ERGO DULCI

LIMINE RELICTO IN TUSCIA AD SERENIS: INVICTISSIMOQUE
MECENATE EX ANGLIA TRANSFU

---

[1] The inscription on Dudley's wife was on her tomb in the crypt, beneath, not in the Church. We quote it in the text. The tablet was probably only a memorial tablet in the Cloister.

[2] This marble is now in the Bargello (Museo Nazionale) at Florence. There is an exact copy of it in white marble on the wall of the inner Court of my Castle of Vincigliata.

GASSET IBIQUE NORTHUMB: WARVICENSUMQUE MAGNANIMO
ROBERTO, DUCI DUDELEO ISSICRATEA

HYMENE ILLUSTRIOR DILECTISSIMISQUE FILIIS ARCTA
AMANTIOR NON SIBI VIXISSET: DUM

VOLITATQUE EJUS UNDIQUE, VIRTUTE SUPER ÆTHERA FAMA,
O INFELIX VITA ÆTATIS XXXXVII

SALUTIS MDCXXXI INTERIIT FLORENTIA CINERES ANIMAMQUE
CŒLUM SEMPER RETINET

ALMA FIDES RETULIT MENTEM AD CŒLESTIA ELATAM
CONDIDIT ÆTERNIS HUNC PIETASQUE LOCIS.

This inscription was probably placed in the Church of St. Pancras, but there is no monument, except the stone with the Bear
and Ragged Staff, already mentioned, which may have served
for Anna Dudley or for her mother Elizabeth.[1]

In the Uffizi Gallery is a portrait of Richard Southwell in
a grand ebony frame with two coats of arms on silver shields,
that of the Medici at the top, and probably the Southwell arms
below, and an inscription as to Holbein painter to Henry VIII of
England. This may have been a present from the English Court
to the Grand-Duke, or may have been brought from England by
Elizabeth Southwell or Dudley, and by them bequeathed to the
Grand-Duke.[2] However the picture may have come there, it

---

[1] Researches as to the Southwell family prove that they have entirely
disappeared from the County of Nottingham where they once held great possessions. In Norfolk the name appears five times as owners of small hold-
ings. In Suffolk, twice in the same manner. In Ireland the name of Viscount Southwell appears in the list of English landed proprietors in 1875, as
a land-owner in Limerick, Kerry, Cavan, Donegal, and Leitrim. In Walford's
County families of the United Kingdom is a notice of Viscount Southwell,
and in Burke's Peerage 1888, a long account of the family; but in the pedigree no mention is made of Elizabeth Southwell, wife of Robert Dudley.

[2] The *Catalogue de la Galerie Royale des Uffizi* by CESARE RIGONI, 1893,
thus describes it: « *765. Holbein Jean le jeune, né à Augsbourg en 1497, mort à
Londres 1543. Portrait de Richard Southwell, conseiller d'État d'Henri VIII,
Roi d'Angleterre. Buste en habit noir et avec un bonnet de la même couleur.
Dans le fond on lit en lettres d'or, X° Julii anno H. VIII. XVIII. ætatis
suæ XXXIII.* »

forms a memorial of the life in the Tuscan Court of Dudley and his wife.

In the National Library of Florence is a copy of Michaud's *Biographie Universelle*, Paris, chez Madame Desplaces, 1855. It contains a short biography of Robert Dudley and his ancestors, full of the usual omissions and inaccuracies. In it the author says : " Il engagea le Grand-Duc Ferdinand à déclarer le port de Livourne, port franc."

Apropos of this port, I have in my possession a MS. patent of the Grand-Duke Ferdinand's, creating the first English Consul at Leghorn, on March 13th 1596. He was appointed at the petition of several English ship-owners, whose names are so mauled in the Italian spelling as to be unreçognisable; and the man chosen as first British Consul was an Irishman written as Capt. Raimondo d'Orchen, which I take to mean Capt. Raymond Dawkins.

In the *Guida storica ed artistica della città e dei contorni di Livorno*, per Giuseppe Piombanti, Livorno, Gio. Marini, Editore, Tipografia Vannini, Casa Pia del Refugio, 1873, Dudley is honourably mentioned as having designed and constructed the new port of Leghorn, and as a most able naval architect and ship-builder. Thus:

Roberto Dudley Conte Warwick, cattolico emigrato Inglese, al servizio del Gran Duca, fu pure abilissimo costruttore navale, il quale per conto del governo, costruì a Livorno alcuni enormi galeoni da 40, da 60 ed anche da 90 cannoni, che furono lungamente il terrore dei Turchi.

The next error in the writers about Dudley may be found in the "Walks in Florence and its environs" by Susan and Joanna Horner, London, 1884, in which at page 437, of Vol. I, there are the following lines: I will italicize the errors.

" Opposite the Palazzo Strozzi, a corner house between two streets bears a shield, with the lion rampant. Here lived and

died Robert Dudley, Duke of Northumberland, the son of Queen
Elizabeth's favourite, the Earl of Leicester, and of *Amy Robsart*,
the unhappy heroine of Sir Walter Scott's " Kenilworth." Queen
Elizabeth, from her mad attachment to Leicester, *is said to have
abetted her lover in the murder of his wife*, and to have disowned
this marriage, so that *the son* was not allowed to bear his heredi-
tary title, *although his possessions were restored to him*, and he
quitted England in *1612*, to seek a refuge in Tuscany at the
Court of *Cosimo II*, who appointed him chamberlain to the
Grand-Duchess, sister of the *German Emperor Matthias*. At her
request the Emperor created Dudley a Prince of the Holy Empire,
with the title of Duke of Northumberland. He was a man of
great learning and accomplishments; his chief studies were
mathematics and nautical science, and he designed the Mole at
Leghorn, besides publishing works of value on navigation, etc."

The many inaccuracies in these lines require especial attention. The shield mentioned is high up on the very narrow part
of the house, or Palazzo, and bears the well-known Rucellai arms.
Underneath it, much lower down, there is an artistic little *tabernacolo* in stone with graceful wrought iron work, containing a
Virgin and child. These objects had probably been placed there
by the Rucellai, and when they sold the adjoining little houses
to Robert Dudley on the 5th of April 1614, were replaced by
him in their former position, in compliance with the good old
Florentine custom, that an inscription, or coat of arms, or work
of art, once exposed to public view on a building, could never
be removed, being considered as public property for ever. Robert
Dudley lived in this Palazzo, but he did not die there; he
died in the Villa Rinieri, now Corsini, just below the Royal
Villa of Petraia, near Quarto, in 1649. He was the son of the
Earl of Leicester, but certainly not of his first wife Amy Robsart,
who never had a child and died in 1560, about thirteen years

before Robert Dudley's birth. His mother was Lady Douglas Sheffield born Howard, who was a widow, when she was married to Leicester, before several well-known witnesses. It is unfair and unjust to condemn Leicester as the murderer of his first wife, Amy Robsart, and most unfair and unjust to accuse Queen Elizabeth of having abetted him in the murder. It is well known that an inquest was held on Amy Robsart's body, and that the verdict was death by " mischance." It is a great mistake to say that Queen Elizabeth discovered Leicester's marriage with Amy Robsart. That marriage was celebrated in the presence of King Edward VI, on the 4th of June 1550, as the young King records the fact in his private journal in the following words:

" 1550, June 4th. Sir Robert Dudley, third (surviving) son of the Earl of Warwick, married Sir John Robsart's daughter, after which marriage there were certain gentlemen that did strive who should first take away a goose's head, which was hanged alive on two cross posts."

This journal in the King's own handwriting is still preserved among the manuscripts in the British Museum, London. On the day of the marriage Sir Robert Dudley, Earl of Leicester, was about eighteen years old, having been born on the 24th of June 1532, the same year in which the Queen, then Princess Elizabeth, was born. It has been said that they were born on the same day in the same year. It is certain, that during their childhood and early youth, they were often together. They were also prisoners at the same time in the Tower of London in the beginning of Queen Mary's reign, 1553. This may partly account for Elizabeth's great esteem for him. On her accession to the throne, Queen Elizabeth advanced Leicester to the highest honours, and gave him the earliest mark of her esteem and affection. In the first year of her reign, she appointed him Master of the Horse, with the fee of one hundred marks per

annum, and in the commission for compounding with such as
might be called to receive the honour of knighthood at the
Queen's command, the name of Lord Robert Dudley was the
first called. In addition to the association of early friendship,
the Queen knew him to possess high qualities which would be
valuable in a public servant, while he was the most accomplished
gentleman in England. He was second only to Cecil in the
strength of his understanding, and second neither to him nor
to anyone else in his attachment to his mistress. It is well
known that the Queen had declared that she would never marry
a subject.

To return to his son Robert Dudley, and the mention of his
possessions. When Leicester died in 1588, his brother Ambrose,
Earl of Warwick, dying soon after, Robert Dudley came into
possession of Kenilworth and the other estates left to him by
his father's will. He enjoyed them, residing occasionally at
Kenilworth, till he left England, not in 1612 but in 1606. Kenilworth and his other estates were confiscated by the Crown, on
his refusal to obey the order of King James Ist, to return to England. They were never restored to him.

When he arrived in Florence the reigning Grand-Duke was not
Cosimo II, but Ferdinand Ist, whose wife was Christina, daughter
of Carlo, Duca di Lorena. The wife of Cosimo II who succeeded
Ferdinand Ist as Grand-Duke of Tuscany, was Maria Maddalena,
daughter of the Archduke Carlo d'Austria, married to Cosimo II
in 1608. It was not the German Emperor Matthias, who created
Dudley, Duke of Northumberland, but Ferdinand II, Emperor
of the Holy Roman Empire, in 1620. Dudley was Grand Chamberlain, as has been before stated in this preface, to the three
successive Grand-Duchesses of Tuscany.

As to the Palazzo Dudley. On the 5th of April 1614, Dudley bought from Lodovico and Ferdinando the sons of Orazio

Rucellai for four thousand scudi, house property in Florence, recorded as " una casa e due casette poste nel popolo di San Pancrazio." On the site, a wedge shaped piece of ground, between Via della Spada and Via della Vigna Nuova, the very narrow end of the wedge facing Via degli Strozzi, Dudley soon after had a Palace built. The principal front consisted of four stories, including the ground floor, with ten windows to each story; this front which looks on the Via della Vigna Nuova, measures about one hundred and thirty five feet. The truncated point of the wedge facing Via degli Strozzi, and on which appear the Rucellai coat of arms and the little *tabernacolo*, is only about six feet wide. It has been said that Bartolommeo Ammannati was the architect, but dates make this doubtful — it is more probable that Dudley himself designed or directed the building of the Palace. It was his town house till his death at Castello in 1649; there eight of his children were born — and there his loving and beloved wife Elizabeth Southwell died on the 10th September 1631.

There are several other short notices of Dudley with the usual inaccuracies. Such as in the " Cyclopædia " by Rees, London, 1829, and the " Encyclopædic Dictionary," Cassel and Co., London, New York and Paris, where is an enigmatical mention of Dudley " (10th Eng.) deriving the name *Dudlei* from *Dodo*, an Anglo Saxon who, about A. D. 700, erected a castle there."

The notice in the *Biografia Britannica* is probably the most favourable to him, though the " Italian Biography " by the Rev. Vaughan Thomas which we have quoted is more full.[1] This writer was Vicar of Stoneleigh, where Dudley's English wife and her unmarried daughter were buried. On the 4th of June 1855,

---

[1] The book was published anonymously for private circulation, by Baxter, Oxford, and seems written quite as much as a testimonial to Lady Dudley — Alice Leigh — as a biography of the husband who deserted her.

he preached the sermon at the annual commemoration of the Leigh family. He confesses in his book that on that occasion he largely pointed out and condemned all that was sinful, licentious, and adulterous in the conjugal and parental conduct of Sir Robert Dudley, in his abandonment of a wife, Alice Leigh, whose virtues claimed not only fidelity but devoted attachment, and children whose infancy as well as number demanded a father's protection and guardianship. " But such observations," he adds, " belong more to the sermon rather than the memoir.[1] "

Litta in his *Famiglie Celebri* noting Mario, Count of Carpegna, who married Teresa Dudley, names her as the daughter of Roberto Duca di Nortumbria, who had fled from England to escape the persecution against Catholicism, and taken shelter with his family in Italy.

This may have been one of the reasons for Dudley leaving England, but not the only one:

1st He was in love with his beautiful young cousin Elizabeth Southwell with whom it would have been impossible to live in England. As to his doing so abroad, it is not my province to judge;

2nd He was utterly disgusted by the treatment received in his attempt to prove by law his legitimacy; the Court of the Star Chamber, and, it is said, King James Ist himself, having sealed up his evidence, and arbitrarily put an end to the suit. After various efforts to obtain justice he got the Royal permis-

---

[1] My dear old friend, and colleague in the House of Commons and in the year 1842 my travelling companion, the late lamented Richard Monckton Milnes, afterwards Lord Houghton (known in his younger days as ' Dicky Milnes,' and ' The Cool of the Evening,' and a frequent guest at my Putney Hill Villa, where he was always called the Poet), told me when I last saw him in Florence in 1883, about two years before his death, that Walter Savage Landor, in conversation with him about Robert Dudley, said : ' He was as great a scoundrel as his father,' alluding probably to his desertion of his wife Alice Leigh and of his daughters by her. It was a short and sharp sentence on such a man.

sion to travel for three years, and in 1605 left England never to return. As we have seen, he did not go alone.

How he atoned for thus leaving behind him a wife, as well as his worries and indignities, by being a most faithful husband and loving father to the family formed under sunnier skies and auspices, this Memoir shall show. He did not leave his English family unprovided for, having left them most of his patrimony, and given liberal dowers to the girls.

There is a very interesting series of portraits which illustrate the life of Dudley, in the magnificent book named "Portraits of illustrious Personages of Great Britain, etc.," by Edmund Lodge, 2 vols folio, London, 1821. This was one of the delights of my boyhood, and is still a delight in my old age.

There is the portrait and biographical notice of Walter Devereux, created Earl of Essex in 1572 by Queen Elizabeth; and of his son Robert Devereux Earl of Essex, by his wife Lettice Knollys, who was our Robert Dudley's stepmother, and his greatest enemy. She was a relative of Anna Bullen or Boleyn, Elizabeth's mother. Robert Devereux was much patronised by his father-in-law, the Earl of Leicester, and in his expedition to Cadiz in 1596, he was accompanied among others by Leicester's son by Lady Sheffield — the subject of our Memoir. In 1599 he was in Ireland, and for his rebellious tumult in London, was tried, condemned and executed in 1601, our Dudley being also implicated.

Lodge also gives us the portrait of the Earl of Leicester, Robert Dudley's father, who, some historians say, caused Essex' death that he might marry Lettice his widow. She obtained such influence over him as caused him to do his son the great injustice of sometimes affirming and sometimes denying his legitimacy, and in the end leaving him the princely Castle and domain of Kenilworth, but with the sting and blot of illegitimacy.

Lodge also gives a portrait of Henry, Prince of Wales, son of James Ist, whose early death, before he had paid Robert Dudley the stipulated price of Kenilworth, involved the latter in such long and tiresome litigations with the English government.

Craik has as a frontispiece to his " Romance of the Peerage," Vol. III, a portrait of Robert Dudley himself, taken from the original miniature by Holland, now at Penshurst. It is the bust enlarged from the full length figure in Harding's Historical Portraits. In his advertisement Craik adds that no other representation of Dudley exists, except an equestrian figure engraved by Pierre Daret, the only known impression of which is in possession of the Rev. William Staunton of Longbridge House, Warwickshire.[1]

Here I think some misapprehension exists. Pierre Daret engraved, it is true, an equestrian portrait of Dudley's son Cosimo, the Colonel of the guard to the Grand-Duke Cosimo II, which we have reproduced. Cosimo Dudley died in 1630[2] and it is possible this has been mistaken for the portrait of his father. Many years ago, I had a correspondence about Pierre Daret's portrait with the illustrious French historian Mignet, but without result as to any portrait of Robert Dudley by him.

And now a word of explanation as to Robert Dudley's own books in my possession.

Long ago I bought from Signor Pietro Bigazzi, together with many other books which had belonged to Dudley, the first two volumes and the fourth of the *Arcano del Mare*, the first edition of his great work which was published at Forence in 1646-47, The third volume was wanting, perhaps lent to some friend

---

[1] It is described in Merridew's Catalogue of engraved portraits of Nobility, Gentry etc. connected with Warwickshire.

[2] See *Tableaux historiques où sont gravés les illustres François et étrangers de l'un et de l'autre sexe,* par PIERRE DARET et LOUIS BOISSEVIN, gr. in 4to, 1652-1656.

who had forgotten to return it. Two or more years after this, Signor Bigazzi brought me, as a New Year's gift, the missing volume of this very same incomplete set. He had discovered it on the low wall or ledge of the Palazzo Riccardi, and bought it from the salesman who had permission to sell his books there. My joy on thus unexpectedly receiving the missing part may be easily imagined by collectors and lovers of old books. The four volumes thus happily reunited after a long separation were in the old binding with the arms of a Cardinal of the Medici family. The third had naturally suffered from ill treatment and exposure on the *muricciuolo* [1] of the Palazzo Riccardi.

I had previously bought from Signor Bigazzi the two great folio volumes of the second edition of the *Arcano del Mare*, published after Dudley's death. Both editions are fully described in the Memoir.

It seems probable that the *Arcano del Mare* was only a *résumé* of several previous works by Dudley. One of them is the MS. volume, quarto size, of which I possess the original, mostly in Dudley's own hand. It is called the *Direttorio Marittimo*, and was written in very faulty Italian for the use and instruction of the officers of the Tuscan fleet. In it most of the subjects enlarged upon in the *Arcano*, are treated concisely, including "great circle sailing" and all kinds of navigation; the administrative management of a fleet, and its manœuvres in a naval battle, etc. The book is in ancient covers of thick paper, and preceded by a dedication to the Grand-Duke, and by a sketch of Dudley's own naval life, written in his own hand with all his corrections and underlinings.

---

[1] Several of the ancient palaces of Florence have these ledges or stone seats along their walls: they were originally for the convenience of dependents, who used to wait or rest there. They are now much used by salesmen. The one on the Palazzo Strozzi is a flower stall.

His *Catholicon,* spoken of by Craik and Vaughan, I have never seen, though I possess a copy of Dr. Mario Cornacchino's amusing old book on the Warwick powder, which was to the seventeenth century what Holloway's pills are to the nineteenth. For a description of the volume I refer you to the Memoir.

His famous political tract " A discourse to correct the Exorbitances of Parliaments and to enlarge the King's Revenue " is so curious that in August 1863 I made an exact copy of it in the library of the Oxford and Cambridge Club, Pall Mall, London. It was taken from the " Historical Collections of Private Passages of State, etc. 1618-1629," by John Rushworth of Lincoln's Inn, London, 1721. Vol. I. Appendix 12.

For its influence in England see Part IV of the Memoir, where this copy is inserted entire.

Whether Dudley took his ideas of political economy from the Italian government then in force and approved of by him; whether the book was a kind of Machiavellian satire on the Tuscan government; or whether the Grand-Duke found Dudley's maxims more worthy of following than the English did, cannot be proved. But certainly many of the measures advised by him are to this day in force in Italy, and are not, for modern life, good measures. For instance Dudley advised that a Fortress should be in every town, the governor of which is not to be chosen from that town; that passports should be demanded for all travellers; that inn-keepers must take down the names of all those lodging with them; that a tax should be put on salt, which is to be a government monopoly; a decimal tax on men's estates; the examining and stamping the weights every year; taxes on every office and trade; and " to make two hundred men titulate, and they to pay for their titles." Now all these are in the Italian scheme of government, even the last. *Vide* the Order of St. Lazzaro.

Among my Dudley books is a dainty little volume styled
" *La Assontione di Maria Vergine* in Venezia appresso i Vari-
schi, 1622." It has an artistic title page, on the top is the cognizance of the crowned Bear and Ragged Staff, with an angel
on either side, and Christ and the Madonna as supporters.
Below is the Dudley coat of arms.

It is dedicated " All' Ill. et Excell. Sig. Roberto Dudlei Duca
di Northumbria et Conte di Varick et Leicester dedicata. Con
licenza de' Sup. et Privilegio, da D. Mauritio Moro Canonico.
Venetia da S. Giorgio d'Alega, lì 20 Dicembre 1622. " In the
dedicatory address is a great laudation of Robert Dudley and
of his wife, and of all their most noble and illustrious ancestors
and families, especially a branch of the Southwells, one of
whom, Baron Don Roberto, settled in Venice, and whose son,
Don Henrico, was Canon of St. Mark's, and a poet withal.

And now a word about the homes of the Dudley, and what
is left of them to the present day. The family home in the
Vigna Nuova is still to be seen, and is so fully described in
the text as to need no description here. The Villa Rinieri,
Dudley's country house and the place of his death, is now the
handsome Villa Corsini, at Quarto, just under the Royal Villa
of La Petraia. It has beautiful grounds and gardens with se-
cular ilex and cypress trees, whose shadows certainly fell on
Robert Dudley and his children when they walked there.

In 1858 I spent a day at Piombino, the married home of Maria
Princess of Piombino, Dudley's eldest daughter, and enjoyed a
refreshing swim in the clear blue sea of the tiny bay. It was
then a very small port, opposite Rio in the Isle of Elba. Probably in the seventeenth century it was a much more important
place, and 'enlivened by the palace of the Appiani family. It
was here that Cosimo Dudley died in 1631.

In October 1864, I also visited the Castle of Olivola, the

home of Maria Maddalena, Marchesa Malaspini, Dudley's second daughter. The Castle, which is well situated on high ground between Sarzana and Fivizzano, still existed in a deserted and neglected state. The large marble coat-of-arms of the Malespini still holds its place over the principal entrance. It looked to me more like an English country house than an Italian feudal stronghold.[1] A few poor looking houses and a church stand near it. In a small room in the Castle, once an oratory, there still remained a white marble slab, bordered by a strip of reddish Porto Venere marble with the following insription :

MEMORIÆ SACRUM.

CAROLUS HERBERTUS ILL^{mi} ET
EXCELLENT^{mi} VIRI PHILIPPI
COMITIS PEMBROKIÆ ET
MONTIS GOMMERICI E T C FILIUS
PRIMOGENITUS MORTALES HIC
EXUVIAS DUM CHRISTO
JUBENTE RESURGANT
IMMORTALES RELIQUIT
ANNO DOMINI 1635
EXEUNTE ÆTATIS SUÆ XVI.

This inscription which records the burial place of the young Earl of Pembroke, who died at Dudley's house in Florence, was removed a few years ago from Olivola[2] by the late Earl of Carnarvon, and is now preserved at Highclere Castle.

The other Dudley possessions at Fiesole, of which Don Carlo's son Don Antonio, a cleric, was the last possessor of the name,

---

[1] Until the French Republican invasion at the end of the last century almost all that part of the country was possessed by the Malaspini, as feudal Lords under the Emperor; and each of the family had his castle or stronghold.

[2] Olivola now belongs to Mr. Browne, the former well-known British Consul at Genoa, who also has a marine Villa at Porto Fino near Lady Carnarvon's Villa, Alta Chiara — High Clere.

are now reduced, as I have said at the beginning of this preface, to peasants' houses on my *podere*, retaining very little of
their former state, except a few bits of stone work which mark
their former style.

This rambling preface is much more lengthy than I had
intended to make it, but I could not resist the desire to lay
before the reader everything that appeared to me interesting
about Dudley, his family and descendants.

The following Memoir will be a mere chronicle of the principal events in Dudley's life. It has no pretension to being a
complete biography, but it is founded on facts, and supported
by good evidence. My hope is that it may give as much pleasure to the reader as it has given me in the writing of it.

In the Appendix, I have reproduced copies in the original
language of all the most important manuscripts and documents,
which I trust may prove of use to some future historian.

LIFE

OF

SIR ROBERT DUDLEY

ROBERT DUDLEY, Earl of Leicester.

PART I.

YOUTHFUL VOYAGES.

R<small>OBERT</small> D<small>UDLEY</small> was born at Shene, Richmond, in,
or about the year 1573. His father was Robert Dudley,
Earl of Leicester, Minister and favourite of Queen Elizabeth; his mother was Lady Douglas Sheffield, born
Howard, widow of Lord Sheffield.

I am not going to enter at length on the moot question of Dudley's legitimacy, on which point he was
very unfairly treated. Proofs were not wanting that
Leicester and Lady Douglas had been married in the
presence of well-known witnesses, but the marriage
was not publicly acknowledged. Various reasons have
been assigned for this concealment, some political and
others private; the most probable seems to be the one
given by the author of ' Leycester's Commonwealth,' [1]
i. e. fear of the Queen's displeasure, and the outward

---

[1] From " Leycester's Commonwealth, conceived, spoken and published with most earnest protestation of all dutifull goodwill and affection toward this realm." Printed 1641, pag. 21-22.

maintenance of his boast that he was privately married to her Majesty.

The same contemporary author writes, in speaking
of Leicester's subsequent marriage to Lady Essex: " But
for this controversie, whether the marriage be good or
no, I leave it to be tried hereafter between my young
Lord of Denbigh (Lady Essex' son by Leicester) and
Master Philip Sydney, whom the same most concerneth;
for that my Lord was contracted to another Lady before, that yet liveth (whereof Master Edward Diar and
Master Edmond Tilney both Courtiers, can be witnesses), and consummated the same contract by generation of children."

That prophesied trial did truly come off in 1605,
and Lady Sheffield, as well as three or four other witnesses swore to the marriage having taken place at
her house of Esher in Surrey by a lawful Minister of
the Church, Sir Edward Horsey giving her away.

During his earliest years the boy Dudley lived with
his mother, but when he was about five years old she
gave him up to his father's charge. This was in 1578,
the year in which the unacknowledged wife was driven
to profit by the freedom forced upon her, and for protection to marry Sir Edward Stafford of Grafton. In
the trial of 1605 she stated as her reason for this
" that her life had been repeatedly threatened, and
attempts had been made to poison her, and that her
hair and her nails had fallen off; in consequence of
which she felt no safety for her person, unless she put
herself in such a situation as to render herself perfectly
secure." [1]

---

[1] *Report of the Barony of Lisle*, pag. 254.

The Earl of Leicester may have forced her into this marriage; he certainly took advantage of it to celebrate publicly his union with Lady Essex, who had practically been his wife privately for some time previous. Consequently his son Robert was placed at school, or more probably resided in the house and under the care of Sir John Dudley, a kinsman of the Earl of Leicester, who lived (says Lysons, in his *Magna Britannia*) at Stoke Newington, and not at Newington Butts as stated by others. Lysons in his mention of Sir John Dudley repeats the tradition of Leicester himself having visited his little son there. Owen, or Evan, Jones, who was subsequently witness for Sir Robert Dudley in the well-known trial of 1605, confirms that statement.

In 1583 the boy was at a school, or with a private tutor at Offington, near Worthing in Sussex, under the charge of his uncle Ambrose, Earl of Warwick, who had a residence at or near Worthing. The memory of his having lived there is still preserved at Worthing, in the name of Warwick House.

In 1588 he was at the University of Oxford. The entry of his name appears in the book of Christ-Church College with the title *Comitis Filius* (son of an Earl) 7th May 1588.

In the same year, 1588, he served at the camp of Tilbury as Colonel under his father the Earl of Leicester, who was *Generalissimo*. This fact is stated by himself in the *Arcano del Mare* and in his MS. volume the *Direttorio Marittimo*.

In 1588, the Earl of Leicester died at Cornbury, when on his way to Kenilworth. In his last will dated Middleburgh, 1st August 1587,[1] Leicester with a folly

---

[1] See Appendix, n. I.

equal to his injustice called his son 'his base son' though he left him eventual heir, after the death of Ambrose, Earl of Warwick, of Kenilworth and of other estates. The inserting of the fatal word 'base' was probably due to the unbounded influence obtained over Leicester by his third wife Lettice Knollys, the widow of Walter Devereux, Earl of Essex. For if Leicester in his last will had owned his son Robert by Lady Douglas Sheffield, to be his legitimate son, his subsequent marriage with Lettice Knollys, Countess of Essex, as an inevitable consequence became null and void, and she would have lost her great position as Leicester's lawful wife and widow.

As to Lady Sheffield's suspicion that some system of slow poisoning was tried upon her, it is curious to observe that Leicester was more than once suspected of having persons, who stood in his way, removed by poison, to name two of them, the husband of Lady Douglas Sheffield, and the husband of Lettice Knollys, Countess of Essex. Giulio Borgherini, an Italian follower of Leicester's, commonly called Doctor Julio, was supposed to be the provider of the poison.

The death of the Earl of Essex on August 21st 1576 is reported by the author of Leicester's Commonwealth (page 23-24), who adds " and so he died in the way of an extreme flux, caused by an Italian recipe, as all his friends are well assured, the maker whereof was a Chyrurgeon (as is believed) that then was newly come to my Lord from Italy,[1] a cunning man and sure in operation. . . . . Nor must you marvaile though all

----

[1] Here the author is mistaken, Dr Julio having been one of the witnesses of Lady Sheffield's marriage some years previously.

these died in divers manners of outward diseases, for this is the excellency of the Italian Art for which this Chyrurgeon Doctor Julio was entertained so carefully, who can make a man dye in what manner and show of sickness you will, by whose intructions no doubt but his Lordship is now cunning."

Not so cunning however but that on Leicester's death there were whispers of his having been himself poisoned.

It is certain that his widow Lettice Knollys was afterwards married to Sir Christopher Blount Kt. and lived till the year 1634. The same consideration as to her position, also accounts for her fierce and successful opposition to Sir Robert Dudley's attempts in 1605 to prove the marriage of his father and mother, and in consequence his own legitimacy.

In 1589 his uncle Ambrose, Earl of Warwick, died, and Dudley came into possession of Kenilworth, and of the other estates left to him by his father's will.

In 1581 he had engaged by a contract *per verba de presenti*, in the presence of good and faithful witnesses to marry Frances Vavasour, one of Queen Elizabeth's maids of honour. The Queen however refused her consent on account of Dudley's youth, and Frances Vavasour subsequently married Thomas Shirley, of the Ferrers family.[1]

After this early matrimonial disappointment Robert Dudley seems to have given his mind to travels, and

---

[1] See Appendix, n. II. See also the attestations of Edward Barker *Causarum Ecclesiasticarum sive Majestatis Registrarius ac Notarius Publicus*, London, 3 November, 1592, and of Guittelmary Auberie *Legum Doctor Alma Curia Cant. et de Arcubus.* London *Officialis principalis. Datum Londini 6 die Novembris anno Domini 1592*, relating to Dudley's matrimonial contract with Frances Vavasour.

for those days went far and wide. From a boy he always had a love of the sea, and for its development he shall speak for himself. In the Proem to his Italian book the *Direttorio Marittimo*[1] after a dedication to the Grand-Duke he says: " Setting aside many superfluous circumstances which have occasioned the author to turn his attention to the theory and practice of the art of navigation, suffice it to say that he is Nephew of three Grand Admirals of England (or *Generalissimi* of the Sea, which is one of the highest offices held under that of the Crown) and that he had from his youth a natural sympathy for the sea, and this in spite of his having in 1588 held the very honorable post of Colonel in the land forces, which he exercised under the command of his father, the General in Chief and Grand Master of England. He determined at any cost to enter the marine army, on which at that time the reputation and greatness of England depended. He had also a great desire to discover new countries, therefore from the age of 17 he gave himself to the study of navigation, and of marine discipline and war. In fact he wanted to blend naval command together with military emprise by land, in India and other parts to which navigation should take him. Therefore he built and manned ships of war, in which he sought to place the best pilots that were to be found, and in whose great knowledge and experience he trusted implicitly. One, the famous mariner Abram Kendal, might be called

---

[1] Written in Italian by Dudley himself and of which I possess the original MS. copy. The only fragment of title page remaining to it is headed *Direttorio Marittimo di Don Roberto Dudley, Duca di Nortumbria, fatto per ordine del Serenissimo Gran Duca di Toscana suo Signore.*

his master, from him he learned enough navigation for an Admiral. But although Queen Elizabeth then reigning in England would not allow such a mere youth to break his maiden lance in an emprise requiring so much knowledge of the world, and in which many veteran Captains had fared so ill,[1] and lost both men and ships, she contented him by allowing him to make a voyage. Thus it came to pass that in 1594 he began this voyage to the West Indies, to discover and open the way to the Empire of Guiana or *Walliana* (sic) in America, much renowned in those times as a great and wealthy nation; which he did with such success, — being both General of his men and Admiral of his ships, — that he made himself master of the Island of Trinidad, discovered Guiana,[2] fought and captured the galleons of the enemy, returning at the year's end with much useful spoil.

" After this he was engaged in so many honourable actions by sea and land in the service of the Crown, that not being able to take the desired voyage to China, he sent his ships and men there under command of Captain Wood, a very brave sailor. He took the command of the great English fleet in 1596, in the absence of his uncle, the Earl of Nottingham, High Admiral. The year following (1597), he was Admiral of the English vanguard in the battle of Cadiz in Spain,[3]

---

[1] Apropos of Elizabeth's feeling on this subject I have in the Appendix, n. III, reprinted a correspondance between Queen Elizabeth and King James on the subject from Rymers Fœdera. Tom. XVI, pag. 18-19.

[2] He made a map of Guiana, which he published in the *Arcano del Mare.*

[3] Dudley thus reports this emprise in his *Arcano del Mare* under the head of Cadiz: *In questo golfo è porto di Cadez: nel 1597 del*

when they burnt the fleet from the Indies, and took
the city. Then he besieged Faro in Algarna (Algarve)
in Portugal, and next took the command of the English
galleons sent to the rescue when Calais in France was
taken by His Serene Highness the Arch-Duke *A. Men-
toza* (Mendoza). In the which and divers other actions
and voyages he has learned what he knows of the art
of navigation, and the practice of command and marine and military discipline combined.

" In especial he practised the science of navigation
by grand circles with practical longitude, as explained
in the *Arcano del Mare.*"

Such is the summary of his nautical life, which
Dudley gave the Grand-Duke of Tuscany, in the book
of sailing directions prepared for the Tuscan fleet. He
gave a much more detailed account of his maiden
emprise, the voyage to Trinidad, in a letter to the
Rev. Richard Hackluyt, Prebend of Westminster, the
great writer on sea voyages in the time of Elizabeth
and James I[st].[1] Hackluyt heads this

---

*mese di giugno l'armata Inglese fece giornata con l'armata Spagnuola
e dell' Indie, e gl' Inglesi restorno vincitori e presono la Città, alla
quale fazzione fu presente l'autore, il quale conducera la vanguardia
dell' armata Inglese.*

[1] This Mr Hackluyt was a well-known man in his day, as may be
judged by the following letter from Queen Elizabeth to the Archbishop
of Canterbury, dated

　　　　　" At Greenwich Sunday, 18th of May,
　　　　　　　in the forenoon, 1600.

" A LETTER TO THE LORD ARCHBISHOP OF CANTERBURY,

" We are moved to recommend unto your good favor, Mr Hackluyt, a learned preacher, that hath not only taken great pains in his
calling, and served a long time Sir Edward Stafford, Knight, being
then Her Majesty's Ambassador in France in a dangerous time, but
hath bestowed his time and taken very great pains in matter of navigation and discoveries, a labor of great desert and use, wherein

" A voyage of the honourable gentleman Mr Robert Dudley, now Knight, to the Isle of Trinidad and the coast of Paria, with his return home by the Isle of *Granta* (Granada), Santa Cruz, *St. Juan de Puertorico* (Porto Rico), Mona Zacheo, the shoalds called Abreojos, and the Isle of Bermuda. In which voyage he and his company tooke and sunke nine Spanish ships whereof one was an armada of 600 tunnes. Written at the request of Mr Richard Hackluyt."

After a certain prologue Dudley relates: " I weighed ancker from Southampton road the 6th of November 1594. Upon this day, my selfe in the " Beare," a ship of 200 tunnes, as Admirall; and Captaine Munck in the " Beare's Whelpe," Vice-Admirall; with two small pinnesses, called the " Frisking " and the " Earewig," I passed through the Needles, and within two days after bare in with Plimmouth. But I was enforced to returne backe.

" Having parted company with my Vice-Admirall, I went alone wandering on my voyage, sailing along the coast of Spaine, within view of Cape Finisterre and Cape St. Vincent, the north and south capes of Spaine. In which space, having many chases, I could meet

---

there may be after occasion to employ him, and therefore our desire is for the good of her Majesty's service that he might be provided of some competent living to reside in these parts. And because we are given to understand that the benetice of great Allhallows, in Thames Street, is like to be void, (being in your Lordship's gift), we do earnestly pray your good Lordship, that at our mediation, you will be pleased to bestow the same, if by the decease of the incumbent it shall be void, on this learned and painful minister. Wherein your Lordship shall not only have due and honorable consideration of his deserts and pains, but give us occasion to think ourselves beholden unto you in granting your goodwill unto him at our motion and entreaty. So etc...

" P. C. Reg. Eliz."

with none but my countreymen, or countrey's friends. Leaving these Spanish shores, I directed my course, the 14ᵗʰ of December, towards the Isles of the Canaries. Here I lingered twelve dayes for two reasons : the one, in hope to meete my Vice-Admirall ; the other, to get some vessel to remove my pestered men into, who being 140 almost in a ship of 200 tunnes, there grew many sicke. I tooke two very fine caravels under the calmes of Tenerif and Palma, which both refreshed and amended my company, and made me a fleet of 3 sailes. In one caravel, called " Intent," I made Benjamin Wood Captaine ; in the other one Captaine Wentworth. Thus cheared as a desolate traveller, with the company of my small and newe erected Fleete, I continued my purpose for the West Indies.

" Riding under this White Cape two daies, and walking on shore to view the countrey, I found it a waste desolate, barren, and sandie place, the sand running in drifts like snow, and very stony ; for so is all the countrey sand upon stone (like Arabia Deserta, and Petrea), and full of blacke venemous lizards, with some wild beasts and people which be tawny Moores, so wilde, as they would but call to my caravels from the shore who road very neere it. I now caused my Master Abraham Kendall to shape his course directly for the isle of Trinidad in the West Indies ; which after 22 dayes we descried, and the 1ˢᵗ of February came to anker under a point thereof, called Curiapan, in a bay which was very full of pelicans, and I called it Pelican' Bay. About 3 leagues to the eastward of this place we found a mine of Mercazites, which glister like golde (but all is not golde that glistereth), for so we found the same nothing worth, though the Indians did assure us it was Calvori, which signifieth gold with them. These Indians are a fine shaped and a gentle people, all naked and painted red, their commanders wearing crowns of feathers. These people did often resort unto my ship, and brought us hennes, hogs, plantans, potatos, pinos, tobacco, and many other pretie commodities, which they exchanged with us for hatchets, knives, hookes, belles and glasse buttons.

" The country is fertile, and ful of fruits, strange beasts, and foules, whereof munkeis, babions, and parats were in great abundance.

" Right against the northernmost part of Trinidad, the maine was called the high land of Paria, the rest a very lowe land. Morucca I learned to be full of a greene stone called Tacarao, which is good for the stone. Caribes I learned to be man-eaters or canibals, and great enemies to the Islanders of Trinidad.

" In the high land of Paria I was informed by divers of these Indians, that there was some Perota, which with them is silver, and great store of most excellent cane-tobacco.

" This discovery of the mine I mentioned to my company, who altogether mutinied against my going in search for it, because they something feared the villany (sic) of Abraham Kendal, who would by no means go.

" I gave them their directions to follow, written under mine owne hand. But they went from me, and entred into one of the mouthes of the great river Orenoque.

" I was told of a rich nation, that sprinkled their bodies with the powder of golde, and seemed to be guilt, and that farre beyond them was a great towne called El Dorado, with many other things.

" In my boate's absence, there came to me a pinnesse of Plimmouth, of which Captaine Popham was chiefe, who gave us great comfort.

" I stayed some sixe or eight dayes longer for Sir Walter Ralegh (who, as we surmized, had some purpose for this discovery), to the ende that, by our intelligence and his boates, we might have done some good: but it seemed he came not in sixe or eight weeks after.

" And after carefully doubling the shouldes (shoals) of Abreojos, I now caused the Master (hearing by a Pilote that the Spanish Fleete ment to put out of Havana) to beare for the Meridian of the yle of Bermuda, hoping there to finde the Fleete. The Fleete I found not, but foule weather enough to scatter many Fleetes; which companies left mee not, till I came to the yles of Flores and Cuervo: whither I made the more haste, hoping to meete some great Fleete of Her Majestie my Sovereigne, as I had intelligence, and to give them advise of this rich Spanish Fleete: but findinge none, and my victuals almost spent, I directed my course for England.

" Returning alone and worse manned by half than when I went foorth, my fortune was to meet a great Armada of this Fleete of some 600 tunnes well appointed, with whom I fought board and board for two days, being no way able in all possibilitie with fifty men to board a man of warre of sixe hundreth tunnes. And having spent all my powder, I was constrained to leave her, yet in such distresse without sailes and mastes, and hull so often shot through with my great ordinance betweene winde and water, that being three hundred leagues from land, I dare say, it was impossible for her to escape sinking. Thus leaving her by necessitie in this miserable estate, I made for England where I arrived at St. Ives in Cornwall, about the latter end of May 1595, scaping most dangerously in a great fogge the rocks of Silly.

" Thus by the providence of God, landing safely, I was kindely entertained by all my friends, and after a short time learned more certaintie of the sinking of that great scippe, being also reputed rich by divers intelligences out of Spaine.

" In this voyage, I and my Fleete tooke, sunke, and burnt nine Spanish ships; which was losse to them, though I got nothing."

In 1596 when on his voyage to America, or perhaps before sailing from England, he made some nautical instruments, as may be seen from the following inscriptions. In the *Gabinetto Fisico* in the Specola, or Natural History Museum of Florence, there is a copper instrument (a compass?) with the inscription ' Sir Robert Duddeley was the Inventor of this instrument 1596 ' — and another much larger brass instrument to find the time of the ebb and flow of the tides in divers places, it had a brass base 1 *braccio* (1 ft. 11 in.) in diameter, and is inscribed ' Sir Robert Duddeley was the inventor of this instrument.' If the reader can understand what this invention was like from Dudley's description of it in mixed English and Italian, on a loose sheet of paper among my Dudley MSS., I here reproduce it for his benefit. Perhaps the accompanying illustration may elucidate its complexities.

Strumento per trovar l' ora dei flussi del Mare in diversi luoghi. Tondo di ottone — diametro 1 braccio Fiorentino. — ' Sir Robert Duddeley was the inventor of this instrument.'

Nel mezzo: ' The cen. of the ecliptick' — ' The cen.
of excentr.'; *sul cerchio medio:* ' The prosthaphereses
(sic) of the Sunn.' — ' The distance of the Moone from
the earth in semidiameters of the earth '; *sul cerchio
esterno:* ' The yearly motion of the Moone anomilæ

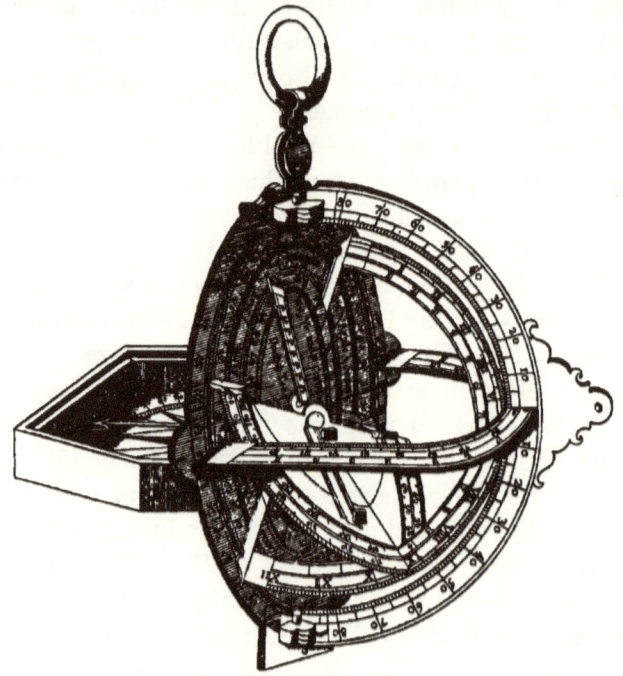

DUDLEY'S NAUTICAL INSTRUMENT TO FIND THE EBB AND FLOW OF THE TIDES.

from the Apogeon of the Sun great Epicicle by 360
and Meridian of London.'

' The yearly motion of the Moone middle place from
the Sunnes, by 360 for the merid. of London according
to the table of Renaldus which differeth 8. 37 from
Maginus.' *Il cerchio esterno di circa 1 ¹/₂ soldo di B° F°*

è fisso — la parte dentro questo cerchio gira — di più vi è una scaletta graduata, che gira sulla parte movibile del tondo.

Sulla faccia dove vi è la scaletta: ' The oblique zodiack only used with the howers to give the tyme and tydes.'

These instruments had probably been brought by Dudley to Florence in 1606 and placed by him in the *Gabinetto Fisico,* with the date of their invention by him.[1]

---

[1] The *Saggio Istorico della Real Galleria di Firenze,* Florence, 1779, says (pag. 154, vol. II) : " The collection of ancient scientific instruments in the *Gabinetto di Fisica* was increased in 1654 by some brought from Germany by Prince Mathias, brother of Ferdinand II, and by others which Robert Dudley, Duke of Northumberland, and English gentleman, had left the Grand-Duke when he died."

DOUGLAS, Lady Sheffield.

PART II.

LITIGATIONS AND SELF-EXILE.

I~n~ 1601 Dudley fell under the displeasure of Queen Elizabeth, for taking part in the rebellion of the young Earl of Essex. The Earl had been under arrest in his own house for some time, having offended the Queen though it is not precisely known for what reason. Lotti, the Italian resident at London, opines that he had made some negotiations with the King of Scotland which were displeasing to Her Majesty of England.[1] Tired of being a prisoner he protested, and the matter was placed by the Queen in the hands of Parliament. But this was too slow for the young rebel, who got his friends together, Dudley and Blount among them, and with 1100 followers and partizans, marched into London. The Earl of Essex, Dudley, Blount, and others were taken prisoners. The Earl was subsequently beheaded, as we know to the Queen's eternal remorse. Dudley got off easily, being shortly after released.

His much journeying threw Robert Dudley into com-

---

[1] See Lotti's account of this in Appendix, n. IV.

munication with other great navigators of the day,
among whom was Thomas Cavendish, who had three
young and charming sisters. With one of these the
young sailor, fresh from his voyages, fell in love, and
being a 'heretik' (i. e. protestant), and deeming himself
free from Frances Vavasour, he married her. The
bride died soon after, in 1596 without issue, and in
the same year he married Alice second daughter of
Sir Thomas Leigh, Knight and Baronet of Stoneleigh,
Warwickshire.

From 1596 to 1605 Dudley was living partly in
the country at Kenilworth, and partly in London.
Alicia Leigh during that time bore him four daughters:

First Alicia Douglassia, baptized at Kenilworth
25th September 1597, who died May 1621, ætatis 24.
By will nuncupatory she bequeathed to her mother
£ 3000 to lay out for pious and charitable uses.

Frances, the second daughter, lived with her mother
in Dudley House, Saint Giles, London, till she married
Sir Gilbert Knyveton of Bradley, Derbyshire.

Anne, the third daughter, married the great lawyer,
Sir Robert Holbourne, Solicitor general to Charles Ist.
She died about 1663.

Catherine, the fourth and youngest daughter, married
that distinguished Royalist in the time of Charles Ist,
Sir Richard Leveson, K. B., of Trentham Hall, Stafford-
shire, ancestor of the present Duke of Sutherland.

These years of Dudley's married life with Alice Leigh
were years full of worries to him. He was under the
Queen's displeasure for his share in the Essex affair.
It was also the time in which he was fighting at long
odds for his honour, his name and nobility.

Since he had become heir to Kenilworth he wished

to prove that he had inherited it as his right, and not
as a father's tardy reparation to a base-born son. For
this cause he attempted by proceedings at law to prove
himself the legitimate son of Robert, Earl of Leicester,
and of Douglassia late Lady Sheffield, born Howard,
widow of Lord Sheffield. There seemed some hope of
success, and the Ecclesiastical Court — which, as the
plague was raging in London, was that year held at
Lichfield — was still sifting his evidence, when on February 10th 1603, Lady Lettice, late Countess of Essex,
Leicester's widow, filed a bill in the Star Chamber,
through Sir Edward Coke, against Sir Robert Dudley
and others for defamation. On October 18th of the
same year Lord Henry Sydney of Penshurst, who had
married Mary Dudley, Leicester's sister, stopped the
proceedings at Lichfield, and brought all the depositions
to the Star Chamber.

Here Robert Dudley's efforts could avail nought,
although, as we have before said, Lady Sheffield and
many witnesses swore to her marriage at Esher. All
the documents proving this were sealed up by order of
the Council of the Star Chamber; while the evidence on
the side of Lettice Lady Essex's marriage with Leicester
was taken alone and unquestioned. On this partial
evidence Lady Sheffield, Doctor Babington, and Sir
Thomas Leigh — Dudley's father-in-law — were all
found guilty of conspiracy

This one-sided law-suit ended on May 13th 1605, in
a verdict against Dudley, his whole evidence being sealed
up and put away, and in vain did he try to get the
judgment reversed.[1] The Essex family together with

---

[1] See Lotti's letter about it. Appendix, n. V.

the Sydneys, and their most powerful party were too
strong for him. The trial evidently created opposite
impressions in royal circles, for in 1604 James Ist, who
ratified the decree of the Star Chamber, promulgated
an act " to restrain all persons from marriage, until
their former wives and former husbands be dead." That
Charles Ist took a different view of Dudley's case from
that of his father we see by the plain wording of
his patent creating Alice Leigh Duchess Dudley, one
phrase of which runs : " And whereas our dear father
not knowing the truth of the lawful birth of the
aforesaid Sir Robert (as we piously believe) granted
away the titles of the said Earldoms to others, which
we now hold not fit to call in question, nor ravel into
our deceased Father's actions..... And yet we, having
a very deep sense of the great injuries done to the said
Robert Dudley and the Lady Alice Dudley and their
children, are of opinion that in justice and equity these
possessions so taken from them do rightly belong to
them, etc., etc.[1] "

The unfair sentence of the Star Chamber seems
to have completely unhinged Dudley's character, and
brought on that crisis in which to revenge his slighted
honour he cast off all allegiance to England, her laws,
and even her domestic claims on him. Even her religion, for he turned Roman Catholic, and then finding,
or feigning to find, that his union with Alice Leigh
was adulterous and against the Roman Catholic law
of marriage (his former wife Frances Vavasour not
being dead at the time), he repudiated her. This at
least was Dudley's own excuse for the repudiation of

---

[1] See Appendix, n. VI. The patent of Charles Ist.

Alice Leigh, and subsequent marriage with Elizabeth Southwell. It is a case of conscience which will be judged differently according as it is looked at from different points of view. No doubt his life with Alice Leigh after his character and rank were abased by the decree of the Star Chamber, was no longer a happy one; for we see from her subsequent behaviour that she was a woman who held greatly to rank and station.

At length in 1606 he took that decisive step which led him to the Grand-Ducal Court of Tuscany and exercised a ruling influence on all the rest of his life. Irritated and rendered desperate by this harsh and unjust treatment, he, at the end of 1605, obtained the royal permission to travel in foreign parts for three years, and went, never to return; moreover he did not go alone. He was accompanied by a young cousin of great spirit and beauty named Elizabeth Southwell, eldest daughter of Sir Robert Southwell of Woodrising, Norfolk.[1] Her mother was eldest daughter of Charles, second Lord Howard of Effingham, Lord High Admiral. Through this connection with Lady Sheffield's family the young people were first cousins once removed.

A very interesting *relazione* (report) in the Medicean Archives contains a graphic account of this part of Dudley's life. It was written on July 26th 1611 by an Englishman in Paris, and is addressed to the Father Confessor of the Duchess of Tuscany, who had evidently set his reverence to obtain information about

---

[1] Sir Robert Southwell was one of the most distinguished naval commanders in the year of the Invincible Spanish Armada, 1588.

the then new members of her Court. The informant is very cautious, he signs himself with illegible hieroglyphics, and says that for the future his signature will be R. Tomasine. He supplicates that what he writes on English matters shall be communicated to no one but the Cavalier Vinta (Minister of the Grand-Ducal Court), and he especially hopes that the Earl of Warwick will not know that he has written, for " he holds him in great honour and is his faithful friend," but — he adds, " the less secrets are divulged the more they remain secrets."

After giving Dudley's pedigree and early life, and an account of the trial, he goes on in very good Italian: " In which law-suit this Sydney was much favoured by the Earl of Salisbury, now *Sicill* (Cecil) while on the part of Dudley were the Count of Hertford and all the House of Howard. But the great influence of Cecil obtained the consent of the King, who was present when the sentence was given in favor of the Sydneys, and against this Robert Dudley.

" After which sentence being *sdegnato moltissimo* (extremely indignant) the said Robert Dudley, who but few years before had been so happily married to a daughter of the good knight Sir John *Lis* (Leigh), requested and obtained leave from the King to leave England for three years, and having caused nearly 40,000 scudi of his own estate to be secretly conveyed to France, he departed, at the age of 37 years.[1] He was followed by a young lady of the Court, a most beautiful girl of the *Havar* (Howard) family, 19 years old, and this under the pretext of religion, both of

---

[1] A mistake, he was 32.

them having professed the Roman Catholic faith. In
Lyons, where he resides at present, he is much honored,
and gives it to be understood that he will return to
England no more. His young relative is constantly
seen with him in public, as a kind of protest that
there is no guilty concealment between them.[1] "

So runs the report from France. That this elope-
ment in high life caused a great sensation in England
we gather from other documents. The Italian minister
Lotti (whom Lord Herbert of Cherbury calls ' my good
friend Loty') wrote from London to the Secretary of
the Grand-Duke of Tuscany on July 13th 1605 : " The
Queen (Anne of Denmark) is much put out because
a married cavalier, Sir Robert Dudley, who they say
is a natural son of the Earl of Leicester, has last night
carried off a maid of honor of whom he was enamoured.
Strict orders were promptly given out, but at present
we have heard no news. This gentleman is about
35 years of age, of exquisite stature, with a fair beard,
and noble appearance. The fact has created great
scandal."

(The first and last parts are in cypher.)[2]

On the 20th of July, Signor Lotti again writes:
" That Court Lady, niece of the Lord High Admiral,
who they say ran off with Sir Robert Dudley, himself
nephew of an Admiral, has been stopped at *Cales* (Calais) by the Governor of that city; the expedition from
here arriving almost at the same time as the fugitives.
But as he found that she had taken this step, not for
love, but with the object of entering a monastery and

---

[1] We find from other sources that she dressed as his page.
[2] See Appendix, n. VII.

serving God in the true religion, I do not know whether
the French will let her be brought back by force; on
the contrary it is believed they will allow her to follow
out her holy inspiration." (Oh! naughty Elizabeth
Southwell, to be a week or two later walking about
the streets of Lyons in no conventual guise.)

The King ignored the love story, but expressed
himself disgusted in the extreme at Dudley's secession
from the Protestant faith. Here Lotti adds in cypher:
" The chief reason is that his Majesty does not want
Catholic subjects, especially when they are brave and
worthy men.[1] "

Having proved himself a free man according to
his new religion, and perhaps still more according to
his own desires, Dudley lost no time in legalizing as
far as possible his union with Elizabeth Southwell.
He presumed on their position as new converts to
obtain the Pope dispensation from the laws of con-
sanguinity, without by the way mentioning the little
impediment of a wife and four children in England.
The dispensation given, they were duly married at
Lyons, in spite of his wife Alice, who wrote to express
her willingness to turn Roman Catholic and join him,
bringing her children with her.

All this is told in a letter from Antonio Standen
addressed *Al molto illustre Sig. Belisario Vinta Cav. di
San Stefano, mio Sig. osserv. Livorno,* and dated Rome,
January 27th 1607. It speaks also of King James' anger
against Dudley for his marriage and assumption of the
title of Earl of Warwick.[2]

---

[1] See Appendix, n. VIII.
[2] See Appendix, n. IX.

As to this Antonio Standen, there is a letter from him to the Grand-Duke of Tuscany: dated — *Grasinne* (Gray's Inn or Gravesend?) *ne' borghi di Londra alli 7 luglio 1595.*[1] There is also a notice of Standen, by no means flattering, on the page facing the letter. It proves him to have been a spy of Queen Elizabeth's, living at Florence and professing Catholicism.

---

[1] The letter is in the Archivio Mediceo, Filza 4185.

PART III.

DUDLEY AS SHIP-BUILDER.

Dudley did not stay long in Lyons. He had a great wish to live in Florence, and thither he wended his way with Elizabeth as soon as they were married.

There is a document from him in the Medicean archives, written in French, wherein he craves the Grand-Duke's protection, as he wishes to establish himself in Florence, and enter the service of his Serene Excellency. He then sets forth his attainments, especially in the matter of ship-building and nautical and military command.[1]

The Grand-Duke though pleased with his appearance, and delighted with his marine talents, nevertheless took every means to obtain information about him before giving him the *entrée* to his Court. There is a 'minute' of the Florentine Secretary, to Lotti, Minister at London, dated March 17th 1607, asking for information about Dudley, and protesting that the

---

[1] See Appendix, n. X.

Grand-Duke in protecting him has no intention to offend the English King, etc. Information was also requested from Lyons, and from London by private means. The Medicean archives (filza 4185) contain several of the *relazioni* in answer to these enquiries, from some of which we have already quoted. There is also a rough draft of a letter from the Grand-Duke of Tuscany to the Earl of Northampton, March 17th 1607, saying : " The Earl of Warwick as your Lordship is aware has come to reside in these my dominions that he may be able to live a quiet life, according to the religion which till now he has always observed. Besides the information I have received of his merits and valour, I have the more willingly received him, on account of his relationship with your illustrious Lordship, and knowing from him the love you bear towards him." He then says a good word for Dudley's loyalty towards King James, to whom he is a *fedel vassallo*, and begs the Earl to act a father's part to Dudley, and maintain him in the good grace of his Majesty.'

As soon as the Grand-Duke had satisfied himself about Dudley's antecedents, at least as much as was revealed to him, he took him into his service ; and we find that in 1607 Dudley had already begun ship-building for the Grand-Duke. Targione (*Aggrandamento*, vol. I, pag. 79, etc.) says : " In the Court Diary kept by Cesare Tinghi I find that in 1607 a vessel with a square sail, and also oars, was built from the designs of the Earl of Warwick, and that a galleon also designed by him was launched at Leghorn on March 20th 1608, and baptized with the name of *San Gio-*

' See Appendix, n. XI.

vanni Battista" (St. John Baptist). *Apropos* of this vessel, Dudley, in his Architecture, has the following marginal note in Italian, after one of his *simetrie* or mathematical proportions for ship-building: "Of this symmetry the Duke made the Galleon *St. Giovanni Battista* for the Grand-Duke Ferdinand. She carried 64 *pezzi grossi* (great guns), was a rare and strong sailer, of great repute, and the terror of the Turks in these seas. Alone and unassisted she captured the Captain galleon of the Great Lord (*Gran Signore*) twice her own size and valuing a million. She also, without assistance from the others, fought the Grand Turk's fleet of 48 Galleys and 2 'Galliazze,' and made the *Generalissimo Bassia* (Bashaw) of the sea in person to fly, as she very nearly captured his Galley."

Dudley was certainly living much at Pisa and Leghorn in the years 1607-1608, where he seems to have had constant employment in the arsenal. Lotti writing from London March 13th 1607[1] says: "His Excellency (Sir Thomas Challoner, tutor of Prince Henry) showed me the design for a ship made at Leghorn by the Earl of Warwick, and he also showed me another which he said was more perfect than any."

It seems that Dudley wanted to get his old instructor in ship-building, Mathew Baker, of the Deptford Docks over to Italy to assist in building the Italian Fleet. Here is a letter of Signor Lotti from London, May 23rd 1607, written all in cypher:[2] "In my last letter of the 16th inst. I told your Highness that I had been at Deptford, and under pretence of knowing something about ship-

---

[1] Archivio Mediceo, Filza 4188.
[2] Archivio Mediceo, Filza 4188. Original in Italian.

building induced Mathew Caccher[1] to come and spend a
morning with me in London. I then thought he would
accept the offer of going over to Italy in the service
of your Highness. But notwithstanding that he is ill
satisfied here, and being now old no longer suits the
heads of the profession, and that he has so little employment, that for two years he has not drawn a penny
of salary — knowing also that with you he would have
good pay, yet he decidedly, though much to his regret,
excuses himself from coming, solely on account of his
great age, he being 77 years old, and looking even
more. He tells me if I will go to Deptford again, he
will give me the models of some of his ships, hoping
thus to be useful to your Highness even here. Asking
me about his pupil Sir Robert Dudley, he expressed
how willingly he would have taught his profession in
Italy to oblige him. Then he told me there was a
young man whom he had instructed, — but as yet he
was unknown, or he would not be allowed to leave
the kingdom, — and he would see if this youth would
accept service under your Highness..... We are expect-
ing the return of that Naval Captain who brought
orders from Sir Robert Dudley, and will send every
thing (i. e. the arms bought in England for the Grand-
Duke) under his care....."

Lotti's letters to the Grand-Duke at this time did
not much assist Dudley's standing at the Tuscan Court.
He writes much about a Captain Janvier, one of Dudley's master mariners — probably the one spoken of

---

[1] A letter to Lotti April 10th 1607 from the Tuscan Court offering
this man the appointment, at double the salary he received in England, gives the name as Matthew Baker. See Appendix, n. XII, Lotti
must have misread it.

above — who had promised information about Dudley's French marriage, but never seems to turn up to give it. There is great mystery about this, but it ends in the revelation of the whole story of Dudley's wife left in England and the consequent illegality of his present marriage; of the English King calling the Pope to account for the dispensation given on false evidence, and the Pope's anger thereupon. In fact Lotti takes every thing with the English colouring (as did his successor Salvetti, the next Italian " resident " in London) and puts the very worst construction on it all.

On February 4th 1608 he writes in cypher : " The King of his own accord spoke of Sir Robert Dudley and said : ' If he had been a traitor to my own person and state, I should expect from his Highness the Grand-Duke some real sign of friendship; but as he has only erred in lightness and dishonour, I should not wish to drive him out of His Serene Highness's state; yet that he should receive Dudley in his house, and honour him as he does, seems very strange to me. He (Dudley) has a wife and children here, the Pope has annulled his marriage to the woman he has with him,[1] and I, for my part, hold him incapable of any honorable action.' "

This comes rather strongly from the King who only a few months earlier, October 17th 1607, had sent Dudley, — so Lotti writes, — an order of recall to England, with a promise of an Earldom, and the title of Earl of Warwick.[2] If he were such a miscreant, why did James hold out these inducements for his return to England ?

---

[1] The King mistakes here, the Pope did not annul the marriage.

[2] Archivio Mediceo, Filza 4188 (new numeration). Letter from Lotti, London, to Cavalier Vinta, Florence. See Appendix, n. XIII.

The mother of Robert Dudley also figures in this same letter, and in another of October 24th. In the first Lotti says that the Countess of Stafford often applies to him for news of her son; and in the latter, he encloses a letter from her to Dudley, adding this mysterious little sentence: " I cannot clearly say, not having official notice from the court, but I well understand that there are attempts towards a compromise made by the Viscount de Lisle the Queen's chamberlain, who is the party opposing the pretentions of the said Earl of Warwick."

This compromise was never made. Dudley would not accept an Earldom as a compensation for acknowledging himself illegitimate, and his mother no true wife; and till this slur was taken off he refused to return to England.

Perhaps he realized that a worthy future was opening before him in Italy. As a naval man he had at once seen the great adaptability of Leghorn as an international port, and also opened the Grand-Duke's eyes to its capabilities. Within a few years Leghorn, thanks to Dudley, had risen to importance, and was rapidly becoming a great commercial port.

" I have heard from some living who have visited those parts," says Anthony Wood, " that this our author Robert Dudley was the chief instrument of causing the said Duke not only to fortify it and make it a *scala franca*, that is, a free port, but of setting an English factory there, and of drying the fens between that and Pisa. At which time also our author induced many English merchants that were his friends to go and reside there."

His work at Leghorn is thus referred to by Dudley

in his *Arcano del Mare: Di quivi verso mezzogiorno si trova Livorno, il quale è porto di gran considerazione per commercio e la spiaggia è buona, ma il Molo è d' invenzione dell' autore, ed è buonissimo porto, e sicuro per navi e galere per tutti i venti.* On page 136 of the *Arcano* is a plan for the fortifications of the port and mole of Leghorn, and on page 138 is another sketch under which Dudley has written: " The scalle of Brace; each Brace 2 English feet " (The scale of Braccie, each Braccia, etc.).

In his " Military Architecture " we find this plan thus mentioned by Dudley: " The 5th simetrie regular, of 7 *Bollowards* (*baluardo* — large bastion) somewhat differing from the former conteyning the situation and new Porte of Livorno, as myselfe both invented and dessined it for his heyghnes (sic) the great Ducke; and withall shewing how this regular forme would well have agread for the fortefiing the same Towne and Ports, and in my opinion is more perfect than it."

The Italian archives of these three years 1607-1609 show the great interest the Grand-Duke Ferdinand took in Dudley. There are letters from the Tuscan Court giving Lotti instructions to try and re-instate Dudley in the favour of the King, adding that " here he is known as a worthy knight, and of the utmost goodwill, and that he could not possibly entertain any idea of disloyalty or ill-faith towards King James or his state." Again: " It seems to us that this Knight shows himself every day more worthy of our protection, and especially of our efforts to prove in Rome the validity of his last marriage. We will therefore that you do your best to elucidate the matter in his favor as far as you can for truth's sake."

Lotti, as we have seen, took the English view —
that is the view held by the powerful and interested
party of Sydney and Essex, — and did little on Dudley's
behalf, so little that in 1608 Dudley asked the Duke
to legalize his marriage ; his wife also wrote a supplica-
tion to the Duchess pleading her right on the score
of the illegality of her husband's former marriages,[1]
and the Pope's permission granted for this union with
herself. Whatever the Grand-Duke thought of the
conflicting evidence laid before him, he was politic
enough to take Dudley's side, and retain a most valuable
master of the marine ; and when Ferdinand Ist died
in 1608, Cosimo II who succeeded him remained equally
Dudley's friend. During this time Dudley's home in
Florence was in *Via dell'Amore,* where he was a tenant
of Cavalier Annibale Orlandini ; and here in 1609, his
first child by his wife Elizabeth Southwell was born,
and named Maria, and in 1610, a second child, Cosimo,
was born.

About this time Dudley wrote or began to write
his first book on military and naval Architecture, for he
always dignifies ship-building by this term. This exists
in three large half-bound volumes in manuscript, in
the *Specola* or Museum of Natural History, Florence,
where Dudley's nautical and mathematical instruments
are preserved. The first two volumes treat of the building of ships, and were written in English.

A note, proem to the third volume, which speaks
of seven sorts of *simetries* (symmetries), supposed to
be written by Dudley's master-mariner Abram Kendal,
says : " As to the art of Architecture, in regard to

---

[1] Archivio Mediceo, Filza 4185.

the above said symmetries, the Duke has written an
entire volume with figures of many kinds of vessels,
but it is written in the English language. About the
fortifications of Ports, and the method of doing so, he
has also written in English, for at that time, about 1610,
the Duke did not know enough of the Italian tongue
to write that volume in the *Volgare,* but perhaps he
will do so when he has the leisure. He has also written
a larger volume than these, on the true and real art
of navigation, but this was written in England, with
many curious mathematical and astronomical figures,
and other things never before seen, such as nautical
Instruments for the observation of the variations of
longitude and latitude, and others for the horizontal
and spiral Navigation, and about the Great Circles.
Of these, however, common sailors understand little, as
also about the Marine Management and discipline, and
about sea fighting and squadrons, which are amply
treated in these volumes."

In this rare MS. we find that Dudley heads the
first part " First Chapter of my Booke touching the
34 simetries, following: their use and qualleties." It is
difficult to say whether Dudley's orthography and dic-
tion were more original in writing English or Italian.

Here is his heading, several years later, to the third
volume in Italian: *Il 3zo volume di Vascelli di Guerra
secondo l' inventione di me Duca di Northumbria et della
mia esperienza per più di 40 anni. In quale li disegni
stesso bastano, senza altro discorso lungo.* The idiom, be
it observed, is entirely English, though the words are
Italian.

Here is his own account of the second volume:
" The second volume or Tombe (Tome) of my Worke

touching Marinarie, and Conteyning 2 Bookes, — the
one of the archetecture of al sorte, and of vessels of
warre. The other of the fortefiing or ordering of
Ports, Invented by R. Dudley, Earl of Warwick and
Leycester sole heyre to John, Ducke of Northumberland. "

In the fourth page of the second volume the author
thus praises his favorite 12th *simetrie*. He had by this
time got beyond the original seven.

" The 12th Simetrie is the reall Thirds, which of all
proportions is most perfecte for vessels with 2 Deckes,
being thirdes in lenth and breadth, thirds in *Rache* (sic).
third in draught, thirds in flower ; and the proportion
according to my vessel, is the longest and greatest of
burthen and force, it is possible to make ; being called
by me *Gallione Perfecta ;* and in burthen will be
neare 1200 tonns. This vessell is of so much force in
fight eather to offende, as wite cann not adde more
to the force, and of sayle excellent beyonde all other
Galleons. She can carie 90 of my Demicanns,[1] which
sorte of peace is only of greate importance in a sea
battayle and of so much consequence is this force, as
the greatest Gallion in Englande carieth not 18 Demi-
cannons : these vessels are cheafly fitt to be the Royall
' Gallions Perfecta ' of a great Kinge's settled navie, and
not be imployed but uppon great occasion to defende
the State or such like being of so greate charge so
great a strenth to a state as not fitt otherwise to be
adventured uppon lesse occasion."

By which we see that Dudley had supreme faith

---

[1] Demi-cannons, an invention of Dudley's for use on the Tuscan
galleons.

in his own ships, though his enemies sometimes detracted from their credit. The last volume begins:

" Haveing written in former times 4 bookes of marinarie, as before mentioned; I thought it most necesserie to finish this fifth being of so great importance, both for strenth of Princes, and saftie of merchante goodes as nothing more utill, as by the discourses following will easely by explayned; especially being a worke not hetherto perfected to anie great purpose (more than vulgarly knowne) by anie, the curiositie whereof made me more paynfully serch into the debth of this arte and with good succes have accomplished my desiers, and promises by Practes herein, both in the time of Don Ferdinando great Ducke of Toscana of famos memorie as allso by his worthie sonne Don Cosimo now greate Ducke of Toscana, from both of them having receaved more favours and obligations then I coulde meritt, or necessarie here to be mentioned: and therefor not to diverte the reader from the matter, I will only secure him that whatsoever is conteyned in this worke is different from the orders of all others in these Simetries, as well from those in England as in these other p^{ts} and not taught me by anie, but invented merely (with God's assistance) by the practise, experiens, and knowledge it hath pleased his Infinite Goodness to imploy in me, and afforde by my Practise, contemplations, and studies herein ; and therefor doe desier the practise and imploymente thereof — may be cheafly for God's service to the suppression of all as I intend Infidelitie."

It is probable that this early and unpublished treatise was the germ of the future *Arcano del Mare*.

In 1610 also, Dudley is named in a *privilegio* (pa-

tent) which shows his activity of mind and inventive
genius. It is thus headed :

X Ottobre 1610.

*Al Conte Ruberto di Warwich privilegio di nuova in-
venzione per aumentare la seta.*[1] (To Earl Robert of
Warwick, a patent for a new invention to improve silk.)
Whether this new invention to improve the quality
and increase the quantity of silk, as well as improve its
manufacture and design, has anything to do with that
branch of industry having continued to flourish in Italy
till now, one cannot say. It gave him the exclusive
right of using the invention at Pisa for twenty years.

---

[1] Archivio Centrale Florence, Class IX, n. IX, stanza 3, armadio XII.

Part IV.

DUDLEY A FLORENTINE COURTIER.

In 1611-1612 Dudley was negotiating for a marriage between Prince Henry, eldest son of King James Ist of England, and a Princess of Tuscany. The negotiations were conducted partly by Ottaviano Lotti, whose despatches we have quoted in the last chapter, and by Sir Thomas Challoner, who had been Prince Henry's tutor. Dudley had probably suggested the marriage, in order to propitiate the English court and to serve his patrons the Medici.[1] It may be observed, that the youngest sister of Elizabeth Southwell, who married Sir Edward Rodney in 1614, was a lady of the privy chamber to Anne of Denmark, wife of James Ist of England, and may perhaps have advised and assisted Dudley in the affair.

Dudley was at the same time engaged in negotiations with Prince Henry for the sale to him of the great Kenilworth estate. All these aspirations were

---

[1] See Appendix, n. XIV.

doomed to be disappointed by the death of Prince Henry in 1612.

In the Kenilworth affair, as in his law-suit, Dudley was treated harshly and unfairly. His estates were seized by the Crown, and granted to others, as were also the titles of Leicester and of Warwick. The patent of King Charles Ist creating Alicia Dudley, born Leigh, Duchess Dudley, dated 22nd May 1644, Oxford,[1] bears witness to the injustice done at this time to Robert Dudley. The said patent was probably drawn up by Holbourne, Solicitor general to Charles Ist, who was son-in-law to Alicia Dudley.

In spite of his wrongs, Dudley and his wife attended the Florentine Court as Earl and Countess of Warwick, and indeed took a prominent position there. In 1612 Dudley appeared as Judge in a *Barriera,* or Tilting tournament, followed by a Masquerade, held in Florence on the 17th and 19th of February 1613.

The fête is fully described in a book printed by Bartolommeo Sermartelli in 1613. For those who would like to know how Dudley and the Florentines amused themselves we will quote it.

On February 3rd a grand game of *calcio* (football) on Piazza Santa Croce, which all the Court had attended, was followed by a ball at the Palazzo Pitti. The guests danced till the third hour of night (about nine o'clock) when suddenly was heard in the Palace a great sound of drums and trumpets; and not knowing what this portended, every one remained breathless (*restò sospeso l' animo*) when behold, a herald with a great number of torch bearers entered the Hall. He was dressed in

---

[1] See Appendix, n. VI.

military costume, with a wand in his hand. . His sur-
coat was of cloth of gold with the arms of Eros and
a broken thunderbolt beautifully embroidered on it.
This herald was accompanied by 10 pages carrying
torches, and richly dressed in white and gold *Erme-
sino* [1] with plumed caps of a new and bizarre shape.
Having entered the room with a proud warlike mien,
the herald spoke thus : " The good Knight Fidamante
and the Knight of Immortal Love, Champions of omnipotent and insuperable Love, moderator of heaven and
earth, tamer of the fiercest beasts, have sent me to
this company of famous heroes, to present a challenge
which they are ready to support with the lance, and
with the pen." With these words he threw down
some papers, which a dwarf, who was with him, pre-
sented to their Royal Highnesses, and the cavaliers,
and departed.

The challenge came from Prince Ferdinand De Medici
and Don Paolo Giordano Orsini, who offered to fight
any other knights, for the good cause of the wrongs
of Love, and of Venus, who had come to Florence from
Cyprus and found themselves neglected.

The tournament was held on the 17th of February
in the theatre of the Palazzo Pitti, a room about
25 yards square, which was ornamented with statues
and frescoes ; it had a stage and scenery at the end,
and boxes and raised seats all round.

The knights fought in the centre. Ten Senators
were deputed to elect 20 gentlemen as umpires among
whom Sir Robert Dudley, who was famous in all knightly

---

[1] A light Persian silk fabric so called from Ormuz, whence it was
first imported into Europe.

exercises, was one. Two large boxes were erected at opposite ends. The Grand-ducal party were in one box, and the umpires in the other, among these were Signor Francesco del Monte, General of the Ducal infantry; Marchese Pireteo Malvezzi, Master of the horse to H. R. H.; *Il Signor Conte di Veruich* (Warwick), Englishman; Signor Conte Giulio, Estense; Tassone, Honorary Secretary; the Grand-Duke's Secretary; Don Giovanni De Medici; Pier Capponi, Constable of the order of St. Stephen; and several other cavaliers of the same order.

Then follows a detailed account of the tournament, with a description of the knights' dresses, their songs, and grand deeds, their fanciful names, and the celestial gods and goddesses that appeared to help and to hinder the champions as they did in old Homer's days. The poems and dialogue were written by Ottavio Rinuccini. After the tournament all the actors made a torchlight procession through the city.

On the 16th December 1612 Dudley's fourth child was born and the Archduchess Maria Maddalena, after whom she was named, was her god-mother.

This Archduchess was the daughter of the Archduke Charles II, and wife of Cosimo II Grand-Duke of Tuscany. Her being god-mother to the daughter of the Dudley's shows how much they were esteemed at Court.

To propitiate King James Ist of England it is said that Dudley wrote and sent to him in 1613 the pamphlet 'For bridling the impertinence of Parliament.' Craik[1] says that Wood gives the title as 'A discourse

---

[1] CRAIK's *Romance of the Peerage*, vol. III, pag. 133–137.

to correct the Exorbitances of Parliaments, and to enlarge the King's revenue.'

No great notice of this paper was taken till the commencement of the next reign, when, in the year 1629, it was suddenly raised into notoriety by an information being filed by the Attorney general in the Star Chamber, against certain individuals for dispersing copies of it. The accused individuals were no less distinguished persons than the Earls of Bedford, Somerset, and Clare, Sir Robert Cotton, the great antiquary and collector, John Selden and Oliver St. John, all eminent Parliamentary leaders of the popular party. They were charged with an attempt to make the Government odious by pretending that there was a design to adopt the measures recommended in the paper, etc. The prosecution was stopped by the King's order, on its being discovered what the paper really was.

The prosecution had disastrous consequences for Sir Robert Cotton, who died 6th May 1613.

The *Biographia Britannica* describes Dudley's tract ' as being in all respects as singular and as dangerous a paper as ever fell from the pen of man.' It was printed and published by the opponents of the court in 1641 immediately after the execution of the Earl of Strafford, with a title attributing it to the pen of that nobleman : ' Strafford's plot discovered,' etc.

Horace Walpole, who believed Dudley to have been the legitimate son of the great Earl of Leicester, observes when speaking of this paper in his ' Royal and Noble authors,' that, " considering how enterprising and dangerous a minister Dudley might have made, and what a variety of talents were called forth by his misfortunes, it would seem to have been fortunate both for himself and his country, that he was unjustly deprived of the honors, to which his birth gave him pretensions."

Dudley may have considered it an act of homage to the Grand-Duke to recommend his political measures in England, for the tract is little more than a description of Italian polity after all. We here give it entire as proof of this.

HOW TO BRIDLE THE EXHORBITANCES OF PARLIAMENT
BY ROBERT DUDLEY, EARL OF WARWICK.[1]

The proposition for your Majesty's service, containeth two parts: the one to secure your state, and to bridle the Impertinency of Parliaments: the other, to increase Your Majesty's Revenue, much more than it is. Touching the First, having considered divers means, I find none so important to strengthen Your Majesty's regal authority, against all Oppositions and Practises of troublesome Spirits, and to bridle .them, than to fortify your kingdom, by having a Fortress in every Chief Town, and important Place thereof, furnished with Ordinance, Munition, and faithful Men, as they ought to be, with all other Circumstances fit for to be digested in a Business of this Nature; ordering withal, the Trained soldiers of the country to be united in one Dependency with the said Fort as well to secure their Beginning, as to succour them in any Occasion of Suspect, and also to retain and keep their Arms for more Security, whereby the Countries are no less to be brought in Subjection, than the Cities themselves, and consequently the whole Kingdom, Your Majesty having by this Course the Power thereof in your own Hands. The Reasons of the Suggests are these: 1st That in Policy, there is a greater Tie of the People by Force and Ne-

---

[1] From the *Historical collections of Private Passages of State,* etc. (1618–1629), by JOHN RUSHWORTH of Lincoln's Inn, Esq. London, 1721; vol. I. Appendix, pag. 12.

cessity, than merely by Love and Affection, for by the One, the
Government resteth always secure; but by the Other, no longer
than the People are contented; 2nd It forceth obstinate Subjects
to be no more presumptuous, than it pleaseth your Majesty to
permit them; 3rd That to leave a State unfurnished, is to give
the Bridle thereof to the Subjects, when by the contrary, it
resteth only in the Prince's Hands; 4th That modern Fortresses
take long Time in winning, with such Charge and Difficulty, as
no Subjects in these Times have Means probable to attempt
them; 5th That it is a sure Remedy against Rebellion, and
popular Mutinies, or against foreign Powers, because they cannot
well succeed, when by this Course the apparent means is taken
away, to force the King and Subject upon a doubtful Fortune
of a set Battle, as was the Cause, that moved the pretended
Invasion against the Land, attempted by the King of Spain in
the Year 1588; 6th That Your Majesty's Government is the more
secure, by the People's more subjection, and by their Subjection,
Your Parliament must be forced consequently to alter their Style,
and to be conformable to Your Will and Pleasure; for their
Words and Opposition import nothing, where the Power is in
Your Majesty's own Hands, to do with them what you please,
being indeed the chief Purpose of this Discourse, and the secret
Intent thereof, fit to be concealed from any English at all, either
Counsellors of State or other. For these, and divers other weighty
Reasons, it may be considered in this Place, to make Your Majesty
more powerful and strong, some Orders be observed, that are
used in fortified Countries, the Government whereof imports
as much as the States themselves, I mean in Times of Doubt
or Suspect, which are these; Imprimis: That none wear Arms
or Weapons at all, either in City or Country, but such as your
Majesty may think fit to priviledge, and they to be enrolled;
2nd That as many High-ways as conveniently may be done, be
made passable through those Cities and Towns fortified, to
constrain the Passengers to travel through them; 3rd That the
Soldiers of Fortresses be sometimes chosen of another Nation,
if subject to the same Prince; but howsoever, not to be born
in the same Province, or within forty or fifty Miles of the Fortress, and not to have Friends or Correspondency near it;

4th That at all the Gates of each walled Town be appointed
Officers, not to suffer any unknown Passenger to pass, without
a Ticket, showing from whence he came, and whither to go.
And that the Gates of each City be shut all Night, and keys
kept by the Mayor or Governor; 5th Also Inn-keepers to deliver
the Names of all unknown Passengers that lodge in their Houses;
and if they stay suspiciously at any Time to present them to
the Governor. Whereby dangerous Persons seeing these strict
Courses, will be more wary of their Actions, and thereby mis-
chievous Attempts will be prevented. All which being referred
to your Majesty's wise Consideration, it is meet for me withal
to give you some Satisfaction of the Charge and Time to perform what is purposed, that you may not be discouraged in the
Difficulty of the one, or Prolongation of the Other; both which
Doubts are resolved in one and the same Reason, in respect
that in England each chief Town commonly hath a ruinated
Castle, well seated for strength, whose Foundation and stones
remaining, may be both quickly repaired for this Use, and with
little Charge and Industry made strong enough, I hope, for this
Purpose, within the Space of one Year; by adding withal Bul-
warks and Rampiers for the Ordnance, according to the Rules
of Fortification. The Ordnance for these Forts may be of Iron,
not to disfurnish your Majesty's Navy, or be at a greater Charge
than is needful.

To maintain Yearly the Fort, I make account an ordinary
Pay, three thousand Men will be sufficient, and will require
Forty thousand Pound charge per Annum, or thereabouts, being
an Expense that inferior Princes undergo, for their necessary
Safety. All which prevention added to the invincible Sea-force
your Majesty hath already and will have, will make you the most
powerful and obeyed King of the World. Which I could likewise confirm by many Examples, but I omit them for brevity,
and not to confuse your Majesty with too much matter. Your
Majesty may find by the Scope of this Discourse, the Means
shewed in general to bridle your Subjects, that may be either
discontent or obstinate. So likewise am I to conclude the same
Intent particularly, against the Perverseness of your Parliament
as well to suppress that pernicious Humour, as to avoid their

Oppositions against your Profit, being the second Part to be discoursed on: And therefore have first thought fit, for better prevention thereof to make known to your Majesty the Purpose of a general Oath your Subjects may take for sure avoiding of all Rubs, that may hinder the Conclusion of these Businesses. It is further meant, That no Subject, upon Pain of High Treason, may refuse the same Oath, containing only Matter of Allegiance, and not scruples in Points of Conscience, that may give Pretence not to be denied. The Effect of the Oath is this, That all Your Majesty's Subjects do acknowledge you to be as absolute a King and Monarch within your Dominions as is among the Christian Princes; and your Prerogative as great; Whereby you may and shall of yourself, by your Majesty's Proclamation, as well as other sovereign Princes doing the like either make Laws, or reverse any made, with any other Act, so great a Monarch as yourself may do, and that without further consent of a Parliament, or need to call them at all in such Cases, considering that the Parliament in all matters, excepting Causes to be sentenced at the highest Court, ought to be subject unto your Majesty's Will, to give the negative or affirmative Conclusion, and not be constrained by their Impertinencies to any Inconvenience, appertaining to your Majesty's royal Authority, and this, notwithstanding any bad Pretence or Custom to the contrary in Practise which indeed were fitter to be offered a Prince elected, without other Right, than to your Majesty, born successively King of England, Scotland and Ireland, and your Heirs for ever; and so received not only of your subjects, but also of the whole World. How necessary the dangerous supremacy of Parliaments' Usurpation is to be prevented, the Example of Lewis the Eleventh, King of France, doth manifest, who found the like Opposition as your Majesty doth, and by his Wisdom suppressed it. And, to the Purpose here intended, which is not to put down altogether Parliaments and their Authority, being in many Cases very necessary and fit, but to abridge them so far, as they seek to derogate from your Majesty's regal Authority, and Advancement of your Greatness. The caution in offering the aforesaid Oath, may require some Policy, for the easier Passage at first, either by singular or particular Tractaction,

and that so near about one Time over the Land, as one Government may not know what the other intendeth, so it may pass
the easier, by having no Time of Combination or Opposition.
There is another Means also more certain than this to bring to
pass the Oath more easily, as also your Profit, and what else
pretended; which here I omit for brevity, requiring a long
Discourse by itself, and have set it down in particular Instructions to inform your Majesty.

The second Part of this Discourse is, touching your Majesty's
Profit, after your State is secured. Wherein I should observe
both some reasonable Content to the People, as also consider
the great Expenses that Princes have now-a-days, more than
in Times past, to maintain their Greatness, and safety of their
Subjects, who, if they have not Wit or Will to consider their
own Interest so much indifferently, your Majesty's Wisdom must
repair their Defects, and force them to it by compulsion, but
I hope there shall be no such cause, in Points so reasonable
to increase your Majesty's Revenue, wherein I set down divers
Means for your gracious self to make choice of either All or
Part at your Pleasure, and to put it in execution by such
Degrees and Cautions, as your great Wisdom shall think fit in
a Business of this Nature.

Imprimis: The first Means or Course intended to increase
your Majesty's Revenues or Profits withal is of greatest Consequence, and I call it a Decimation, being so termed in Italy,
where in some Parts it is in Use, importing the Tenth of all
Subjects' Estates, to be paid as a yearly Rent to their Prince,
and as well monied men in Towns, as Landed men in the Countries, their Value and Estates esteemed justly as it is to the
true Value, though with Reason; and this paid yearly in money.
Which Course applied in England for your Majesty's Service,
may serve instead of Subsidies, Fifteens, and such like, which
in this Case are fit to be released, for the Subject's Benefit and
Content, in recompense of the said Decima, which will yield
your Majesty more in certainty, than they do casually by Five
hundred thousand Pounds per annum at the least. Item, That
when your Majesty hath gotten Money into your Hands by some
Courses to be set down, it would be a profitable Course to in-

crease your entrada,[1] to buy out all Estates and Leases upon your own Lands in such Sort, as they be made no Losers whereby having your Lands free, and renting it out to the true Value, as it is most in Use, and not employed as heretofore, at an old Rent, and small Fines, you may then rent it out for at least four or five Times more Money, than the old Rent comes unto. So as if your Majesty's Lands be already but sixty thousand Pounds per Ann., by this Course it will be augmented at the least Two hundred thousand Pounds per Annum, and to buy out the Tenants Estates will come to a small matter by the Course, to make them no Losers considering the Gain they have already made upon the Land. And this is the rather to be done, and the present Course changed, because it hath been a Custom used merely to cousen the King. Item, Whereas most Princes do receive the Benefit of Salt in their own Hands, as a Matter of great Profit, because they receive it at the lowest Price possible, and rent it at double gain yearly, the same Course used by your Majesty, were worth at least One hundred and fifty thousand Pounds per Annum. It is likewise in other Parts that all Weights and Measures of the Land, either in private Houses, Shops, or publick Markets, should be viewed to be just, and sealed once a Year, paying to the Prince for it, which in England, applied to your Majesty, with Order to pay sixpence for the Sealing of each said Weight or Measure, would yield near Sixty thousand Pounds per Annum. Item, Though all Countries pay a Gabella[2] for Transportation of Cloth, and so likewise in England; yet, in Spain, there is Impost upon the Wools, which in England is so great a Wealth and Benefit to the Sheep-Masters, as they may well pay you five Pounds per Cent of the true Value at the Shearing, which I conceive may be worth One hundred and forty thousand Pounds per Annum. Item, Whereas the Lawyers' Fees and Gains in England be excessive, to your Subjects' Prejudice, it were better for your Majesty to make Use thereof, and impose on all Causes sentenced with the Party, to pay five Pounds per Cent of the true Value

---

[1] Dudley means *Entrata,* income.
[2] Gabella, an Italian word for dues of Custom.

that the Cause hath gained him, and for recompense thereof,
to limit all Lawyers' Fees and Gettings, whereby the Subject
shall save more in Fees and Charges, than he giveth to your
Majesty in the Gabella which I believe may be worth, one year
with another, Fifty thousand Pounds. Item, Whereas the Inns
and Victualling houses in England are more chargeable to the
Travellers, than in other Countries, it were good for your Majesty
to limit them to certain Ordinaries and raise besides a large
Imposition, as is used in Tuscany, and other Parts; that is, a
Prohibiting all Inns and Victualling-houses, but such as shall
pay it; and to impose upon the Chief Inns and Taverns, to pay
ten Pounds a year to your Majesty, and the worst five Pounds
per Annum, and all Ale-houses twenty Shillings per Annum,
more or less, as they are in Custom. Of all Sorts there are so
many in England, that this Impost may well yield One hundred
thousand pounds per Annum to your Majesty. Item, In Tuscany,
and other Parts, there is a Gabella of all Cattel, or Flesh, and
Horses sold in Markets, paying three or four per Cent of what
they are sold for, which by conjecture may be worth in England
two hundred thousand Pounds per Annum, using the like Custom
upon Fish, and other Victuals (Bread excepted) and for this
Cause, Flesh and Fish and Victuals in the Markets, to be prised
and sold by Weight, whereby the Subject saveth more in not
being cousened, than the Imposition impaireth them. Item: In
Tuscany is used a Taxation of seven per Cent, upon all Aliena-
tion of Lands to the true Value. As also seven per Cent upon
all Dowries, or Marriage-monies. The like, if it be justly used
in England, were worth at least One hundred thousand Pounds
per Annum; with many other Taxations upon Meal, and upon
all Merchandises in all Towns, as well as Port Towns, which
here I omit, with divers others, as not fit for England. And
in satisfaction of the Subject for these Taxes, your Majesty may
be pleased to release them of Wardships, and to enjoy all their
Estates at eighteen years old, and in the mean Time, their
Profits to be preserved for their own Benefit. And also in For-
feitures of Estate by condemnation, your Majesty may release
the Subject, as not to take the Forfeiture of their Lands, but
their Goods, High Treason only excepted; and to allow the

Counsel of Lawyers in case of Life and Death; as also not to
be condemned without two Witnesses, with such like Benefit,
which importeth much more their Good, then all the Taxations
named can prejudice them. Item, Some of the former Taxations
used in Ireland and in Scotland, as may easily be brought about
by the first Example thereof used in England, may very well
be made to increase your Revenue there, more than it is by
Two hundred thousand Pounds per Annum. Item, All Offices
in the Land great and small, in your Majesty's Grant, may be
granted, with Condition, to pay you a Part Yearly, according
to the Value. This, in Time, may be worth (as I conceive) One
hundred thousand Pounds per Annum: Adding also Notaries,
Attornies, and such like, to pay some Proportion Yearly towards
it, for being allowed by Your Majesty to practise, and prohibiting else any to practise in such Places. Item, To reduce your
Majesty's Household to Board-wages, as most other Princes do,
reserving some few Tables: this will save Your Majesty Sixty
thousand Pounds per Annum, and ease greatly the Subject
besides, both in Carriages and Provision, which is a good Reason,
that your Majesty in Honour might do it. Item, I know an
assured course in your Majesty's Navy, which may save at least
Forty thousand Pounds per Annum, which requiring a whole
Discourse by itself, I omit; only promise you to do it, when-
soever you command. Item, Whereas your Majesty's Laws do
command the strict keeping of Fasting-days, you may also prohibit
on those Days to eat Eggs, Cheese and White-meats, but only
such as are contented to pay Eighteen Pence a Year for the
Liberty to eat them, and the better Sort Ten Shillings. The
Employment of this may be for the Defence of the Land, in
maintaining the Navy, Garrisons, and such like, much after the
Fashion of a Crusado in Spain, as your Majesty knoweth, being
first begun there, under the Pretence to defend the Land against
the Moors. And the same used in England, as aforesaid, may
very well yield, one Year with another, One hundred thousand
Pounds, without any disgust to any, because it is at every One's
Choice to give it or no. Lastly, I have a Course upon the Ca-
tholicks, and very safe for your Majesty, being with their good-
liking as it may be wrought, to yield you presently at least

Two hundred thousand Pounds per Annum, by raising a certain
Value upon their Lands, and some other Impositions; which
requiring a long Discourse by itself, I will omit it here, setting it down in my Instructions; It will save your Majesty at
least One hundred thousand Pounds per Annum, to make it
Pain of Death, and confiscation of Goods and Lands, for any
of the Officiers to cousen you, which now is much to be feared
they do, or else they could not be so rich; and herein to allow
a fourth Part Benefit to them that shall find out the cousenage.
Here is not meant Officers of State, as the Lord Treasurer, etc.,
being Officers of the Crown. The Sum of all this Account
amounteth unto Two Millions, or Twenty hundred thousand
Pounds per Annum. Suppose it to be but One Million and a
half as assuredly your Majesty may make by these Courses set
down, yet it is much more than I promised in my Letter, for
your Majesty's Service. Besides, some Sums of Money in present,
by the Courses following: Imprimis: By the Prince's marriage,
to make all the Earls in England Grandees of Spain, and Principi, with such like Priviledges, and to pay Twenty thousand
Pounds apiece for it; 2nd As also, if you make them Fœditaries
of the Towns belonging to their Earldoms, if they will pay for
it besides, as they do to the King of Spain in the Kingdom of
Naples. And so likewise Barons, to be made Earls and Peers,
to pay Nineteen thousand Pounds apiece, I think might yield
Five hundred thousand Pounds, and oblige them more sure to
his Majesty; 3rd To make choice of Two hundred of the richest Men in England in Estate, that be not Noblemen, and make
them Titulate, as is used in Naples, and paying for it; that is,
a Duke Thirty thousand Pounds; a Marquess Fifteen thousand
Pounds: an Earl Ten thousand Pounds, and a Baron or Viscount
Five thousand Pounds. It is to be understood, that the antient
Nobility of Barons made Earls, are to precede these as Peers,
though these be made Marquesses or Dukes; this may raise a
Million of Pounds and more unto your Majesty. To make Gentlemen of low Quality, and Francklins, and rich Farmers, Esquires,
to precede them, would yield your Majesty also a great sum of
money in present. I know another Course to yield your Majesty
at least Three hundred thousand Pounds in Money, which as yet

the Time serveth not to discover until your Majesty be resolved to proceed in some of the former Courses, which till then I omit. Other Courses also, that may make present Money, I shall study for your Majesty's Service, and, as I find them out, acquaint you withal. Lastly, To conclude all these Discourses, by the Application of this Course used for your Profit, That it is not only the Means to make you the richest King that ever England had, but also the Safety augmented thereby to be most secure, besides what was shewed in the first Part of this Discourse, I mean, by the Occasion of this Taxation, and raising of Monies, your Majesty shall have Cause and Means to imploy in all Places of the Land so many Officers and Ministers, to be obliged to you for their own Good and Interest, as nothing can be attempted against your Person, or royal State, over Land, but some of them shall in all probability, have Means to find it out, and hinder it. Besides, this Course will detect many Discorders and Abuses in the publick Government, which were hard to be discovered by Men indifferent. To prohibit gorgeous and costly Apparel to be worn, but by Persons of good Quality, shall save the Gentry of the Kingdom much more Money, than they shall be taxed to pay unto your Majesty. Thus withal I take my Leave, and kiss your Gracious Hands, desiring Pardon for my Error I may commit herein.

Such was Dudley's advice to King James after a few years study of political finance at the Court of Tuscany. Fortunately his suggestions did not suit the English Government.

Since Dudley's arrival in Tuscany several changes had taken place. The Grand-Duke Ferdinand had died, and Cosimo II succeeded him. His wife was Maria Maddalena, daughter of the Archduke Charles of Austria, and she made Dudley her Grand Chamberlain.

In 1613 also Paolo Vinta, Prime Minister to the Grand-Duke, died, and was succeeded by Curzio Picchena. They both wrote many letters and despatches

regarding Dudley, to the Grand-Duke's agent Amerigo Salvetti who succeeded Lotti as Italian resident
in London.

On the 6th of April 1614, Dudley bought from Lodovico and Ferdinando, brothers, sons of Orazio, the son
of Luigi Rucellai, for the sum of four thousand scudi,
some house property in the parish of San Pancrazio in
Florence, where he built for himself a palace. On his
death in 1649 this passed to his descendants of the
Dudley and Paleotti families, was sold by them, and
is now the property of the Bordoni family. The site
is a wedge shaped piece of ground between the Via
della Spada, and Via della Vigna Nuova, with the very
narrow end facing Palazzo Strozzi. The illustration we
give is from an old water-colour showing in its original
position the loggia of the opposite Palazzo Corsi-Salviati
(now belonging to the Marchesa Arconati-Visconti born
Peyrat), before the Via de' Tornabuoni was enlarged.
It was removed to the other end, of the front of that
palace in the year 1864.

The principal front, consisting of four stories (including the ground floor which was let out for shops)
with ten windows to each story, looks on Via della
Vigna Nuova, and measures about one hundred and
thirty five feet in length. The truncated part of the
wedge facing the Via degli Strozzi, and on which
appear the Rucellai arms and a little tabernacle, is
only about six feet wide. It has been said that Bartolommeo Ammannati was the architect, but dates
render that doubtful. It is more probable that Dudley
himself designed or directed the building of the palace.
It was his town house till his death in 1649; there
eight of his children were born, and there his loving

DUDLEY HOUSE, AND LOGGIA CORSI BEFORE THE ENLARGEMENT OF VIA TORNABUONI, A. D. 1864.

and beloved wife Elizabeth Southwell died on September 10th 1631.[1]

In 1614 Lord Herbert of Cherbury was entertained by the Dudleys in Florence, as may be seen in his own account of the visit mentioned in the preface to this Memoir. In Lord Herbert's relation there is an evident mistake as to dates. He speaks of Dudley as having the title of Earl and Duke of Northumberland given to him by the Emperor. It is matter of notoriety that Dudley was not made Duke of Northumberland by the Emperor Ferdinand II before the year 1620. Lord Herbert also mentions, not very respectfully, " the handsome *Mrs Sudel,* whom he (Dudley) carried away with him out of England, and was there (in Florence) taken for his wife."

---

[1] In n. XV of the Appendix to this Memoir, there is an account of the purchase and sale, and a description of the palace and its successive owners.

PART V.

DUDLEY AS MASTER OF MARINE.

D<small>OMESTIC</small> events did not entirely absorb Dudley's mind at this time. He was much occupied at Pisa and Leghorn, in the building of ships, and in new inventions for their more speedy locomotion. He had enemies also, probably some Italian ship-builders or merchants who, jealous of his success, tried to throw discredit on his vessels, one of which had been named *St. Cosimo* after the Grand-Duke.

We will give a free translation of a postscript to a letter written by Dudley to Cav. *Sciolli* (or Cioli), Grand-Ducal Secretary, on March 31st, 1618.

" Since writing the above, I have received your Excellency's letters and doubt not that they[1] will write even more and worse things about the new galley, for I know their intentions. I am ready to assert in their presence that the new galley floats as well, and is

---

[1] The pronoun 'they' here is not explained, the persons referred to being evidently known to Cioli. See Appendix, n. XVI.

swifter than the *St. Cosimo,* but that if they want it to
answer the helm, they should not over-weight it with
more stones or sand, than they put in the other boats.
I do not believe that they do this from ignorance, it
being a common and well-known fact that too much
weight puts a vessel too deep in water. When a boat
is once proved to float well, and answer the helm, it does
not lose the qualities, therefore they must account for it
in this case. And further I reply, that even if it were
true that it sinks so deep as to impede its speed, I
certify his Royal Highness that in two days I would
remedy the defect by a stratagem of my own, which
has never been revealed. Of this you may be quite
sure. As to what Madame says of the *St. Cosimo,*
though it is my own building, I say with truth it
is the very best work, and her ship-masters could
not do better than imitate it. Yet even that at-
tracted such jealousy and hindrance, that it was kept
on the stocks two years before it could be brought
to perfection; so we must have patience also with this
new one, and let the envy and ill-feeling work off a
little, till people better recognize the quality of the
ship. I who know both one and the other, and have
seen them both tried, assure you that if the *St. Cosimo* is good, this one will never be bad. True, the
St. Cosimo has this advantage — I watched over the
building of it till the hull was perfectly finished, while
for this I merely gave the design, and only inspected
the work when it was ready for trial."

He goes on at length to explain the causes of this
envy which existed in nautical quarters, and says it is
only through spite, that the ship was over-laden with
stones, and left behind at Marseilles. This enmity and

opposition had little effect on Dudley's career as a ship-
builder, for on May 10th 1618, he wrote to the Grand-
Duke through Cioli that he had been detained so long
at Pisa to overlook the building of a new ship designed by him: " You may tell his Serene Highness, my
Signore, from me, that the vessel will in my opinion
be all that I wished it to be. I have also thought
of a " curiosity " in the matter of a new form of oars,
which row with more force and yet facility. I hope
these will prove a great success. I have sent oars
of the kind to be tried on a galleon at Leghorn
and they write me word that they succeed very well.
Before returning to Florence I shall go down to Leghorn and see the effect, and also inspect the *Sassaja*
and *Petaccia* as lately commanded by his Serene Highness. I beg you also to thank his Serene Highness
for the letter written by him in favor of my cause at
Rome to Monsignor Torelli, Deputy Judge, who has
given the sentence in my favor, as I desired, and which
is of great importance to me." [1]

Regarding the *Sassaja* and *Petaccia* which were
in 1617 placed under Dudley's hands for repair, we
have an interesting letter to Cioli from Cosimo da
Castiglione, a sea Captain, showing how those vessels
became damaged in a fight with the Spaniards.

It seems that as the *Petaccia* and *Sassaja* were
ready to sail for Elba, twenty Englishmen from Duppar's ships,[2] under a renegade Fleming named Rhys,

---

[1] It does not seem that this cause at Rome had anything to do
with the later one in the Curia Apostolica, which was in 1627. See
Appendix, n. XVII.

[2] This famous Duppar had orders from the King of England to
make reprisals on the Spanish vessels, which orders were renewed
in 1626. He had however no right to board the Duke of Tuscany's ships.

boarded the Grand-Duke's vessel, the *Petaccia*. The Captain flew to the helm and put his men on guard, but the assailants threw several of them into the hold, and disabled others. Then cutting off three anchors and setting sail, they tried to escape with the ship, but in so doing they collided with the *Sassaja* and ran aground.

By this time the harbour, and the fortress of the port were aroused, soldiers and guards were despatched, and a general *mêlée* ensued, resulting in Rhys being captured with 47 of his men, who were thrown into the prison at Leghorn to await the Grand-Duke's orders.

In another letter dated from Leghorn May 20th 1618, Dudley reports on the two new galley ships he has built at Leghorn, and of the success of his own new oars, which the *comite* (crew) and the galley slaves find a great improvement, as they are less fatiguing to use, and make more way; they also economise in the expense of tow or rope (*stroppi*) which in the course of a year mounts up to 600 scudi. "In fact," he says, "the *comite* and galley slaves, who are the best judges of the mysteries of the art of rowing, oppose no difficulties of any kind, but I have given orders that the trial be fairly continued all this year, to make sure of it before I put the plan into execution for the vessel I have in the docks at Pisa, which is not far enough advanced to permit my return to Florence to attend to other business of His Serene Highness.' I pray your Excellency to procure me from H. S. H. the

---

[1] Archivio Mediceo, Filza 1376 (new numeration). See Appendix, n. XVIII.

favour of the loan of one of his carriages for the
journey thither, which if graciously conceded, I desire
may be sent to Pisa on Saturday evening next, the
26th inst."

The Grand-Duke must have sent his carriage, for on
the 30th of the same month of May, Dudley writes to
excuse himself for having kept the carriage — which he
spells *caroce* instead of 'carrozza,' — so long. He says
he has been ill of a fever arising from a cut by some
instrument, and the doctor would not hear of his travelling. This fever he cured with a wonderful powder
of his own invention. As we shall see below, he had
medical proclivities, and his Will reveals the fact that
he kept a private medicine chest, which he calls his
cerusicheria.

This trait in the versatility of Dudley's tastes is
curiously shown in a medical book written in 1620 by
Marco Cornacchini, Professor of medicine at Pisa, and
dedicated *ad Illustrissimum D. Robertum Dudleum comitem
de WARVICH.* The whole book sings the praises of,
and gives the method for using, a certain curative
powder invented by Dudley, which, according to Cornacchini's title page, seems to cure everything. It runs
*Methodus qua omnes humani corporis affectiones ab humo-
ribus copia, etc., tuto, cito et jucunde curantur.* We are
told that when Dudley himself was ill of that fever
we have mentioned on his way from Pisa, he put it
to flight by means of this powder alone, and also
that he cured his "most illustrious spouse" of a fever
in the same way. Then Cornacchini runs over a list
of grand ecclesiastics, gallant knights, and sober citi-
zens who have been healed of their various mortal
diseases by this potent panacea. After this he gives

various methods of administering this powder in different doses and different times, for the various complaints.

It seems to have been composed among other ingredients of Antimony, Scammony, and Cream of Tartar. From this we see that Robert Dudley the second had the same taste for medicaments as his father Robert Dudley the first, but that he used his recipes for life and not for death. In the Italian dispensaries this powder is sometimes called *Pulvis Comitis Warvicencis*, sometimes *Cornacenni Pulvis*.

The enthusiastic Cornacchini in his dedication tells Dudley he possesses the one kind of true nobility, that of glorious deeds, and that his clearing the Italian seas of barbarous and evil pirates was not a greater benefit to mankind than his fighting and exterminating the evil humours which molest humanity and cause disease.

That Dudley was also devoted to the exact sciences as well as the learned ones we gather from his works.

Targioni[1] says " he rendered himself famous for his mathematical genius" and in a letter from Salvetti, dated September 1624, he mentions that " he has sent by Braccio an English friend of Dudley's (probably Tracy) a quantity of instruments for perspective; and that he will forward the rest as soon as he finds an opportunity." As we have said,[2] the Gabinetto di Fisica in the Florentine Museum contains several nautical instruments invented by Dudley.

----

[1] TARGIONI, *Aggrandimenti,* vol. I, pag. 79.
[2] See pag. 39–41.

PART VI.

DUDLEY APPEALS TO THE ROMAN ECCLESIASTICAL COURT.

—

From this time the Dudley documents in the Italian archives are full of letters from Amerigo Salvetti, who had succeeded Lord Herbert's "good friend Loty" as Italian resident in London. They contain frequent mentions of Dudley, who was by no means forgotten in England.

On the 6th of September 1618, Salvetti writes to Picchena that Viscount de Lisle had been made Earl of Leicester, to the prejudice of this Earl of Warwick (meaning Dudley);[1] adding that Baron Riche, who at the same time had been made Earl of Clare, finding that Clare had been a Royal title, had petitioned to have it changed to Earl of Warwick, and that orders had been given to make out the patent, with the said change. He regrets that Dudley has no one to take

---

[1] See Appendix, n. XIX.

his affairs in hand for him in England, where he is at a disadvantage.

This granting of the titles of Leicester and Warwick was naturally felt and resented by Dudley as a personal affront and injury. His state of mind may be exemplified by the three following anagrams composed by him: 1. *Robertus Dudleus Trude sed sublevor*. 2. *Detrudes sublevor*. 3. *Re delusus deturbo*.[1] The last anagram relates probably to his intended reprisals against the English skippers and merchants at Leghorn, and must have been a later one.

On the 16th November 1618, Salvetti writing to Sig. Picchena, the Grand-Duke's Minister, names a certain Doctor Dempster whose attitude towards Robert Dudley does not seem to be quite loyal. Salvetti writes, on November 9th, that " he has not seen Doctor Dempster for some time, but he hears from the merchant Burlamacchi, that Dempster wanted to borrow money from him, that he might return to the service of the Grand-Duke. As he had no order, the money was not lent to him. He had before this tried in vain to obtain a loan from Sig. Gaetani." Again on November 16th: " Dr. Dempster is in this city (London), but whether on account of its great size or that he does not choose to show himself, I can neither obtain a sight of him, nor learn where he is to be found. Sig. Gaetani has seen him, and he says he should not leave England till he had drawn a certain L. 300 sterling for which he said he had the order from the King."

On the 23rd he says: " Dr. Dempster must be with you by this time, for I hear that he left London last

---

[1] See the genealogical (Dudley) trees in the ' Uffizio della Nobiltà e Cittadinanza ' Firenze.

week for the sea, without saying a word of adieu to any one, having first drawn 200 scudi of the L. 300 on his Majesty's order." From another letter it appears that Dempster spoke strongly against Dudley, his birth and titles etc. In it, Salvetti having given a full account of Dudley's family from his grand-father John Dudley, who died on the scaffold, to his own life and vicissitudes (in which however he makes some mistakes), adds: " This is all the information I can give you, for I cannot furnish spurious news as does Dr. Dempster, who more often speaks to satisfy his own passions, rather than to assert the facts of the case."

Doctor Dempster was the author of *Etruria Regalis* (of which there is a copy in the Palatine library Florence), published at the expense of Mr. Coke. Dr. Dempster may have been envious of Dudley's accomplishments, and of his great favor at the court of Tuscany, which was indeed very high.

Dudley in 1619 was Grand Chamberlain to Maria Maddalena, sister of the Emperor Ferdinand II, who was then Grand-Duchess of Tuscany, having been married in 1608 to Cosimo II.[1] She was, together with Christina of Lorraine, widow of the Grand-Duke Ferdinand Ist (who died in 1608), joint regent of Tuscany, during the minority of her son Ferdinand II, who lived till 1670.[2]

In 1620 the Duchess Regent Maria Maddalena used her influence with her brother the Emperor, on her Grand Chamberlain's behalf, and obtained for him a patent giving the title of Duke of Northumberland to

---

[1] Cosimo died in 1621 aged about 31.
[2] Maria Maddalena of Austria died in 1631. Christina of Lorraine died in 1637.

him and his heirs male. The heading of the diploma
which is dated March 9th 1620, declares that Robert
Dudley denounces the English Duke of Northumberland, because he has himself been endowed with the
title by Frederick Emperor of Bohemia.[1] The taking of this title was a defiant answer to the new
creations of the Earldoms of Leicester and Warwick
in England before referred to. He went further: he
took Sig. Salvetti's hint about the disadvantages of having no agent in England, and in September 1620 he
placed his affairs there in Salvetti's own hand.

An Italian letter of September 3rd 1620 from the latter runs thus: " I have received a letter from the Earl of
Warwick in which he prays me to undertake, together
with an English gentleman the management of his
affairs in this Kingdom. He has procured an authentic
mandate, but as I have no kind of instructions from
your Excellency, I cannot decide without the express
command of my most Serene Sovereign, to mix myself
in other people's affairs, especially affairs of such a nature as these, in which one would daily be obliged to
treat with persons of State. This I should not dare to
do, without authority from head quarters nor could
I hope by so doing to serve your Highness's interests.
But if the Earl in his *procura* will nominate me as agent
by appointment of his Serene Highness, not only will
I serve him, but will show more diligence than I have
even before shown. I supplicate your Excellency to
inform me of the wishes of my Serene Lord, which I
shall always observe." [2]

The Grand-Duke lost no time in sending his man-

---

[1] See Appendix, n. XX, for the diploma in full.
[2] See Appendix, n. XXI.

date to his London agent, and Salvetti writes to Picchena on October 29th 1620, to say he will do his best to serve the Earl, though he wonders at the strange humor which causes him to style himself Duke of Northumberland, a whim which very much militates against his chances of success in England. He adds: "I have not heard whether his Majesty has yet been informed of this, but any way I seem to see him hurling his thunder-bolts" (*mi par di vederlo fulminare*). Again on August 6th 1621, Salvetti repeats that he is sorry this *vanità* (ambition) for new titles so misleads Dudley that he loses the real for the unreal.

There is a letter from Salvetti to Picchena, as to *quel titolo tanto vano di Duca*, etc. which, however, he has officially notified to Signor Cav. Calvardi (Calvert), Secretary of State. The letter also treats of Dudley's genealogy.

He indeed had a plurality of uncertain titles. In a letter dated November 4th 1622, Salvetti writes: "The enclosed letter for the Earl of Warwick is from Mr. *Trasi* (Tracy) and I beg your Excellency to inform me on a point I am desirous to know, whether in your court, he takes the name of Duke Dudley, as he has for these last few months signed himself here."

Salvetti's agency appears of slight aid to Dudley, for his letters do nothing but complain year after year of the difficult task imposed on him.

As Sig. Lotti had done before him, Sig. Salvetti now took his view of the matter from the English side; and, as we know, Alice Leigh and her powerful friends with the English court at their backs, had wrested all rights from him, and he got neither recognition nor compensation.

At length irritated to the extreme by the continuance year after year of this persecution, and the harsh measures taken against him, Dudley had recourse to a very strong measure. He applied to the *Curia Ecclesiastica* of Florence for a decree to enable him to make reprisals against the English who frequented the port of Leghorn, and owned mercantile houses there; hoping in this way to repay himself what he considered as the debt of the King of England towards him.

A letter from Dudley in Italian to Cav. *Sciolli* (Cioli) is preserved in the Medici archives dated

" From my house, January 2nd 1627.

" MOST ILLUSTRIOUS AND RESPECTED SIGNORE,

" Seeing no hope from England of my affairs being settled, even though so often through your kindness recommended to the King by his Serene Highness, we must now come to the last remedy to obtain justice, which as His Highness denies it to none, he may the more readily concede to me." Then follows a veiled explanation of what he demands, and an assurance that if Cioli helps him to succeed, he (Cioli) may be sure of a gift of 400 ducats for himself. Moreover Sir Robert Dudley's wife will send a handsome present to Madame Cioli " as soon as His Highness has consented to the restitution demanded." Another letter is dated Pisa March 23rd 1627, and contains the following passage. (We must give it in the original of which please observe the style and spelling; Dudley had not mastered the Italian language yet.)

" Importa assai haver questo bon essempio delle represalio concessa ed eseguito in Livorno contro li Mar-

cellesi soditi del Re di Francia, Principe molto poten-
tiore et utile per la Toscana che Inglitarra può esser." [1]
The letter shows his still firm intention to get permission
to make reprisals on the English shipping and the
English merchants frequenting Leghorn, in order thus
to recover the value of his estates in England, which
had been confiscated by the Crown. Cioli was one of
the confidential advisers of the Grand-Duke of Tuscany,
but he did not agree to this proposition; consequently
Dudley applied to the Ecclesiastical Court of Florence
and actually obtained a sentence in his favor. It appears however that the sentence was not carried into
effect, and that no reprisals were made. [2]

Salvetti writes from London on October 2nd 1626:
" There are rumours whispered of some sentence I don't
know what, which that Robert Dudley, or Duke as he
calls himself, has procured from the Ecclesiastical Fo-
rum, declaring himself creditor of this Kingdom for
L. 200,000. I hope this is not true, or it will prevent
merchants from putting into port at Leghorn with
their ships and effects, etc." [3]

It is certain that the Grand-Duke perceived the ri-
diculous aspect of this affair, and assured Salvetti in
London that " the English merchants of that city need
fear no surprises." But the Duke of Northumberland,
deceived by the flatteries of the Ecclesiastics, rather
than desist from his vain emprise, transferred the cause
to Rome, before the *Auditore della Camera Apostolica,*
which, confirming the sentence of the Florentine *Curia,*

---

[1] See Appendix, n. XXII. The English at this time did a good
deal of sea skirmishing against foreign ships.
[2] For this extraordinary sentence see Appendix, n. XXIII.
[3] See Appendix, n. XXIV.

published an esecutive mandate that the state of Tuscany should proceed to reprisals.

Here is a translation of the announcement sent to Florence of that extraordinary decree of the Ecclesiastical *Curia* dated November 17th 1627.[1]

" This letter of Gregorius Navo, Auditor general of the Camera Apostolica, commands by the same the Grand-Duke Ferdinand and all the other Ministers of Justice under pain of 1000 gold ducats, that they shall confiscate, and sell all or any of the goods of English Parliamentarians and the English residents, *in solidum*, excepting only professed Catholics; to the end that they may give and re-pay to Robert Dudley, Duke of Northumberland, son of another Robert Dudley; to Cosimo Dudley, Earl of Warwick, his son; and to Elisabeth *Sathuella* (Elizabeth Southwell), wife of the above-said Robert, and to all other children which are, or shall be born to the above *coniugi*, eight millions of Pounds sterling; with other two hundred thousand pounds as interest for the same, by reason of the unfair occupation and confiscation made of the above-named Dukedom; and this according to the sentence promulgated by Pietro Niccolini, Vicar general of the Archbishop of Florence, and confirmed by the before mentioned Gregorius Navo." The sentence, a long Latin decree, was, says Galluzzi,[2] affixed to the doors of the Duomo.

So much was the Grand-Duke irritated by the insolence of the Roman *Curia* and by Dudley's resort to it, that the latter would have suffered the penalty of his temerity, had not consideration of his services to

---

[1] R. Archivi del Bigallo – Archivio diplomatico.
[2] *Storia del Granducato di Toscana*, di RIGUCCIO GALLUZZI, vol. III, pag. 155.

the Medici family served to moderate the Grand-Duke's indignation. He also owed much, on this occasion, to the intervention in his favour of the Grand-Duchess Christina.

Galluzzi says that the insolence and aggressiveness of the *Curie* were partly caused by the excessive number of monks that inundated the state, and to whom Madame Christina's inconsiderate piety gave undue influence. Fortunately in this case her own influence was used to remedy the mistakes of her clerical allies.

Not daunted even in this last failure of his desire for revenge, Dudley returned once more to his efforts to obtain justice through Salvetti, who had before proved but a broken reed.

This time however he made his wife, the Duchess of Northumberland, the acting party. She sent in an official claim for the money due to her husband on the sale of Kenilworth to Prince Henry, which, his death intervening, had never been paid.

Salvetti wrote many letters in the end of 1630 and the early part of the year 1631,[1] alluding to the *negozio* of the Signora Duchessa, which as being in its nature, an " old and much worn subject," will be extremely difficult to revive, and he regrets he cannot " console " her with any hopes of success.

As early as September 1630 he thanks the Duchess through Cioli for sending him money for his expenses in the case; and on November 22nd 1630, he says: " With the enclosed I give the Duchess of Northumberland an account of her *negozio,* which I fear will be little to her taste, as it becomes every day more dif-

---

[1] See Appendix, n. XXV.

ficult. Treating as it does of extorting from the Royal Exchequer the sum of 12,000 scudi which her Grace claims, I confess I have not the courage to demand it, knowing the straitness of means in these parts. Besides, the debt is no longer legal as the Duke is in a continued state of contumacy, and now has no friend at Court, like the *Maggiordomo*,[1] I have but the faintest hopes of coming out of it with honour, nevertheless I will not abandon the negotiations as far as my faithful service can go, etc." The death of the Duchess, in 1631,[2] did not stop Salvetti's efforts. His diplomacy must have succeeded in spite of his repeatedly bemoaning its being so *scabbroso*, for on July 30th 1632 he sends four official papers for Dudley to sign and return to him, and on August 26th 1633 writes jubilantly: "Sig. Guadagni will pay the Duke of Northumberland 8000 scudi for which I have this day sent him the order. I beg that I may have a receipt in full, and I am very happy to have succeeded well in these intricate negotiations and to have done something to serve your Excellency."[3]

That the Grand-Duke was pecuniarily interested in the success of this claim (probably he had advanced money to Dudley on the strength of it) we gather from his letter to Salvetti in September 1632 : "We have heard with pleasure that your negotiations on behalf of the Duke of Northumberland have succeeded,

---

[1] The *Maggiordomo* was the Earl of Pembroke, always Dudley's friend. Salvetti writes through Mr. Tracy to inform the Duchess of Northumberland of his sudden death on April 26th 1630. His son died in Dudley's house in Florence in 1635.

[2] See Appendix, n. XXVI.

[3] See Appendix, n. XXVIII.

so that you hope soon to consign the money which will serve to re-imborse ourselves etc." [1]

There was a little self-interest too in Salvetti's activity in this case, which was certainly not undertaken for the love of Dudley. He lets this out in a letter to Cioli dated January 2nd 1632, where he says that if the Duke of Northumberland wishes to recompense him for all he is doing, he might do so by using his influence at the Tuscan Court to get him (Salvetti) recalled from exile, he being now 60 years old, and longing to go back to his native land after so many years absence. He did not however obtain his wish; whether from Dudley's want of diplomacy, or the Grand-Duke's reluctance to ask favours of the Republic of Lucca, who had exiled Salvetti, does not appear.

---

[1] See Appendix, n. XXVII.

PART VII.

DUDLEY AS A FATHER.

During all this stormy time Robert Dudley's family circle in the Florentine home was ever widening. In 1620 an eighth child was born, and by 1631 the olive branches round his table were increased to twelve.

Their maintenance seems to have caused some anxiety to Dudley, who was a proud and careful father, and very fond of his children, except in the one sad instance of the unmanageable Carlo. Several of his notes reveal that the cost of their education and maintenance in Court offices was a serious weight on his finances, at least until his cause in England had been gained.

As a proof of this I give a translation of part of a letter written by Dudley to Cioli, during his more straightened days.

It seems that the Cardinal had gone to Rome, and taken the young Ambrogio as his page. "If I had known I would have begged him not to do so, especially as my daughter Donna Teresa shows the intention of taking the veil, and I do not know if it can be done with moderate decorum, even with all I possess. Some one must have arranged all this without my knowledge, for I am not accustomed to offer things beyond my power. My income, thanks to the grace of His Serene Highness, is about 157 scudi a month. From this I pay more than 50 scudi every month for my son Don Carlo, and give Don Ambrogio 40 scudi a month, besides 17 to his tutor; think then what remains to keep a Duke of Northumberland with three boys besides, and moreover a daughter who wants to take the veil. Then there is the expense of dressing Don Ambrogio for Court, and you know it costs a hundred scudi to buy a new suit of a style worthy the high service of so eminent a prince. Then there is the great expense of a tutor to look after him, otherwise such an inexperienced youth would spend his month's allowance in a day. Were the case different, I should be ashamed to ask anything of you, but I have no land or private income, and scarcely means enough to put my daughter into a convent, and this I can assure the Rev. Cardinal and your Excellency. Therefore I throw myself on the kindness of the Cardinal, assuring him that the good will to serve him is not wanting on my side." [1]

In spite of poverty and expenses, Dudley managed to keep up his rank and importance. In 1630 Pope Urban VIII (Barberini) by a *Bolla* (Bull) created Dudley a *Patrizio Romano,* and gave him the power to form an order of knighthood. This Bull according to Wood was inserted in the *Ceremoniale di Roma* for the year 1630.

---

[1] See Appendix, n. XLI.

A manuscript book entitled *Habiti delli Duchi et Principi dell' ordine Cesareo armati secondo l' inventione*

THE GRAND MASTER OF THE CESAREAN ORDER.

del Signor Duca di Nortumbria, contains the rules of the order. In it there is a little full-length water colour drawing of the master of the order, armed, robed, and crowned, which is probably a portrait of Dudley himself. There is also an extremely rare portrait, engraved by Pierre Daret, of "Don Cosimus Dudleus Nortumbriæ Princeps, Comes Warwichi, Filius, et heres Roberti Ducis Nortumbriæ. A. D. 1625, ætatis suæ 15." Both these portraits are reproduced in this Memoir.

THE BADGE OF THE CESAREAN ORDER.

Dudley ruled that his order of nobility should contain 72 members, who were to be elected solely for their great military merit and bravery. The Emperor was to be Grand Master *in perpetuo*. Thus the order was named *L' ordine Cesareo armati* (Imperial military order). The first rank were called Princes, the second Dukes, the third Cavaliers. The Princes had 12 cavaliers under them with *decurioni*, and in their service were 300 foot soldiers and 100 horsemen. The badge of the order was a white enamelled collar bearing alternated three signs: — The double headed Eagles of the Emperor, the cross, mounted on the world, and the crossed sceptres, with Charles V's motto " nil ultra."

In the MS. of the *habiti delli Duchi et Principi del-l'ordine Cesareo* etc., we find that the Princes and Dukes wore ducal coronets, red velvet gowns, and cloaks of the same lined with ermine. The inferior officials had their cloaks and dress of less costly crimson, lined with tufted stuff. They wore a chain and cross instead of the badge, and carried no sword.

The *cavaliere centurione* wore the same red cloak, but under it a steel cuirass, greaves, and mailed gloves. His helmet had red plumes. Whether this order was ever really instituted, or how long it existed, there is nothing in the archives to show.

In 1629 came the first break in Dudley's large family circle. Young Donna Anna died at the early age of 18 years.

This young girl was buried in San Pancrazio, and Richa (*Delle Chiese,* vol. III, pag. 324) has preserved her epitaph which is now lost.

D. O. M.

QUÆRIS SCIRE QUID MOLIAR – RESOLVOR DONEC REDEAM
APPETIS QUID FUI – ANNA DUDLEA, ANGLO DANOQUE
REGALI STEGMATE NATA – EXPETIS QUÆ LABILIS VITÆ
COMITES – PULCHRITUDO, VIRGINITAS, VIRTUS, RELIGIO
O MORTALIS CADUCITAS. LETHO RELICTIS LARIBUS.

ROBERTUS DUDLÆUS ET ELIZABETH SOUTHWEL
NORTHUMBRORUM VARVICENSIUMQUE DUCES
HOC MÆSTISSIMI PARENTES ANNO 1629
MIHI FILIÆ DULCISSIMÆ POSUERE.

14

' DISCE, TIME, QUID ERGO VIATOR

' FORMA CHARIS VIRTUS UBI NUNC NORTHUMBRIA PRINCEPS

' VIRGO SUB HAC SECUM CONDIDIT ANNA PETRA.' [1]

The Dudley joys and sorrows were closely mingled. The following year 1630, the first wedding in the family took place. A marriage was arranged, probably through the Grand-Duchess, between the Prince of Piom-

---

[1] The author of the Italian Biography has thus translated the in-scription:

TO GOD THE GREATEST AND THE BEST.

WHAT NOW EMPLOYS ME, DO YOU WISH TO KNOW?
TILL I RETURN I AM MOULDERING HERE BELOW.
PERHAPS YOU WISH MY NAME AND RANK TO TRACE;
I ONCE WAS ANNA, OF LORD DUDLEY'S RACE;
FROM ROYAL DANE AND NORMAN MY DESCENT;
MY DAYS ON EARTH WITH FAITHFUL FRIENDS I SPENT.
ASK YOU THEIR NAMES? RELIGION, VIRTUE, TRUTH,
WERE MY COMPANIONS FROM THE DAWN OF YOUTH;
AND BEAUTY TOO, AND PURITY OF MIND,
WITH FAITH UNSHAKEN, AND A TASTE REFIN'D.
SHORT MY SPAN OF LIFE, IT SCARCE WAS DAY
WHEN MY SUN SET, AND NOW MY BED IS CLAY.
MY SORROWING PARENTS BORE A DUCAL NAME,
NORTHUMBERLAND AND WARWICK DEAR TO FAME;
TO ME THEIR CHILD BELOV'D THOSE PARENTS GAVE
THEIR GRIEF'S LAST PROOF, AN HONOURABLE GRAVE.
MDCXXIX.

He says the triplet at the end defies translation, either as a piece of Latin, or an inscriptional statement. In answer to this declaration I venture to offer the following prose version:

Learn, fear, what then traveller?
Beauty, grace, virtue where are they now?
A Northumbrian virgin Princess Anna has concealed them
with herself beneath this stone.

Among the "Verba barbara" in the Calepino Lexicon there appears Charis (χαρις) festivitas gratia beneficum, and so I have taken it. See *Septem Linguarum Calepinus*, etc. Patavii, Typis Seminarii, MDCCLII, apud Joannem Manfre, Superiorum permissu et privilegio.

bino and Donna Maria Dudley, Princess of Northumberland, daughter of Robert Dudley, Duke of Northumberland which is thus announced :

*Di 3 Novembre 1630 si pubbriò denuntiando il matrimonio da
contrare tra gl' Ill.mi et Ecc.mi Sig. D. Orazio Appiano Aragona,
Principe di Piombino, da una parte; e Donna Maria Dodlea Principessa di Nortumbria, Figlia dell'Ecc.mo Sig. D. Roberto Duca di Northumbria etc.*

This was certainly a good match for the young
lady, whose *dote* (marriage portion) cannot have been a
large one. Litta tells us the Appiani were Lords of Pisa
from 1392 to 1399, and Lords of Piombino from 1399
to 1635. Orazio was the last of the Appiani ruling in
Piombino. The principality had been disputed since
the death of Cosimo Jacopo in 1603.[1] At length it
was judged that Orazio was the only one of the family
with any plausible right to it, and he was invested
by the King of Spain on January 5th 1626. It was
however decreed that he should pay a laudamus of
500,000 florins. This, though repeatedly cited, he was
never in a condition to pay, consequently he was
declared *decaduto,* and in 1635 his principality was
given to Niccolò Ludovisi of Bologna, nephew of Gre-
gory XV, and husband of Isabella of Binasco, who man-
fully paid down a million florins as a thank-offering.

The next event to be noticed is a sad one, followed, very shortly, by a sadder one, both of which
must have been very heavy blows for Dudley, throw-
ing a black cloud and sorrowful recollections over all

---

[1] The Court of Spain would have given it in 1611 to Isabella
Countess of Binasco. Finally the Emperor Ferdinand II established
that the Spanish should hold it, with the compact of making it a feudal
estate for the one of the Appiani, who was judged by the Imperial
tribunals to be the rightful claimant.

the remainder of his life. The first of these melancholy
events, the death of Dudley's heir, is thus noticed by
Paolo Verzoni (M. S. M., vol. I, pag. 18):

*A dì 8 di Luglio 1631. Ricordo come questo giorno sono venute
nuove della morte del primogenito del Sig. Duca di Vueruich seguita
a Piombino, dove era andato a visitare la sua sorella, moglie del Principe di Piombino.*

This ill-fated young man died on a visit to his
sister Maria, a few days before he arrived at the age
of twenty-one. His early death may perhaps be attri-
buted to the *peste,* a sort of plague, which was then
making many victims in Tuscany, or it may have been
malarial fever, owing to the unhealthy air of the country
round Piombino. Whatever may have been the cause
of his death, it was a sudden and fearful infliction on
his father, who often spoke of him as his great hope,
being a good son, and not wild like Carlo. It fell
especially heavy on his mother, who, but three months
before, had given birth to her last and twelfth child.

Only two months later the unhappy lady followed
her beloved son to the grave. Her death is thus recorded by Paolo Verzoni (pag. 21):

*A dì 10 7bre. Ricordo come in questo giorno è morta in Firenze
la moglie del S. Duca di Veruich, c sotterrata in S. Pancrazio.*

This is another of Verzoni's mistakes; the Register
of San Pancrazio runs thus:

*A dì 13 7bre 1631. Morse l'Ill.ma ed Ecc.ma Donna Elisabetta
moglie dell'Ecc. Sig. Duca di Nortumbria, e si depositò vicino alla
porta maggiore della Chiesa accanto all'Ill.ma fu già D. Anna sua
figlia.*[1]

---

[1] There is nothing left of the Duchess' tomb in Saint Pancras but
a shield with the Dudley arms on it, of which I have a copy at Vincigliata Castle. There is no inscription extant, and archæologists
dispute whether this fragment is part of the tomb of Dudley himself
or his wife. See Appendix, n. XXVI.

Whatever may be said of her departure from England with Dudley, the act that ruled and coloured all her after life, and which may be excused with the reflection, that she thought it justified by Roman Catholic reasoning, it is certain, that in addition to her beauty, she had many good and great qualities, which made her loved and admired by all who knew her, and rendered her an especial favourite at the Grand-Ducal Court of Tuscany.

For the twenty-four years of her life passed in Italy, she was a faithful wife and a loving mother.

The grief of Robert Dudley in this bereavement may be better imagined than described. But fortunately for him his attention was partly diverted from his sorrow, by the work in which he was engaged for the Grand-Duke. He was, also, busied with the composition of his great book *Arcano del Mare,* which was destined to become famous; besides which he had duties to perform to his numerous children which he did not neglect.

In 1633 he was occupied in arranging a marriage for his daughter Maria Maddalena, thus announced :

A dì 30 Gennaio 1633 si pubblicò il matrimonio da contrarsi tra gli Ecc.mi et Ill.mi Signori Don Spinetta Malaspina, Marchese d'Olivola, da una parte; e Donna Maria Maddalena Dudlea Principessa di Nortumbria.

The marriage took place in the presence of Queen Christine of Sweden. This also was a good match for the young lady. The Malaspina family, divided into several branches, possessed great part of the Lunigiana of which they were the feudal Lords under the Emperor. Litta tells us that Spinetta Malaspina was made Marquis of Olivola by the investiture of the Emperor

Ferdinand III, and on April 15th 1630 he was named high Steward to Christine Queen of Sweden, who, as we have said, had been present at his marriage.

This marriage brought him in contact with the English families who had fled from their native country to save themselves from the persecution which was there carried on against the Roman Catholics. He had long known the old Earl of Pembroke and formed an especial friendship with his son young Charles Herbert, a lad of sixteen, who had visited the Malaspinas at Olivola and frequented the Dudley's house in Florence where he died in 1635. It has been thought that as his tomb is at Olivola, his death took place there, but that is disproved by the following letter from Lorenzo Poltri to Salvetti in London, giving the official announcement. It is dated January 8th 1636.

" The Earl of Pembroke has died in this city after only five days' illness, no remedy having availed. The illness was adjudged to be small-pox. The Duke of Northumberland has done everything that was possible, but finally his hour was come. His Highness (the Grand-Duke) sent his own physician several times, and has heard with much grief of this grave event, sympathizing with the sorrow which this ill-news will bring the Earl his father, with whom His Serene Highness begs to condole sincerely . . . . The body was sent for interment to Olivola in Lunigiana, the place of Marchese Spinetta Malaspina, son-in-law of the Duke of Northumberland, and was conducted by Sig. Carlo Coberel (?) and another gentleman of the neighbourhood, they being furnished with passports in case of any molestation which might happen on the journey. I regret much that it is my duty to give you this news, but we must resign ourselves to events, and I beg to kiss your hand, etc." [1]

Various letters written by Dudley throw interesting lights on his domestic life. In one on July 9th 1638 he begs the Grand-Duke to award a *commenda* in a religious-knightly order (Knights of St. Stephen) vacated by the death of Cav. Carlo Piccolomini, to his son Antonio, whom he wishes to bring up for the navy. The spurs were bestowed, but the young Cavalier did not long enjoy his knightly honours, for on November 19th of the same year, Dudley laments the death, at the early age of 18, of this young son Antonio, who he says was his great comfort being so obedient.[2]

In other letters he complains bitterly of the bad conduct of his now eldest son Carlo, who in 1638 was about 24 years old, and very contumacious.[3] Indeed the chronicle of his sins in these family letters is a long and serious one. His father must have found him difficult to manage for some years; that there was a strong resentment between them, one gathers from a letter of Donna Isabella Aragona Appiana[4] to the Duke of Northumberland dated Boldrone June 4th 1637, saying she is sorry to bring the Duke ill-news, but friendship demands that she should warn him against his son Carlo, who since his return from prison has shown very strong ill-will to his father, saying he shall certainly be obliged to kill him: "The woman M. A. whom he keeps

---

[1] See Appendix, n. XXIX.
[2] See Appendix, n. XXX, XXXI, XXXII.
[3] See Appendix, n. XXXIII to XL.
[4] The Countess Appiani must have been staying for the summer at Dudley's Villa at Castello in Via del Boldrone, close to the Convent where Teresa was. She was a relative, probably mother of that young Count Appiani who married Anna Dudley.

in his house," says the Countess, "is afraid of her life
to remain, he is so wild and furious. The peasants
around say that even before his incarceration he used
to threaten that he would have his father's life, and
that he would take the silver away from the house,
and run away from Florence."

Evidently Dudley acted on this warning, for on
June 15th the young man was sent under military
escort to Olivola, his sister's Villa. This did not prevent him carrying out his puerile threat, for on January 24th 1628, Dudley writes to Cioli, from his Villa:
"I write to-day to beg your Excellency to inform His
Serene Highness that Don Carlo with several men armed
with guns entered my house, while I was at Mass, and
carried away all the silver which was not locked
up, to the value of 300 ducats. His Highness knows
that I was aware of these evil designs and of others
even worse. I hope some serious mark of displeasure
from the court will be shown for so grave a crime
against his father, and defiance to the laws of his
Prince . . . . He came, as far as I can gather,
from Lucca, and has probably returned there with his
booty. I place myself entirely in the hands of His Serene Highness, etc., etc."

Another letter goes into details, and reveals that,
when the family went to Mass, the Duke first made
sure that the whole house was securely locked up,
leaving only an old woman servant in it. She proved
unfaithful, and must have opened the door to Don Carlo.

The Duke thinks his son must have consorted with
bandits, for, against his father's express command, he
persisted in retaining in his service a Genoese outlaw,
and when he entered the house he was accompanied

by nine men armed with pistols. A warrant was issued against Carlo, but the trouble was to find the fugitive. A certain Francesco Luchesini, a maker of clay images, wrote on February 9th in very queer Tuscan to the Duke to say that his son had just seen Don Carlo pass by in a postchaise, with his servant on horseback, going down a bye road, adding that "if the Duke will give something to the bearer, he may learn more about it."

Next we hear that Don Carlo had twice been seen passing Castello, armed with his arquebus. Then he came with two armed men and boldly took up his quarters in the village Church, for in those days the altar was as a city of refuge.

He had written two letters to his brother Don Ambrogio as if from Genoa, showing the intention of going to Marseilles. In them he complained of his father's mistake in treating his sons on the English system in Italy. In fact he darted about here and there, but his association with the brigands had evidently taught him how not to be caught.

The Duke was in despair, and wrote letter after letter to the Grand-Duke through Cioli, saying he had done his utmost, and used every means in his power to keep his unhappy son in order.

From several letters we find that Carlo declared himself a rebel, and stoutly refused to go to the fortress, or the Bargello at the Grand-Duke's bidding. Indeed he so far defied the Grand-Duke as to entrench himself in the centre of Florence, in the Church of the SS. Annunziata. At length in 1638 he was caught, and as he would not go to prison, was put in the convent of *San Domingo a Fesula* (as Dudley

15

writes San Domenico di Fiesole), where the monks were
at their wits' ends to know what to do with him.
They dared not let him go out, and they could with
difficulty keep him there. At length tired of confine-
ment, the ill-advised youth came to terms: "If his father
would give him a new suit, suitable to the occasion,"
he stipulated, " he would go to Germany and enter the
service of King Matthias."

The Duke of Northumberland said he would willingly give the suit of clothes, but that he was sure it
was only a ruse of Don Carlo, and as soon as he was
free he would leave Germany and come back again.
In the end he was really taken to the Bargello, within
the strong walls of which he had to await the Grand-
Duke's pleasure.[1] This even was done with arrogance;
he wrote to make stipulations that he should have a
servant of his own free to come and go, and that he
himself should not be confined to one room.

The devout Donna Teresa did not after all carry
out her girlish wish to take the veil, for in 1645 we
learn that she was married with great state to the
Duca della Cornia. Probably Robert Dudley, having
obtained the money demanded from the King of England, was more able to keep her in the world, and give
her a worthy dower.

---

[1] See Dudley's letters in Appendix, n. XXXIV to XXXVIII.

Part VIII.

DUDLEY'S MAGNUM OPUS.

And now Robert
Dudley having mar-
ried his daughters,
and placed his sons
in some of the Eu-
ropean Courts, was
able to give the years
of his mature life to
science and litera-
ture. He still endea-
voured to keep his
hold on Tuscan ma-
rine matters, for in
September 1638 he
wrote from his Villa
to the Prince Giovan
Carlo de' Medici, who
had just been created
High Admiral of the
Tuscan Navy, to offer
his homage and swear

TITLE PAGE OF A BOOK DEDICATED
TO ROBERT DUDLEY.

his fealty, saying, that "if his nautical experience of many years merited employment in the service of his Highness, he, though old, would be always ready to obey the Admiral's commands." [1]

In 1646 his great work, which may well be styled his "Magnum Opus," was published. Here is an exact copy of the first title page:

DEL

L' A R C A N O

DEL MARE

T O M O   P R I M O

DIVISO NEL LIBRO PRIMO E SECONDO.

And of the second title page:

DELL' ARCANO

DEL MARE

DI D. RUBERTO DUDLEO DUCA DI NORTUMBRIA

E CONTE DI VVARVICH

LIBRI SEI;

NEL PRIMO DE' QUALI SI TRATTA DELLA LONGITUDINE PRATI-CABILE IN DIVERSI MODI, D' INVENZIONE DELL'AUTORE.

NEL SECONDO, DELLE CARTE SUE GENERALI, E DE' PORTOLANI RETTIFICATI IN LONGITUDINE E LATITUDINE.

NEL TERZO, DELLA DISCIPLINA SUA, MARITTIMA E MILITARE.

NEL QUARTO, DELL'ARCHITETTURA NAUTICA SUA, DI VASCELLI DI GUERRA.

NEL QUINTO, DELLA NAVIGAZIONE SCIENTIFICA, E PERFETTA, CIOÈ SPIRALE O DI GRAN CIRCOLI.

---

[1] See Appendix, n. XLII.

AL SERENISSIMO
FERDINANDO SECONDO
GRAN DUCA DI TOSCANA

Suo Signore.

(Here, in the original, is placed an engraving of a mariner's compass.)

In FIRENZE, Nella Stamperia di Francesco Onofri.
1646. Con licenza dei SS. Superiori.

After the second title page comes the diploma of the Emperor Ferdinand, creating Dudley, Duke of Northumberland, etc., folded to fit the page.

The first volume is divided into two books; in each book there are many engravings of nautical and scientific instruments and plans.

The printing of a book was no easy matter in those days.

At page 55, which is the end of the first book, there are the following notices:

" Il Sig. Canonico Vincenzio Martelli veda se nella presente opera si contenga cosa che repugni allo stampato e riferisca appresso. Nel dì 5 d'Agosto, 1645," shewing that there existed a censorship of the press, and that Queen Christine's all powerful priests regulated it. The Canon however was merciful, and gave in Italian the following verdict: " I have read with all diligence this truly admirable and most useful work entitled the *Arcano del Mare;* and not having found in the said book anything repugnant to the Catholic Religion or to good customs, I judge it worthy to be printed. This 12th day of August, 1645. Vincenzo Martelli, Canonico Fiorentino."

Under this is printed also in Italian :

" In accordance with the present report, we judge
that the book may be printed, the usual formalities
being observed. August 18th, 1645."

Then Padre Maestro Alessandro Peri, Florentine
Theological Doctor of the Order of San Francesco, re-
examined this book on 21st of August, and referred
his report, approving it in much the same form as
Padre Martelli, passing it on to Fra Giacomo Cima,
Inquisitor General of Florence.

Lastly came Fra Jacobus, Inquisitor General and
Alessandro Vettori, Senator, Auditor to the Grand-Duke,
as the State Censors; and finally the book went to press
on 26th of August, 1645. Such were the formalities
and permissions required before a book could be printed
in the middle of the seventeenth century.

Dudley's plan according to the preface was to di-
vide his material into six books. The first, as his title
page sets forth, treats of practical longitude in several
systems invented by the author; the second, of maps and
charts in general and of *portolani*, rectified as to longitude and latitude; the third, of military and marine
discipline; the fourth, of his nautical architecture and
building of war ships; the fifth, of scientific and perfect
navigation, i. e. in spirals or grand circles; and the
sixth, of Dudley's geographical and original maps.

In the discourse on the mathematical sciences which
forms part of the *Arcano del Mare*, Dudley puts the
following quaint ideas into more quaint Italian.

" The omnipotent God," he writes, " has propor-
tioned the world in regard to magnitude, number, and
weight, and the created things in it are generally of
three kinds, i. e. supernatural, natural, and a third

species which one might call mathematical, and of which we shall principally treat in this discourse."

We are further informed that " the supernatural are simple, indivisable, and incorruptible in an ascending scale; natural objects are complex, divisable, and corruptible in a descending scale; but mathematical things are sure and infallible by demonstration; and therefore these are more excellent than natural things, in which there enters an element of conjecture and probability, and which are inferior to the supernatural, to which human intellect cannot reach."

The principle of " Great Circle sailing," adopted by Dudley in 1620 and described in his fifth book, though not primarily invented by him, was greatly improved and made practical by his developments of Nunez and Mercator's first dim notions. A further advance was made about 30 years ago in England by Mr. J. T. Towson, late scientific examiner to the Local Marine Board of Liverpool, who received from the Board on June 13th 1857 a testimonial of £ 1000 for his valuable services in developing the principle of " Great Circle sailing " by which the Australian voyages have been so much shortened.

The fifth book contains 30 pages of print, also many engravings of wonderful nautical and astronomical instruments; and ends with a notice regarding the sixth book, and the intentions of the author therein. He announces that the sixth book will contain 127 geographical charts of the four quarters of the globe on a large scale: 54 being for Europe, 17 for Africa, 23 for Asia, and 33 for America.

" These charts," he adds, " are all finished, and have been seen by the Superiors (ecclesiastical censors of the press); but as the author has modernized the European ones, which are not yet engraved for printing, he judges it better to defer the publication till these are complete. Meanwhile navigators who wish to sail by the most perfect system of longitude, may use the general charts in the second volume, with the corrections in the *portolani* which bring them to the same perfection."

" Most pilots who know the coast," he says, " prefer to use their experience, and for them the general charts in vol. II are sufficient; but for sailing on the high seas by means of practical longitude and great circles, the new charts are of the greatest necessity. Therefore the author promises to publish this sixth book as soon as possible."

It is probable that the publication was delayed as much by want of money to pay the engravers, as by want of time.

The two first volumes of the first edition in the writer's possession (containing up to the fourth book) are printed on rough thick paper bound in light yellowish-brown leather with artistic gilding. In the centre of each side are the Medici arms, surrounded by a Cardinal's hat and tassels; on the back the title and numbers of the parts contained in the volume. They are fine old tomes that would delight a lover of old books.

The third volume is twice the size of the other two in measurement, though not in thickness. It bears the date of 1647.

The fourth is very ponderous and filled with maps.

All these were printed at the Stamperia di Francesco Onofri, MDCXXXXVIII, a year later than the last.

In 1661, twelve years after Dudley's death, a second edition of the *Arcano del Mare* was published in Flo-

rence,[1] at the Sign of the Star, the new press of Giuseppe
Cocchini, by the desire of Jacopo Bagnoni di Anton Francesco Lucini, *con licenza de' superiori*. It is announced
under the usual title, as "a second edition, enlarged
and corrected according to the original by the late most
excellent Duke, which is preserved in the Convento della
Pace[2] by the Bernardine monks of the order of Foligno.
It contains a general index of the whole work, its chap-
ters, figures and instructions to the binder, etc., etc."

The dedication to the Venetian Republic is interesting in many respects, especially for its praise of Dudley,
who, for forty years, had been engaged in the composition of the *Arcano del Mare,* and for Lucini's statement, that he had himself been hard at work in a
Tuscan village for twelve years after Dudley's death,
preparing the second edition of this great work, and
the engravings that illustrate it.

After a stilted dissertation on the marine power of
Venice, and man's power over the watery elements,
Lucini says that "the same nature which gave laws to
man, shall receive them back. Thus by the benefit of
nautical science, many islands thrown by nature far
away in the boundless sea, are now united in reciprocal

---

[1] Lord Leigh of Stoneleigh Abbey took home from Italy a copy
of this second edition. The Bodleian Library has a copy of each
edition, as also has the writer of this Memoir. The Magliabecchian
possesses five volumes. Two of 1646-1647 richly bound with gilded scrolls
and the Della Rovere Arms on the cover; two of 1661 in common
board with parchment backs; and one in green without letter-press,
containing all the plates and maps from the edition of 1661.

[2] The Convent of La Pace near Porta Romana, in which the original
first edition was preserved, no longer exists. The site and the land
around it were used for the erection of the Royal Stables in the time
of the late King Victor Emanuel, when Florence was used as the Capital.
The said volumes are probably the ones now in the National Library of
Florence.

commerce, and the two hemispheres parted by a vast ocean are now one single world, the one part being ameliorated, the other enriched. In this worthy emprise, O my Serene Lords, if one man is more signally eminent than others, it is the Duke of Northumberland, who, to make himself master of marine science, tore himself away from a great house, in which he had princely birth; and sacrificed full forty years of his life in unveiling, for the good of humanity at large, the mighty secrets of the sea; while I," naïvely adds Lucini, " for twelve years sequestered from all the world in a little Tuscan village, have consumed no less than 5000 lbs., of copper in engravings to illustrate it. I deliberated a long time to whom I should dedicate the work which I now offer and consecrate solely *alla Maestà della vostra Pubblica Munificenza*. You who command so large a part of the seas, you whose name is glorious, etc., etc.; " in fact a very long peroration which we will spare the reader.

Lucini calls the two volumes of the second edition of 1661 *amplissimi*, and they deserve the epithet; he might have said *pesantissimi*. Each volume measures in length fifty-five centimetres and a half, in width forty-three centimetres, and in thickness six centimetres.

Each of them weighs seven and a half kilogrammes. The first is however a trifle thicker and a trifle heavier than the second. They are very large, heavy, unmanageable volumes. To be read with ease they require to be placed on a great lectern, like those used for the great missals in Roman Catholic churches. They are bound in the same coloured leather as the four volumes of the first edition, with a little tooling, but without gilding or coats of arms.

The first book of the first volume consists of thirty pages of print and many engravings of instruments, etc., at the end of it is an engraving of two little angels holding the Florentine lily over a great star with the motto *nunquam a sole.*

Then there comes the patent of the Emperor Ferdinand, dated 1620, creating Dudley, Duke of Northumberland.

The second book contains twenty-four pages of printed matter and engravings of maps, and ends, like the first, with the little pictures of angels, etc.

The third book contains twenty pages of print and illustrations of a war galley, and of ships of battle in array, and of land fortifications.

The fourth book consists of twelve pages of print, and flourishing engravings of ships, etc. It ends with an elaborate, fantastic figure of a ship with a mast and a flag and sail, on which is the *impresa* with the motto *nunquam a sole.*

The fifth book contains twenty-six pages of print and many engravings of wonderful instruments for finding the position of the sun and of the stars, also a ship in full sail. It also ends with the *impresa* and motto *nunquam a sole.* All these form one volume.

The second volume contains the sixth book. The title page resembles that of the first volume. It is divided into four parts, consisting of forty-one pages of print and of many plans of the coast line, with notes as to the times of tides in all countries, and pictures of ships and fish, sea-monsters, and savages. It ends with the usual *impresa* and motto, and the initials J.B.A.F.L., that is Jacobo Bagnoni and Anton Francesco Lucini.

In the map showing the Orinoco and a quantity

of islands at its mouth, we find that one of the largest
islands is named Dudleana, so called by Dudley on his
voyage to America.

At page thirty-three there is "an account of the
voyage of Captain Robert Thornton, an Englishman,
sent to those parts by order, and at the expense of
the most Serene Grand-Duke Ferdinand Ist his Lord."
Probably by the advice of Dudley.

"This said Captain," we are told by Lucini, "went
and happily returned, and although he had never before been in those parts, or even in the West Indies,
nevertheless by the aid of the charts and instructions
given by the author's (i. e. Dudley's) own hand, and
by the grace of God, he completed the voyage without
losing a man, and discovered the coast of Guiana
more fully and more exactly than it had ever been
known before. He also discovered the good port of
Chiana, which is a secure, royal harbour, and had never
in times past been seen by Christians; and from here
he brought with him five or six Indians, with the intention of presenting them to their Highnesses of Florence, which he did — the which are those Caribs who
eat human flesh."

These poor Caribs afterwards died in Florence, most
of them of small-pox, which was to them more terrible
than the plague, it being a disease never heard of in their
own country. Only one lived on at the Court for several years, and served H. E. the Cardinal de'Medici, and
learned to speak the Italian language quite easily.[1]

---

[1] Probably this was the Cardinal to whom the four first volumes
of the *Arcano del Mare* were dedicated, — those with the Medici arms
and Cardinal's hat. He had, as we have seen, interested himself in
Dudley's affairs.

These Indians from Chiana often talked to the author (Dudley) and others about the richness and fertility of the kingdom of Guiana, and how they " had been to Monoa the metropolis of the kingdom, the residence of the monarch, who is called the Emperor, for he has many kingdoms under his sway. That city is eight days' journey from the port of Chiana; the Indians make the journey very swiftly on foot, traversing usually about fifty miles a day, and sometimes more. The Indians also said that in a hilly country, near Chiana, was a very rich silver mine which they called Perota; there was also some low gold called by them Calciri, of which they made certain images and half-moons, for ornaments. The above named Thornton confirmed the report, and besides asserted that the spiders of that country spun silk, and that there was much *legno verzino* (rosewood), also wild sugar canes, white pepper, *legno pardo*, pith, balsam, cotton and many other kinds of merchandize which would form an abundant commerce, if it were well planted by Christians. He said the air was very healthy, and the entrance to the harbour well formed for fortifications to command the port; and gave many other particulars of the country already printed by the author in 1637 (misprint for 1647), to which for brevity we refer the reader."

The editor of the second edition goes on to say that a " note of Dudley's: 'look out for a Bornea at 6 ¼,' alluding to the mouth of the Amazon, where ships were at certain times in danger from a tidal wave, saved Captain Thornton from getting his vessel swamped." " From this example," adds Lucini, " the importance of the marginal notes to Dudley's maps may be seen, when on many occasions three words were enough to save

a ship and its crew . . . . Captain Thornton sailed from
Leghorn in the month of September about 1608 and
returned to the same port the end of June following
in 1609 or thereabouts."

After this most interesting relation of Captain
Thornton's voyage[1] there is a long list of Indian
words, with their equivalents in Italian, learned by
Dudley himself on his early voyage to Trinidad in 1595.

In July 1648 Dudley's younger daughter Teresa,
Duchess of Cornia, gave birth to a posthumous child,
her husband having died in the end of 1647. The
child, Fulvio, lived but five months, dying on December 14th 1648. This early death of her little son
must have been a great loss, as well as a great grief
to his young mother, as he being naturally heir to his
dead father, she would have had the management of
his estate during a long minority, whereas now it
passed out of her hands.

She did not remain long disconsolate however, but
on June 25th 1649 she entered into a second contract
of marriage as appears from a notice dated September 2nd 1649, headed: "Actum in Palatio Rurali solitæ
habitationis infrascripti Illustrissimi et Excellentissimi
Domini Don Roberto Dudleo nuncupato vulgariter a
Rinieri in populo Sancti Michaelis de Castello, etc., etc."
This notarial act is a ratification of a *scritta di parentado*
which had been celebrated on June 25th of the same
year, between Robert Dubley and his daughter Teresa,
widow of Fulvio, Duke of Cornia, on one side; and the
Illustrious Count and Knight Mario, son of the late
Count Tommaso of Carpigna, on the other. It is in

---

[1] He must have been one of the English captains whom Dudley
called to Leghorn when he first entered the service of the Grand-Duke.

fact a kind of marriage settlement; we quote it here to shew Dudley's continued attachment to the science of medicine. In it he gives Teresa and her husband the use of his palace in Florence, and a gift of "un suo studiolo di ebano detto la Cerusicheria, con cassette di argento ed altro in esso esistente, riservandosi l'usufrutto perdurante la sua vita" (an ebony cabinet known as the medicine chest, with its silver boxes, and everything that is contained in it, reserving to himself the use of it during his lifetime).

Dudley's enjoyment of his *Cerusicheria* lasted a very short time however, for on the 6th of September 1649, he died at his Villa Rinieri at Castello, as appears in the following notice, reported from Verzoni's MS. by Targioni in the *Aggrandimenti*, vol. III, pag. 42.

1649. A dì 6 Settembre è morto in una Villa vicino a Firenze il Sig. Duca di Nortumbria e Conte di Warwick, Inglese chiamato Ruberto, il quale è stato qui molti anni stipendiato dal Re d'Inghilterra, e tolto lo stato per essere buon Cattolico, ed è stato sepolto nella Chiesa di S. Pancrazio dove fu già sepolta ancora la sua moglie Elisabetta Souterel; et era Persona di gran valore e bontà, e pratichissimo delle cose di Mare, avendo egli stampato qui in Firenze un dottissimo libro intitolato Arcano di Mare.

The mistakes in this statement have already been noticed in the preface to this Memoir, where we have proved that no sign of his interment in San Pancrazio exists. An old MS. however speaks of the Dudley tomb being subterranean.

The author of *Athenæ* says that Dudley "died in the month of September 1649 at Carbello (Castello) three miles from Florence, in a house which the Great-Duke of Tuscany permitted him to enjoy gratis during his life. Whereupon his body being conveyed to a nunnery at Boldrone, near to that place, it was there

deposited; but whether it hath been since conveyed to
the Church of St. Pancras in Florence, wherein his wife
Elizabeth had before been buried, and over whose grave
he had erected a sumptuous Monument of marble, with
intentions to be buried by her, I know not; sure I am
that the body was continuing at Boldrone in 1674, and
may perhaps be there still." Now when we are informed by this author, that he had received the whole
information for the article concerning Sir Robert Dudley from his son Carlo, second Duke of Northumberland,
by letter dated Rome, October 17th 1673, we may be
sure that his printed account is correct; and that the
body had not been conveyed from Boldrone to St. Pancras at the date of this letter.[1]

It is perhaps worth observing that in the register
of deaths in the parish of St. Michael at Castello, in
which parish the Villa where Dudley died was situated,
the pages containing entries of the years from 1612
to 1649 are wanting. It is a question whether they
were lost or stolen, or wilfully destroyed.

This Robert Dudley, Duke of Northumberland, was
certainly a very remarkable man. Nobly born, he
was carefully educated, having had as his private tutor
the well-known Thomas Challoner, who was afterwards
tutor to Prince Henry, eldest son of James Ist of England. Like many other famous men of the time, he
had a longing for the sea and for adventures, indeed
he seems to have been destined from his birth, and
by his own and his wife's (Elizabeth Southwell's) connection with famous sailors, to be the hero of nautical
adventure, and to unveil the secrets of the sea.

---

[1] From the Italian Biography of Sir Robert Dudley.

Through his mother he had in his veins the blood of William first Lord Howard of Effingham, Lord High Admiral, one of the most distinguished naval commanders in the "glorious reign" of Queen Elizabeth. Through his first wife he was connected with the Southwells, Vavasours and Rodneys, all of them bearing most illustrious names in the annals of the British Navy. He was in fact a distinguished soldier and a brave, prudent, and scientific sailor. He was skilled in country sports, and in all knightly games and exercises, a favourite at Court, and *l'enfant gâté des dames* in Society.

Though it is difficult to excuse his abandonment and repudiation of his wife Alice Leigh and her daughters, it is evident that he had convinced himself by Roman Catholic rules and reasoning, that he was justified in marrying Elizabeth Southwell, to whom he was undoubtedly a good and faithful husband.

When he left England in disgust at the harsh and unjust conduct towards him of the Court and his stepmother's party, he began a new and most useful, and most honoured life at the Grand-Ducal Court of Tuscany. He proved himself well versed in architecture, military and naval, and faithfully served his adopted country. He was moreover a learned physician, an admirable author, and to the last an ardent student, active, inventive, and indefaticable, honoured not only at Florence, but throughout Italy.

His new port of Leghorn and his great work the *Arcano del Mare* have made his name famous in all the world.

Don COSIMO DUDLEY.

PART IX.

DUDLEY'S DESCENDANTS.

LADY Alice Leigh, of Stoneleigh Abbey, Dudley's third wife, being left in England on his emigration to Italy, gave her mind to works of charity, and to attending to the welfare of her quartette of little daughters. We take the following list of her good deeds from the headings of her funeral sermon, preached at St. Giles' in the Fields by the Rev. Robert Boreman D.D., March 14th, 1669.

1st. She gave a new Chancel screen to the Church of St. Giles.

2nd. Gave large donations to the restoration of the same, as may be seen by a tablet in the Church.

3rd. Supplied silk hangings with silver fringe for the Chancel, a green velvet altar cloth, two white *ditto*, two altar cushions, a Turkey carpet and a neat " pair of organs," in a case richly gilded; also altar rails, and Communion plate.

4th. She augmented by £20 a piece the yearly income of five poor Vicarages of which Kenilworth was one.

5th. Enriched the said five Churches with silver Communion services.

6th. Bought a Rectory house, and endowed the Incumbent of St. Giles' with it.

7th. Paid a yearly stipend to the sexton of the same Church to toll the passing bell for prisoners condemned to die.

8th. Helped largely to repair Lichfield Church, and rebuilt St. Sepulchre's.

At her death she left the following legacies:

1st. £ 100 to redeem Christian captives from the hands of infidels.

2nd. £ 400 to St. Giles' Hospital.

3rd. £ 200 to apprentice poor parish children.

4th. £ 100 per annum to each of the five poor parishes before mentioned.

5th. £ 50 to be distributed at her funeral.

6th. A gown and a pair of kerchiefs, to each of fourscore and ten widows, who were to attend her funeral, and to receive a shilling each for a dinner afterwards.

7th. £ 5 to the poor of every place where her corpse should rest, between London and Stoneleigh in Warwickshire.

8th. Six pence to every poor body that should meet her corpse by the road.

9th. £ 10 each for the poor of Blackley, Lichborough and Patshill.

10th. £ 50 to be distributed in the parish of Stoneleigh on the day of her funeral.

After this edifying list which speaks for itself upon her tomb, we may omit the Rev. Dr. Boreman's laudation, enlarging on them, and see what great families her daughters helped to adorn.

The eldest of the four, Alicia Douglassia,[1] died young and her effigy lies beneath that of her mother in Stoneleigh Church, with this inscription:

"Here lyeth Alicia, who, dying before marriage on the 22nd of May 1621, left to her mother aforesaid, or to the cause of charity, a handsome patrimony,[2] to be at the disposal of her mother, and to be laid out in works of piety."

How many of the good works recorded on Lady Dudley's tomb were performed with young Alicia's money, there is nothing to shew. Nor can we explain the fact of Robert Dudley's unmarried daughter having an independent fortune to bequeath. It looks as though Robert Dudley had at least done his deserted family pecuniary justice, and given up much of his wealth to provide for them.

To see Dudley's second English daughter, you must go to St. Giles in the Fields, where she, Frances, wife of Sir Gilbert Kniveton of Bradley, Derby, Bart, lies in effigy wrapped in her winding sheet. When first erected, the monument was of the ancient bedstead form, but the Hon. Charles Leigh restored it to its present form in 1738. It seems to be by the same sculptor as the similar tombs of her mother and sister at Stoneleigh.

History says nothing about Sir Gilbert Kniveton, the husband of Lady Frances Dudley.

The two younger sisters married more prominent men. Lady Anne, the third daughter, became the wife

---

[1] Owing to a comma put in the wrong place in the Latin inscription of the Duchess Dudley's tomb, the words Alicia, Douglassia, have been taken to represent two persons instead of one. This is not the case; the child was named Alicia from her mother, Douglassia from her grand-mother, Lady Sheffield.

[2] It was three thousand pounds.

of Sir Robert Holbourne, Solicitor General to Charles Ist, presumably the man who drew out the patent creating his mother-in-law, Alicia, Duchess Dudley. Lady Anne died about 1663.

The youngest, Lady Katherine, who was born at Kenilworth about the time when her father left England, was the only one of the four daughters who survived her mother. She married Sir Richard Levison K. B. of Trentham, evidently a favourite courtier of King Charles Ist, who in the patent before quoted says:

"And we also casting our princely eye upon the faithful services done to us by Sir Richard Levison, Knight of the Bath, who hath married the Lady Katherine, one of the daughters of the said Duke, by his said wife, the said Lady Alice Dudley; and also the great services which Robert Holbourne, Esq., hath done to us, by his learned pen and otherwise (which said Robert Holbourne hath married the Lady Anne, one other of the daughters of the said Duke, by his said wife, the Lady Alice Dudley, etc.)." [1]

We are told by Dugdale, that Lady Katherine imitated her mother in works of piety. [2] She rebuilt the Temple Church at Balshall, Warwickshire, and augmented the Vicarage of Long-Itchington in the same county. She, too, founded some Hospitals and Schools, maintained twelve poor widows whom she clad in grey with the letters K and L sewn on their gowns in blue cloth. She moreover gave £ 100 per annum for the placing out of poor apprentices. She died in February 1673, and was buried by her late husband at Lilshull, Salop.

---

[1] See Appendix, n. VI.   [2] *Baronage,* vol. II, pag. 226.

1. Il s.re I
nipote del
libe

2. La so
ma

3. Sa se
ma
cas

4. Il d
pe
ha

oltra che il g.le
Duca di Nortfolk di 12
non ha debiti di
100 scudi in
Francia o nello stato.
ha sp

5. Ha
e hn

uolte di m
che el ffetto
Italia p neg
mi benefici

8 Si figli suoi,
et nel disseg
Cosimo figlio
che s'insci na
fu el pr° delli
mi tutti altri
el e stimato

9 La dote delli
et. no sura in
di massa ha
La figlia mar.e sol
bon partito p

seculi a finirlo. oltra che e porto tanto esquisi'-
ta. che e adesso nõ solo lachiaua di Toscana ma anco d
le niene ogni'anno l'ótto milliõi di mercantia
ueatura

ni lettore. et ogni' sorte di uir tu̇ p̃ si p̃ loro
ellane et Caualcare et sni'le essarcitẏ et il s.ᵉ Don
uuina' g̃t il ser.ᵐᵒ gran Duca ; nella festa a Cauallo
Presentu dell Duca di Parmu elle norse. et
proppio dell istesso Gran Duca. egli serue s.A.
et entra in Cameva sno teme fanno li Camerivi
dea S.A.S.

uayg.ᵉ sara' secondo la persona con quale si tettere
llo che si da alli primi di fiorenza· t che il Principe
e figlia' al s.ᵉ Duca faluiati
nej di madama ser.ᵐᵃ che cveu a trattuve qualche
fauorisce assai

ıl Duca di NortSunıbxın

In Florence the line of Dudley opened out far and wide, and had ramifications with the best Italian families of the 17th and 18th centuries, but, strange to say, they are at present all extinct.

We cannot do better than give the proud father's own account of his family taken from an autograph statement, in possession of the writer; which we reproduce here in the original. It was written in 1628, when he was called on to prove Don Antonio's nobility of descent.

After explaining the genealogical tree which makes out both Dudley and his wife to be of royal descent, and also his reasons for living in voluntary exile, he continues :

" This Dudley has five sons ' and five daughters :

" Don Cosimo Dudleo, Earl of Warwick and Prince of Northumberland, eldest son, aged (hiatus).

" Don Carlo, the second, aged 14.

" Don Ambrogio, the third, aged 12.

" Don Antonio, the fourth, aged 9.

" Don Ferdinando, the fifth, aged 7.

" The eldest girl is Donna Maria, aged 17.

" Then Donna Anna, aged 16.

" Donna Maddalena, aged 15.

" Donna Teresa, aged 5, and

" Donna Maria Cristina who is at the breast, the which was held at baptism by the illustrious Cardinal Barberini, and the Princess Maria Cristina of Tuscany."

---

[1] He had seven: the fourth son, Giovanni, must have died young, as he is left out of this list. Don Enrico, the seventh, was not yet born. A full list of their births and copies of their registrations are given in the notes to the following pages.

THE HERALDIC QUARTERINGS OF ROBERT DUDLEY, DUKE OF NORTHUMBERLAND.

The sixth paragraph runs: "The condition of the eldest girl is well known to every one, as also her deportment at Court, where she is invited by their Highnesses to all their fêtes, and is much respected by them. She is a great favourite with the Princesses, especially the Duchess of Parma, now married."

Paragraph 9: "The dower of the eldest daughter will be in accordance with the person with whom we treat, and will not be less than that of the highest persons in Florence, or that which the Prince of Massa gave his daughter. This eldest daughter is under the protection of Madama Serenissima, who is seeking a good match for her, and favours her very much."

Paragraph eight informs us that " the sons are well brought up in letters, and every sort of *virtù;* they are taught the arts of design, dancing, riding and other knightly exercises.

" Don Cosimo the eldest attends H. S. H. the Grand-Duke on horseback on festal occasions, and so well comported himself at the marriage of the Duke of Parma, that he was made the head of the Grand-Duke's squadron. He attends His Serene Highness on all occasions, and has the *entrée* of the chamber, being much esteemed and favoured by his patron."

After thus exalting his children, we can well accept Dudley's account of his own doings; he says: "The Grand-Duke treats him as his equal with much respect and courtesy, as a Signore who has rendered him great services;" going on to relate how by his plans and at a very moderate expense, Leghorn has been rendered not only the key of Tuscany for commerce, but also of Italy, to the extent of eight millions of *scudi* of merchandize, that are now annually brought there."

18

We have seen that the Grand-Duchess kept her
word, and that Donna Maria[1] was married with all due
ceremony to the Prince of Piombino; that the bride and
her husband's family kept up very friendly relations
with her father's household; the Appiani family spend-
ing the summer months, which are unhealthy at Piombino, at Dudley's Villa at Castello (now the Villa Corsini in Via del Boldrone), and Maria's brothers and
sisters visiting her in winter at her husband's castle,
where her eldest brother died in 1631.

And now as to the fates of this large progeny.

Cosimo Dudley[2] was indeed a most promising young
man, trained from his youth to courtly service, a great
favourite with the Grand-Duke, who made him Colonel
of his guard, while he was yet very young. He died
in 1631, as we have said, at Piombino, cut off in the
opening of a fine career.

---

[1] The baptism of Donna Maria is thus entered in the 'Registro
all'Opera del Duomo, Firenze.' All children born in Florence were
and are still baptized at San Giovanni, a Church dependent on the
Duomo, very near the front of the Duomo.

Tuesday. July 7th 1609. *M.* (Maria) *del Sig. ruberto di ruberto
d' udoleo* (*Dudley*) *Conte di Warwick inglese et della Sig; Elisabetta di
ruberto Sutel* (*Southwell*) *inglese P. di S. lor.* (*Parrocchia di San Lorenzo*).

She was born on that day at 12 o'clock, baptized the same day.
Her god-mother is named as *la Sig. Maria ticci Inglese.* Ticci is
probably an Italian corruption of the English name Tracy. There
was a friend of the Dudleys named Tracy.

[2] The entry of Cosimo's baptism deserves to be here inserted,
precisely as it was copied from the Registry.

1610 Domen. Addì 18 Luglio. Cosimo *del Sign. Conte Ruberto Du-
daleo, et della Sig. Contessa Lisabetta Dudora di Barliche p: Sto Pa-
golo n. addì 16 N: 1. b. Addì 18. C. il serenissimo Grā Duca Cosimo
secōdo Grā Duca di Toscana et p. S. A. S. illmo Sig. Silvio Piccolomini
d'Aragona.*

Observe the fantastic spelling of the names, observe also that the
god-father was the Grand-Duke, represented by a very noble Italian.

Anna, his next sister, died young, just about the time of her presentation. She seems to have been a gentle and saintly girl of great beauty. Nothing remains of her but her baptismal register [1] and funeral epitaph.

Maria Maddalena, the god-daughter of the Archduchess Maria Maddalena,[2] after her elder sister's marriage took her place at the Tuscan Court, and married into an old and well-known family, the Malespina, whose history we have given at pages 109, 110. Her home at Olivola on the beautiful slopes below the Carrara mountains near Sarzana, was a feudal castle of the Lords of Malespina. Here Dudley sent his wild son Charles when in disgrace with the Grand-Duke, and here is the tomb of the young Earl of Pembroke.

The castle of Olivola remained in possession of Spinetta Malespina and his wife M. M. Dudley till his death in 1655; his will is dated December 7th 1642.

His widow Maria Maddalena Dudley, in 1660, married Giambattista son of Gianantonio Fieschi of the Counts of Lavagna. The English family Heneage is connected with this branch. The names of Fieschi and Dudley are frequent in the Heneage family. There

---

[1] Exact copy of Anna's baptismal register:

1611 mercoledì a dì 26 Ottobre. Anna *del Ill. Sig. Conte ruberto uaruich et la Sig. donna lisabetta . . . . P. di S. Michele Visdomini N. a dì 25 h. 13 b. a dì 26. C. Ill.mo Sig. don Aless: del Sig. Fabbritio Malespina Capitano della guardia di S. A. S.*

Observe the dots following the Christian name 'Lisabetta' put there probably in the Italian scribe's despair of writing the family name 'Southwell.'

[2] *Mercoledì adì 19 Decembre 1612* Madda *del Sig. Conte Ruberto D'Udoleo di uaruich inglese et della Sig. Lisabetta uaruich P. di San Michele Visdomini n. a dì 16 d. h. 7 1/2 b. a. d. 19 d. C. la Sig. Luisa gerini già ne' Marchesi del Monte p. la scr.ma archiduchessa Maria Madda.na*

is in the Medicean archives (filza 5521) a letter from
her to Cardinal Leopold dei Medici asking some Court
office for a certain Cavalier Cesare Conosciuti. It is
signed D*. Maria Maddalena Dudlea-Fiesca.

Carlo,[1] the scapegrace of the family, was, as we
have seen, a thorn in his father's side, and by his
insolence and contumacy made it difficult for Robert
Dudley to maintain his position at the Tuscan Court.
If, like his father, he had been allowed to work off his
youthful energies in travel and adventure, he would
probably have been less hard to manage. As it was,
the trammels of Court life chafed him, and he escaped
them by absenting himself without leave, and refusing
the bonds of etiquette. Unfortunately he fell into bad
hands, and for the sake of lawlessness consorted with
outlaws, the result of which we see in his raid on his
father's Villa. He was but ill prepared to take his
rank as Duke of Northumberland after his father's
death. However he for many years sustained the office
of gentleman of the chamber to Cardinal Giovan Carlo
de' Medici, for which in 1640 he was receiving 192 ducats
a year, besides Christmas gifts of wine and meat, and
afterwards made a grand marriage with Marie Madeleine Gouffier of the ancient house of Gouffier of Poitou.

The founder of the house, Jean Gouffier, was Seigneur of Bonnivet of Lovan-Gouffier, of Bellefaye and

---

[1] Don Carlo's baptism:
*Lunedì 8 Settembre 1614 Carlo dell' Ill.mo et Ecc.mo Sig. Conte
Roberto del Signor Alberto di Varuick e dell'Ill.ma Sig. Contessa Lenter
di Lanceter nominata Lisabetta del Sig. Cav. Ruberto Sotuherch P.
S. Pancrazio a dì 7 do. h 2 b. a dì 8 d. C. l' Ill.mo et Ecc.mo Don
Gio: Medici. C.*

This son Carlo was an unruly and undutiful son to his father,
as we shall shew later.

Bataille, which he acquired in 1341. Jean Gouffier, the second, was Chamberlain to Charles II, then Dauphin. The third Gouffier, Aimeri, added to his family Seignories that of Boisy, and became Baron of Roannois, of Maulevrier, etc., was Counsellor and first Chamberlain to the King, Seneschal of Saintange, Governor of Touraine, and Tutor to King Charles VII, during his minority. After this extraordinary celerity of aggrandisement in their rise, we are not amazed to hear that the house of Gouffier counted among its members, a Cardinal, a Grand Almoner of France, a Marechal, a first Chamberlain, a Grand Master of France, an Admiral, several Seneschals and Governors of provinces, etc. Unluckily after all this prosperity it became extinct in the middle of the eighteenth century. Among the family titles, which are numerous, are those of Comte d'Etampes, Comte de Caravas, Baron de Maulevrier, Duc de Roannez, Marquis de Boisy and Seigneur de Crêvecœur.

This last was the branch to which Carlo Dudley's bride belonged, being the second daughter of Charles Antoine Gouffier, Marquis de Braseux, Seigneur de Crêvecœur, and his wife Françoise de Pisseleu, daughter of the Seigneur de Heilly. Marie Madeleine was, when Carlo married her, already the widow of Sig. Fabroni, Lord of Marradi in the Romagna. As to whether her marriage with Carlo Dudley were happy or not, we have not much evidence. Straws, they say, will shew which way the stream flows, and a few very small straws remain to us, in some fragments from Carlo Dudley's MS. Such as:

La Signora Duchessa mia moglie ha voglia di licenziarsi.
6 Aprile 1648. (My wife the Duchess wishes to go away.)

La Signora Duchessa sta pronta a partire per Lom-
bardia, perchè così voleva il Sig. Duca . . . . . Il Sig. Duca
faceva partire la Nipote. (The Duchess is about to leave
for Lombardy, for such is the Duke's wish . . . . . The
Duke caused his niece to depart.)

4 Febbraio 1650. La Contessa volle andare in casa di
Giuliano Gondi colle sue robe. (The Countess wanted
to go to the house of Giuliano Gondi with all her be-
longings.)

After all these signs of not being able to live in
the same house, the longer manuscript, a petition,
from Rome, dated May 5th 1676, is more intelligible.
It says that, owing to the Duke of Northumberland
being so long separated from his family, and deprived
of his property (this seems to mean exile and confiscation), he beseeches the Grand-Duke to remember
on his behalf the services rendered by his father,
especially in the Port of Leghorn. He pleads that,
without his property, his daughter is losing a great
matrimonial chance, the Princess of Rossano having
proposed a marriage for her with the Prince of Strongoli, but in his present state he has no means of giving
her the requisite dower.

This daughter was Carola, not the famous Christine
who was married in 1663 to Marchese Paleotti. It
may be presumed that the Grand-Duke recalled him
from exile, for in 1685 we have evidence of his living
in his father's house in Florence, under circumstances
which seem to show however, that Carlo, Duke of Northumberland was little less amenable to the decencies of
Court life than Carlo the youth.

A curious old MS. in possession of the author gives
a view of him at seventy years of age, the year before

his death, that is certainly not prepossessing. We are told that on the 17th of February 1685, there was a reception in Casa Corsi, at which the Duke of Northumberland assisted. He had taken a chair which had been placed for the ladies, and Marchese Capponi, master of the ceremonies, asked him to give it up to one of the dames. This he disregarded, till, on the request being repeated, the Duke became enraged, and haughtily said that persons of his rank were entitled to sit where they chose. High words followed till the Duke in a fury put his hand in his pocket. The Marchese, thinking he would draw out his pistols, embraced him with both arms so that he could not move his hands, till other Cavaliers came to his assistance. There was a grand scene, Ladies screaming and running to the door, Cavaliers struggling in the room, angry or alarmed voices on all sides, and suddenly into the midst of it there entered Prince Ferdinand, son of the Grand-Duke Cosimo III. He demanded to know what tumult was going on, and ordered the Marchese Capponi to retire to his own house, and not to leave it till further orders, and told the Duke that one of the Court carriages was waiting for him. Some of his own gentlemen and squires escorted the Duke home, who also had orders not to leave his house till further commands.

Prince Ferdinand sent to inform the Grand-Duke at Pisa, of the fact, who, approving all his son had done, said he would now take the matter into his own hands. He sent the Sergeant general, Bracciolini, to the Duke to obtain his apologies. These Carlo refused to give, and held to his demands of satisfaction from the Marquis. Much time was lost,

but it only rendered the Duke more obstinate than
before, and in fact so contumacious that the *Sbirri* of
the Bargello were placed to guard his house at night.
At length an officer and twelve soldiers from the fortress were sent to say that the Grand-Duke desired
his recalcitrant courtier to transfer his residence to the
fortress. Without a word of remonstrance the Duke
of Northumberland ordered his carriage, walked haughtily into it, and was forthwith taken to the prison at
the fortress, in which Filippo Strozzi found his tomb,
and where Carlo himself had been confined in 1638.
This is the last we hear of Carlo Dudley till his death
in 1686.

Don Ambrogio, who was no doubt named after his
great uncle Ambrose, Earl of Warwick, was a page to
the Grand-Duchess and had, besides his servant, a tutor
to take care of him, "lest he should spend all his
month's allowance at once." [1] A stray note mentions
that he wrote to his brother Carlo from his sister's
house at Olivola, on 15th of July 1637, and another
in his father's hand recording that in 1628 "Don Ambrogio was in love, and paying court to a daughter
of the Rucellai close by." The Rucellai palace is only
a few steps from Dudley's house in the Vigna Nuova.
No such marriage is recorded, nor do we hear of Don
Ambrogio after this, as he died young.

---

[1] This is the registration of Dudley's sixth child, Ambrogio, born
on the 4th April 1617:

Mercoledì 5 Aprile 1617. Ambrogio dl Sig.ᵣᵉ Ruberto Conte di
varvic di rubet dudel e della Sig.ᵣⁿ Elisabetta del S.ᵣᵉ Ruberto . . . . . .
P. S. brancatis n. a. dì 4. h. 19 ¹/₂ b. a. d. 5 d. C. Ill.ᵐⁱᵒ et Ecc.ᵐᵒ Sig.ᵣ
don Antonio Medici p. sua altezza di Medici. C. sua altezza di Mantova p. sua altezza la Sig.ᵣⁱ beatrice Marchesa baglioni ne' Malespini.
(ne' is the abbreviation of nei, and means married into the Malespini
family.)

Don Giovanni his next brother also died young.[1]

Don Antonio[2] was one of the pages of the Grand-Duchess. Dudley evidently intended to make a naval officer of him, but he did not live to fulfil his destiny. In 1636 his father obtained his election into the knightly Order of St. Stephen. A great many ceremonies and formalities had to be gone through before the young man got his spurs. A ponderous legal deed, called an *Atto di provanze,* had to be drawn up, proving that the postulant was of noble descent through all his four grand-parents. Dudley drew up a genealogical tree proving his own descent from King Henry III, and that of his wife Elizabeth from King Edward II of England. Then came acts of notary, registrations, etc., and after all the young man only donned the white robe of Knighthood a few months before his early death.[3]

In the following year we find the name of Conte Don Antonio Dudleo, Cavaliere dell' Ordine di Santo Stefano, as one of the actors in a grand Court pageant, held at the Pitti Palace for the delectation of the Grand-

---

[1] Baptism of the seventh child, Giovanni, born on the 19th jan. 1618:
Masti (maschi) di Gennaio 1618. Dom.ca a, d, 20. Gio. dl Sig.r Conte Ruberto d' Varvich e dla Sigra lisabetta dl Sigr Ruberto suel. P. S. Pancratio N. a dì 19. b. a. d. 21 d. C. il R. A. M. S. Cardinale de' Medici p. S. A. R. S. Sigr Averardo dellmo Raffle Medici. C. la Sigra Principessa Claudia d' Urbino. p. el Sigra Marta Concina.

[2] *dom. a dì 31 Maggio 1620.* Antonio *dell' Ill.mo Sig. Conte Ruberto di ruberto dudleo conte di uaruich et della Sign. Contessa Elisabetta del Sig roberto . . . . . . P. S. Pancrazio. n. d. d. h. 6. b. d. d. C. il Sig. riccardo di Gio.ni deburgo p. l' ecc.mo Sig. Principe don lor.zo Medici C. la Sig. Marchesa leonora concini p. l' ecc.ma Sig. Principessa Maria Medici duchessa d' urbino.*

In 1621 Elizabeth, now Duchess of Northumberland, gave birth to a ninth child.

[3] See Appendix, n. XXX, XXXI.

The armorial bearings of Elizabeth Southwell.

Duchess Vittoria della Rovere. The pageant was called *Le Nozze degli Dei* (Marriages of the Gods). There were thirty gods and goddesses, all courtiers, besides various choruses, such as the twelve nymphs of Diana; seventeen Cyclops of Vulcan; the nine Muses; the chorus of Venus, consisting of fourteen loves, three Graces, " the genius of Smiles" and " Frolic ; " thirty marine gods of Neptune ; forty celestial spirits of Jupiter; twenty infernal Numi of Pluto ; and fourteen nymphs of Juno. There was also a battle between the warriors of Mars and Vulcan. It must have been a grand spectacle, and was probably the last gay scene in which Don Antonio took part.

Don Ferdinando [1] became a monk. In an old letter of Robert Dudley's to Cioli, while enumerating the expenses of maintaining and dressing his large family, he dismisses the priestly son with the words: " Don Ferdinando is in his novitiate and spends almost nothing." He was in the Convent of San Domenico at Fiesole.

At the same time his next sister Donna Teresa [2] was in the Convent of the Crocetta in Via del Boldrone, close to the family Villa at Castello. As we have before said, she wished at an early age to be a nun, but as

---

[1] Baptized and thus registered:

Masti 1621. lunedì a dì 11 8bre Ferdinando del Ill.mo et Ecc.mo Sig. Duca Dudduleo di nortumbria c conte di uaruiche e della Sig. Elisabelt . . . . . . P. di S. Pancrazio n. d di. a. h. 11 C. l' Illust. Sig. Marchese Ferdi. Riano p. il S. G. Duca.

[2] From the birth register of the Baptistery:

Femmine 1623 Giovedì a dì 22 Giugno. Teresia di Don Ruberto Dudleo Duca di Nortumbria c della Ecc.ma Sig. lisabetta del Sig. Ruberto Sotiele. P. S. Pancrazio n. a. di do. h. 2 b. a di. C. il ser.mo Ferdinando Gonzagha Duca di Mantova e p. lui l' Ill.mo Sig Marchese Piero Guicciardini C. la Principessa Margherita Medici e p. lei l'Ill.ma S. Marches Ipolita Malespina.

Observe the family name Southwell written Sotiele.

she grew older and went to Court, she became more worldly. She was almost a greater favorite at the Pitti Palace than her sisters had been, and on September 24th 1645, she was married to the Duca della Cornia of the great Perugia family. This marriage is thus mentioned by Paolo Verzoni, MS., *Mag.*, t. II, pag. 198:

A dì 24 Settembre 1645. Ricordo come questa sera il Signor Duca dela Cornia ha dato l' anello alla sua nuova moglie, che ha preso, che è una figlia del S. Duca di Nottumbria, e l' anello si è dato nel Palazzo dc' Pitti alla presenza dei Serenissimi Padroni, et in quella sera si fece un bellissimo festino in detto luogo per solennizzar quelle nozze.

Although the Duca della Cornia was a widower, this was a very good match for the daughter of the Dudley family. The young lady was then about twenty-two years old. She was especially honoured too, in the Grand-Duke having the wedding ceremony performed in his own Palace, and in being himself one of the witnesses. In the evening the Grand-Duchess gave a *festa* at the Pitti Palace in honour of the bride, and Donna Teresa must have felt very important in being thus made the centre and cause of a Court *Fête*. As we have said, her first taste of married life did not last long. She became a widow before she was a mother,[1] and her child, a boy, named Fulvio, died a

---

[1] In 1648 in MS. (*Mag.*, t. II, pag. 369) of Paolo Verzoni there is the following entry:

A dì 5 Luglio ricordo come questo giorno è stato battezzato in questa città un figlio del già S. Duca della Cornia, il quale morì alli mesi passati, lassato il ventre pregnante, al quale è stato posto nome Fulvio Lodovico Melchior e sono stati tenuti dalla Sig^{ra} Ortensia Salviati a nome della Ser. Gran Duchessa, e da Mons. Nunzio Bentivoglio a nome del S. Cardinale Sforza.

few months after,[1] — a bitter trial for one so young. The trial was aggravated by law worries. Her son dying in infancy, she became his heir *ab intestato*; but the Apostolic Chamber here came in, and decreeing that the family of Cornia, being by this child's death extinct, his properties reverted to the Church. This decree was promulgated in Rome on December 13th 1647, and drawn up by Galoppi the notary who was secretary to the " Apostolic Camera."

The Duchess Teresa strenuously fought for her rights, but never obtained them. The long law-suit was ultimately finished after her death by a transaction between her heirs and the Apostolic Chamber, in which the latter was of course the chief gainer.

These were indeed vicissitudes, but youth helped her through, and with the elasticity of her age, she soon formed other ties. A few months after her child's birth and early death, she married another great man, the Count of Carpegna. Of him Verzoni (pag. 212) records that " on January 12th 1646 the Count Mario Carpegna, first gentleman of the Chamber to the Cardinal Carlo de' Medici, was chosen as High Steward, in place of the Abate Corsi, sent as vice legate to Avignon."

Litta in his *Famiglie celebri* tells us that Mario was of the family of the Conti di Carpegna in Montefeltro, that he was made Knight of St. Stephen on April 3rd 1604, held the post of High Steward to Cardinal Carlo de' Medici at the Court of Tuscany, where he met the beautiful

---

[1] In the MS. (*Mag.*, t. II, pag. 349) of Paolo Verzoni there is the following entry:

A dì 14 Dicembre 1648. Ricordo che questo giorno è passato a miglior vita l' unico figlio del già S. Duca della Corgnia, che era d' età di mesi cinque, chiamato Fulvio Lodovico Melchior, ed è morto in Firenze.

and interesting young widow Teresa Dudley, Duchess
Cornia. He had been elected Gonfaloniere of Rimini,
where his family were inscribed on the Roll of Nobles.
He made his will in Rome, June 3rd 1661, where he
died after having instituted for his descendants, the law
of primogeniture in the person of his eldest son Ulderico Gaetano, leaving his wife guardian of their three
children Vittoria, Ulderico Gaetano, and Anna Maria.
His widow died in Rome August 21st 1698.

It was to give the Count and Countess of Carpegna
a home in Florence near their Court duties, that Dudley
executed that deed on their marriage in 1649, giving
them the use of the house in Vigna Nuova for five years.
By Robert Dudley's will Teresa and her husband inherited
a third share in the family palace, the other two being
held by her only surviving brothers Carlo and Enrico.

Of little Maria Cristina there seems but little to
say, the only view of her we get is Dudley's mention
of her christening,[1] and her being nursed by her mother.

Don Enrico, the youngest of all, appears now and
then in the family chronicles.[2] For instance, in the
letter to Cioli, before spoken of, Dudley says:

---

[1] Thus registered:

*1628 Martedì a dì 20 Giugno Maria Christina dell'Ecc.mo Sig.
ruberto di ruberto Duca di Northumbria e dell'Eccel.ma Signora lisa-
betta . . . . p. di S. Pancrazio n. il d. 18 C. l' Ill.mo c. R. Mons.
Alphonso Giliucci nutio d' appresso il G. D. di Toscana p. l' Ill.mo
S. Card.le Francesco Barberino C. la Marc. Ipolita Malespina p. la
Princ. Maria Christina P. di Toscana.*

Here the civic scribe gives up the task of spelling Southwell altogether and leaves an hiatus.

[2] Don Enrico's birth is thus registered:

*Martedì a dì p. Aprile 1631 Enrico dell' ecc.mo Sig Duca Don Ro-
berto Dudleo Duca di Nortumbria e dell' ecc.ma Sig. Elisabetta di Don
Ruperto Sauthuel P. S. Pancrazio. n. d. d. h. 3. C. il. Sig. Principe
Gia. Carlo Medici p. lui il Sig. Marchese Niccolini.*

"Don Enrico spends five scudi a month," and a little before he remarks: "Don Enrico is kept at Olivola by his sister the Marchesa Malespina."

This good elder sister evidently took a mother's part to the little motherless baby.

We also find his name as page on the roll of the household of Cardinal de' Medici in 1644.

The Medicean Archives (filza 5535) contain two letters dated respectively April 16th and May 7th 1662, written by Don Enrico to the Grand-Duke, praying for a reversion of the decree made by him four years previously, stopping a certain suit for debt, brought by Don Enrico against his brother Carlo, Duke of Northumberland. He says that "he had paid all the expenses of the *Magistrato della Mercanzia,* before which Court the case was brought, and that this long suspension of justice did him much harm." [1] The Grand-Duke seems not to have answered the first of these, as the second is almost identical in substance. This Henry, who in 1652 became Earl of Warwick (all his elder brothers, except Carlo, being deceased), was joint heir with Carlo Duke of Northumberland, of their father's house in Vigna Nuova.

To the third generation the family of Dudley kept up its prestige. The wild Carlo had two sons, Antonio, and Roberto, and two daughters, Christine who was a famous if unprincipled beauty, and another, Carlotta, who was to have married Prince Strongoli.[2]

At the birth of Carlotta on December 1650, we find Carlo Duke of Northumberland writing to ask the Grand-Duke and "Madonna Reale" to stand as sponsors to his

---

[1] See Appendix, n. XLIII.
[2] See Appendix, n. XLIV.

newly-born daughter. On this occasion he is loyal enough. "I who was born under the protection of Your Highness," he writes, "am bound in duty on every occasion most humbly to confirm my ready and obedient service to you. Therefore I beseech you to accept these my dutiful observances, and to permit me to kiss your robe. Your most Serene Highnesses most humble, obedient and faithfull servant,

"THE DUKE OF NORTHUMBERLAND."

This baptism seems to have taken place in the monastery of San Niccolò.[1] Besides the Grand-Duke and Duchess there were present the Grand-Duchess Vittoria della Rovere and Princess Margherita Luisa of Orleans.

Carlo Duke of Northumberland had taken up his residence in Bologna, and there his son Robert retained his home till his death in 1706. He was Chamberlain to Queen Christine. His will, drawn up by Ser Jacopo Mezzavilla, is dated April 29th 1706, and is to be seen in the Archives· of Bologna.

Don Antonio, Carlo's second son, chose the Church as his profession, although he had been made Knight of St. Stephen without the usual formalities. He was

---

[1] Del Migliore thus mentions the baptism:

"E perchè vi son sempre state Donne de le prime case di Firenze, su luogo antiposto, e reputato convenevole alla funzione del tenersi al Battesimo, nel 1661 da Ferdinando Carlo Arciduca d'Austria, con Anna de' Medici, sua moglie, la Carlotta Luisa, nata di Don Carlo Dudley Duca di Nortumbria, conte di Varviche e Lincestre, descendente dal sangue Regio d'Inghilterra, e di D. Maria Guffier de' Duchi d'Aquitania: presenti col seguito della prima nobiltà, le Granduchesse Vittoria della Rovere e la Margherita Luisa d'Orleans. (Passeremo alla Nunziata, di lì poco distante.)" DEL MIGLIORE's *Firenze*, ed. 1734, lib. I, pag. 261.

Canon of the Vatican, and was buried in Rome in 1728 aged 75, in the especial place of sepulture for the Canons. He lived in Via Sant'Agnese in Rome, in the house of his brother-in-law the Marchese Paleotti;[1] until, in 1692, both Carlo and Enrico being deceased, their shares of the family home in Florence passed to him. This same priestly Don Antonio also became possessed, in 1695, of several farms near Fiesole, and in the parish of San Martino at Maiano, left to him by his mother Maria Maddalena Gouffier, Marchioness of Braxeis.

Till 1720 the Canon lived at Viterbo, where he made his will, leaving his nephew Marchese Tommaso Paleotti sole heir to all the Dudley property in Florence, Fiesole, and Maiano. He too seems to have died soon after, for in the year 1728, all these properties lapsed to the Marchese Andrea Paleotti, Canon Antonio's heir at law, the line of Dudley being then extinct.

Carlo's daughter Cristina, who married Marchese Paleotti, was at a very early age a lady in waiting at the Court of Savoy; the chronicler Tioli records under the date of December 23rd 1663, that "the Marchese Andrea Paleotti arrived at Bologna from Turin with his bride Donna Cristina, daughter of the English Duke of Northumberland, who was in the Court of Madama di Savoia at the age of fifteen." He adds that "for beauty, spirit, and *bizzarria*, few or none could equal

---

[1] From information kindly afforded me by the Cavaliere Dottore Odoardo Vecchietti of Florence for which I beg to thank him sincerely, we learn that the Palazzo Paleotti in Bologna is in the Via Luigi Lamboni già San Donato, and that it occupies the site of the ancient Palazzo Bentivoglio, with which family the Paleotti intermarried in the 17th century. Several of the Paleotti were Senators, and one of them a Cardinal.

her, and that neither Prince nor Cavalier could pass without admiration, and wishing to know her."

This beautiful Cristina's daughter, Diana, only sixteen years younger than her mother, inherited her beauty and eccentricity, with some of her grand-father's wildness. She married into the Colonna family, as we learn from Imhoff. In his *Genealogiæ viginti illustrium in Italia Familiarum, etc.*, Amstedolani, ex officina Fratrum Chatelain, anno MDCCX, Imhoff says, in speaking of the great Colonna family of Rome:

"Marcus Antonius secundogenitus præcipitato ex amoris æstu cum fœmina forma magis quam dote prædita, haud tamen ignobili, et maternum genus ad Leicestriæ Comitem in Anglia, gratia Elisabethæ Reginæ, florentissimum, referente matrimonio, fratribus cognatisque stomachum movit, eaque propter procul ab illis ætatem egit, quattuor jam liberorum sequioris sexus pater, sicut accepimus, (Carolo?) natu minimo Innocentius XII Papa inter domesticos suos Præfecti domus (Maggiordomo) dignatione adscito, et Principi Protonotariorum Apostolicorum creato spem galeri rubei injecit, sed morte sua destituit; quam contra illius successor Clemens XI implevit."

For all the particulars of this marriage of Marc'Antonio Colonna and Diana, the favourite daughter of Cristina Paleotti born Dudley, and of the life and adventures of the beautiful, fascinating and profligate Cristina Paleotti herself, consult the very interesting volume *Una illustre avventuriera*, Cristina di Nortumbria, by Corrado Ricci, seconda edizione, Milano, Fratelli Treves, editori, 1891.

It contains a graphic description of the manners, customs and amusements of the high and gay society of Bologna, towards the end of the seventeenth century. It gives moreover the true history of the daughter of Charles Dudley, by his French wife Marie Madeleine Gouffier. In beauty, wit and eccentricity, few or none could equal her, and none were so daring and adventurous.

She soon became the most celebrated beauty in Bologna, and so she continued for many years, through strange adventures and vicissitudes. *Tre volte nella polvere, tre volte sugli altari* (thrice in the dust, thrice on the altars) to the end of her romantic life. Her last and greatest adventure resulted in her success in marrying her daughter to Don Marc'Antonio of the great Roman family of the Colonna, notwithstanding the bitter opposition of the Colonna family. It was even suggested that the marriage was null and void, because the old Constable Colonna had in past years been the successful lover of Cristina, and was father of a child by her. But in the end Diana was publicly acknowledged as the true and lawful wife of Marc'Antonio, a very great match even for one of the Paleotti, and a descendant from the Duke of Northumberland. Cristina's son Tommaso, Colonel of the Guard of the Grand-Duke, was made Knight of St. Stephen in 1724.

Another daughter, Adelhida or Adelaide, had almost as adventurous a life. After a very unfortunate marriage with an Italian named Roffeni, she became protestant and espoused the Duke of Shrewsbury, whom she had met at the house of her cousin the Conte di Carpegna. She was a leader of Society in London, where she held receptions on Sunday and Thursday. She was lady in waiting to the Princess of Wales.

She was much persecuted in London by her wild

brother Ferdinand, who after getting into trouble in
several of the European courts, gave constant alarm
and annoyance to the Duke and Duchess of Shrewsbury.
He was finally hanged at Tyburn on March 28th, 1718,
for the murder of his Italian lacquey Giovanni Niccolò.
He made a special request to the hangman, that he
might be hanged apart from the other prisoners, who
were to be executed at the same time (on black Monday),
so that he might not be defiled, by being touched by
them in their death struggles. The Marchese Neri Corsini, of the day, Inviato of the Grand-Duke in London,
was present at the execution.[1]

The children of Teresa Contessa di Carpegna, also,
attained to high offices at Court. Ulderico Gaetano,
the heir, was a great favourite of the Grand-Duke
Ferdinand II, who honoured him with the collar of
the Order of St. Stephen at the early age of 14.

His two sisters were maids of honour to the Grand-
Duchess, and were distinguished at Court for their intel-
lectual qualities and high education. Vittoria married
a Roman noble named Cavalieri; her son the Marchese Emilio de' Cavalieri was the residuary legatee
of his grand-mother Duchess Teresa.

Anna Maria, the other sister, married another Roman
noble, Marchese Giovanni Battista Naro.

No Dudleys in the line male now remained to carry
on the name. After the third generation they became
extinct in Italy.

---

[1] *Una illustre avventuriera*, pag. 271 to 282.

APPENDIX.

APPENDIX.

I.

The Earl of Leicester's Will.

The Probate bears Date 6ᵗʰ Sept. 1588, and Administration was granted to Lady Lettice Countess of Leicester his Relict, and Executrix.

This is the last Will and Testament of me Robert Earl of Leicester, her Majestys Lievtenant General of all her Forces in the Low-Countries, and Governor and Captain General of all the United Privinces, written with his own hand the First of August in Middleborough 1578. First I take it the to be the Part of every true Christian, to make a true Testimony of his Faith at all Times, and especially in such a Case and such a Time as this is. And, therefore, I do mean here faithfully to make a short Declaration to testify in what Faith I do live, and depart from this World through the Grace of my Lord and Saviour to continue me in the same till the Seperation of this Life and Body. And so I do acknowledge my Creation and Being, to be had and continued by the Providence of our Almighty God, the Creator of all Things both in Heaven and Earth, and do confess, that above all Deeds, that his Divine Majesty hath done for Mankind, is the Gift of his blessed Son, Christ Jesus, to be the Redeemer and Saviour of his People that be faithfull, by whose only Merits and Passion I verily believe and am most assured of the forgiveness of all my Sinnes, be they never so great or infinite and that he only is the sufficient Sacrifice that hath appeased the Wrath of his Father, and that blessed Lamb, which innocently suffered all Torments, to bear the bitter Burden due to us miserable Wretches, for his most tender Compassion over all that have Grace to Believe in him. All which his Graces

Goodness and Mercy I most faithfully take hold on, being so promised by himself, who is the only Truth itself, that I am the Child of Salvation; and to be the Inheritour of his ever-lasting Kingdom, and to meet with him at the joyfull Day of Resurrection, with all the faithful Children, and Saints of God. In this Faith I now live, and in this Faith I trust to change this Life, with continual Prayer to the Throne of Grace, to grant me, during this Pilgrimage of mine, a true, humble and penitent Heart, for the due recognition of all mine Offences, and the willing Amendment of the same, and to fly instantly to the sure Ankerholde my Lord and Saviour, Christ Jesus, to whom with the Father and the Holy Spirit, be all Honour, Glory and Dominion, forever. Amen. Thus being in perfect Health and Memory, and having set down my Faith as a true Christian, and being uncertain of the Hour of Death, I think it my Part to settle my worldly Matters in as good Estate as I can, spe-cially being hastily and suddenly sent over, and likewise having very little Leasure, since my Arrival to get any Time for my private Business.

But first my Will is, to commit this wretched Body of mine, when it shall please God to seperate it from the Soul, to the Order of my dear Friends, that shall be living as my Execu-tors, and my overseers of this my last Will and Testament, and they to take such Order for the Burial of my Body, as they shall think mete, always requiring that it may be done with as little pomp or vain Expences of the World, as may be, being persuaded that there is no more vain Expences than that in a convenient Tombe or Monument I wish there should be. And, for the Place where my Body should lye, it is hard to appoint, and I know not how convenient it is to desire it; but I have always whised, as my dear Wife doth know, and some of my friends, that it might be at Warwick, where sundry of my Ancestors doe lye, either so, or else where the Queens Majesty shall command, for as it was when it had Life, a most faithfull, true loving Servant unto her, so living and so dead let the Body be at her gracious Determination, if it shall so please her. Touching my Bequests, they cannot be great, by Reason my Ability and Power is little, for I have not dissembled

with the World my Estate, but have lived always above any
Living that I had (for which I am heartily sorry) least that,
thro' my many debts, from Time to Time, some Men have taken
Loss by me. My Desire therefore is, and I do charge my
Executors to have due Consideration, that if any Person shall
justly after my Decease make such Complaint, that they may
be satisfied as far as shall be found in any Equity it is due
to them, with Advantage to them beside. I do here appoint
my most dear, well beloved Wife, the Countess of Leicester, to
be my sole Executrix of this my last Will and Testament; and
do require her, for all Love between us, that she will not only
be content to take it upon her, but also to see it faithfully
and carefully performed. And although, albeit there may many
Imperfections be found with the making this Will, for that I
am no Lawyer, nor have any Councel now with me to place
things in such Forme as some are able; yet as my true Meaning
is I trust to express, that accordingly it may be interpreted,
for I mean to make it as plain as I can. And first of all, before
and above all Persons, it is my duty to remember my most
dear, and most gracious Sovereign, whose Creature under God
I have been, and who hath been a most bountiful, and most
princely Mistress unto me, as well in advancing me to many
Honours, as in maintaining me many Ways by her Goodness
and Liberality. And as my best Recompence to her most excellent Majesty can be from so mean a Man, chiefly in Prayer to
God, so whilst there was any Breath in this Body, I never failed
it, even as for mine own Soul. And as it was my greatest Joy,
in my Life Time, to serve her to her Contentation, so it is not
unwelcome to me, being the Will of God to dye, and end this
Life for her Service. And yet, albeit I am not able to make
any Piece of Recompence of her great Goodness, yet will I
presume to present unto her a token of an humble, faithfull
heart, as the least that ever I can send her, and with this
Prayer withall, that it may please the Almighty God, not only
to make her the oldest Prince, that he ever gave over England,
but to make her the Godliest, the Virtuest, and the Worthiest
in his Sight, that he ever gave over any Nation. That she may
indeed be a blessed Mother and Nurse to this People, and

Church of England, which the Almighty God grant for his Christ's Sake. The Token I do bequeath unto her Majesty, is the Jewel with three great Emrodes with a fair large Table Diamond in the Middest, without a Foyle, and set about with many Diamonds without Foyle, and a Roap of fayre white Pearl, to the Number six hundred, to hang the said Jewel at; which Pearl and Jewel, was once purposed for her Majesty, against a Coming to Wansted, but it must now thus be disposed, which I do pray you, my dear Wife see performed, and delivered to some of those whom I shall hereafter nominate and appoint to be Overseers for her Majesty.

Next to her Majesty I will now return to my dear Wife, and set down that for her, which cannot be so well as I would wish it, but shall be as well as I am able to make it, having always found her a faithfull, loving and a very obedient, carefull Wife; and so do I trust this Will of mine shall find her no less mindfull of me being gone, then I was always of her being alive. I do give and bequeath to my said dear Wife, over and beside the Jointure I have made her, the Lease of Drayton Basset, freely to give and dispose at her Will. *Item.* There be certain parcels of Grounds, which I bought of the Earl of Oxford, being sometime belonged to the House of Crambrooke, and I reserved purposely to be joined to the Park of Wansted, as also the Parcel of Ground, called Watermans, which I bought of the L. of Buckhurst; both which I do also freely give and grant to my said Wife forever, with the Mannor of Wansted, already assured unto her. *Item.* I do give to my said Wife, during her Life, all other Lands and Tenements, which I did purchase in the Lordship of Wansted, beside that is passed by Deed, with the House and Mannor, to her before, And because I do give the House and Land of Aldersbroock, which I bought of Fuller the lawyer to my base Son Robert Dudley, I do desire and pray my said dear Wife, that she will be pleased to give him also the great Pond before the Door of the said House, being Parcel of the Mannor of Wansted. Which House and Lands of Aldersbrook I do also grant unto my said Wife, till my said base Son shall accomplish the Age of twenty Yeares. *Item.* I do give unto my said dear Wife all my Goods and Leases whatsoever, toward the payment of me Debts, and her better Maintenance, saving such as I shall hereafter, in this my Will, limit and sett down for other Uses. *Item.* For that there is sixteen-thousand Pounds, due by me, to the Merchants of London, upon Mortgage of the Lordships of Denbigh, and others, and that neither my Leases, nor Goods, able to redeem them, and to pay other my Debts; I do give Power and Authority, by this my last Will, to such as I have made Assurance already, for the same Purpose, as if they want Power and Authority by any such former Act. I do give all power and Authority, that is possible for me to give, either to my Executrix and my Overseers, jointly together, or such of them as shall be living, to sell all my Lands and Leases, with the Parsonage of Warrington, which I have in Lancashire, and were sometimes the Lands of Sir Thomas Butler Knt. and Edward Butler Esq., his son. All which Lands and Leases I do will in any wise to be sold for the Redemption of the Lordships of Denbigh, and Chirk, and the overplus thereof, to go toward the Payment of my other Debts, for the better Ease and Relief of my Executrix, and for that the said Lands of Butlers, were intended at the first, by the said Butler, to be given to my said base Son, Robert, I do in Liew thereof give unto him the said Lordships of Denbighe and Chirke, etc. but after the Death of my dear Lord, and Brother, the Earl of Warwick, to whom, with all other my Lands, during his Life, I do give and bequeath, saving such as I have already granted to my said dear Wife, in Joynture or shall grant unto her, by this my last Will and Testament. The Castle of Kenilworthe, I do likewise give unto my said Brother, with all the Parks, Chases and Lands, during his Life, and the Park and Paddock of Rudfine only excepted, which I always gave unto my Wife during her Life, the Timber Woods of all which I do reserve from any Waste (Reparations necessary excepted) or if it shall please my Lord and Brother to build out the Gallery which I once intended, then to take such Timber as shall be convenient for the same. *Item.* I do will and give all such Stuff and Implements of Household, as I have heretofore stored the said Castle with, all to remain to the said Castle and House, and not to be altered or removed. I do also give two Garnish of silver Vessells to remain, as the rest, to the said Castle, with two Basons and Ewers of silver gilt, with other Plate for a Cupboard, to the value of two hundreth Pounds, over and above the former Parcells of Vessell and Basons and Ewers. *Item.* I do give and grant, by this my Will, the said Castle and Lands belonging to the said Castle, and which I have purchased to the same. Also, after the decease of my Lord and Brother, to my base Son Robert Dudley, as also the free Farm of Rudfyne, I do give also to my dear Wife my House and Mannor of Langley, with all the Appurtenances, and the Use of all the Coppice Woods there, with the Lease of Whitney, until my said base Son accomplish the Years of one and twenty; both which, after, I do give and grant to Robert, my base Son, in such sort as shall be limited unto him, with the rest of the Lands I give him. If he dye before the said one and twenty Year, then my said Wife to enjoy the said Lands and Leases during her Life. I give him also the leases of Grafton Pasture, after the decease of my said Wife. I doe also desire my good Lord and Brother, the Lands aforesaid coming to his hands, that it will please him to give some reasonable Stipend to the Boy, when he comes to more years, for his Maintenance. In the meantime, after the Decease of Gabriel Bleke, and his Wife, I do give and grant to the said Robert, all such Lands and Leases, as I have conveyed unto me from the said Gabriel forever; and the same Lands, Houses and Leases, to enjoy presently after the Decease of the said Gabriel Bleke and his Wife now living. I do give and grant to my said base Son, also, after the Decease of my dear wife, the Mannors of Balsoll, and Long Itchington, in the Countye of Warwick, with all Appurtenances. I do likewise give and grant to my said base Son, the Mannors of Cleobury and Eurnewood, after the Decease also of my said dear Wife. *The Moyety of such Lands as was recovered from the Lord Berkely, I do leave unbestwowed; but to be imploied by my Lord and Brother upon such our next heirs (for that it came by Descent) as he shall find living with him, Sir Robert Sydney if he live to it.* And for all those things which I have granted, whereof my dear Wife hath Interest, either during her Life, or otherwise, if any mine Heirs or Assigns, shall go about to molest or disturb her Estate, and shall molest and any way disturb her from any such Estate, granted to her either by Deed or Will from me that immediately it shall be lawfull for her, during her Life, to enter and seize upon the Lands, that any such Disturber shall presently hold or enjoy from me, whatsoever it shall be. *Item.* If the Lands which was Butlers in Lancashire, cannot be sold in sort to pay and redeem the Mortgage of Denbigh and Chirk, and to make six or seven Pounds more, at the least, toward my other Debts; then it is my Will, that my Overseers shall, and my Executrix also, joyn with them, if so it be need-full to bargain and sell all those Lordships of Denbigh and Chirk, and to make the most of it, and the Overplus to go to the Payment of my other Debts. And then I do give and grant by this Will, all the Lands and Leases in Lancashire, to my sayd Robert my base Son for ever. And for that there is certain of my Lands charged with Rents and Tenths to her Majesty, and that I have certain free Rents in Wales to as great Value or more my humble Request to her Highness, is, that it may please her to discharge those Rents from my other Lands, and to receive the other Rents in Wales for the same, which is no less to her Majesty at all, but as certain as the other. And where my base Son is young and casual, whether these my Gifts shall come unto him or no, if he dye before he is one and twenty Years old, unmarried and without Child, then, if my Lord and Brother be living, I shall require him to dispose of all those Lands, leaving them unto him as my right and lawfull Heir. Save only, that if my said base Son Robert should dye without Issue, and that the Mannor of Denbigh and Chirk be redeemed, I do give and bequeath forever the Lordship of Chirk, to my well-beloved Son in Law the Earl of Essex, as also my House in London called Leicester House; if the said Robert, my base Son dye without Issue to whom I give and grant as other the former Lands, after the Decease of my dear Wife, the said House, and the remainder, if he dye without Issue, to my said Lord the Earl of Essex my Son in Law, and the Heirs of his Body lawfully begotten. And where in one Article before touching my purchased Lands in Wansted, I left my said Lands undisposed, but during the Life of my said wife; I do hereby, also, give and grant those purchased Lands, not passed unto her by Deed before, or not inclosed within the Park of Wansted, to Robert, my base Son during his Life, and the Heirs of his Body, if he have any lawfully begotten; otherwise if he dye without Issue, I do give and grant those Lands purchased in Wansted to the Lord of Wansted, being any of the Heirs of the Body of my said dear Wife, forever. Etc.

II.

Dudley marries Lady Frances Vavasour.

Dalla citata filza 4185 (nuova numerazione). Archivio Mediceo.

Exemplar verum ex lingua Anglicana in Latinam versa literarum testimonialium contractus matrimonialis habiti inter Dominum Robertum Dudley et Franciscam Vavasor.

Ego Edouardus Barker causarum Ecclesiasticarum suæ Majestatis Registrarius ac Notarius publicus, omnibus per presens scriptum testimonium facio: Quod per commissionem specialem a Johanne Archiepiscopo Cantauriensi, quidam testes bonæ extimationis, nominatim Capitaneus Thomas Jobson de Colchester in comitatu, Essexiæ armiger et Thomas Combley de London generosus, testes honestæ famæ, fuerunt iuxta ordinariam et legitimam procedendi formam, coram me ad perpetuam rei memoriam examinati, sicut per eorum examinationes in custodia mea remanentes apparet, Quæ ad hunc effectum testificant: Quod honorabilis Robertus Dudley de Kenelworth, fuit per verba de presenti et mutuum consensum legitime contractus Dominæ Franciscæ Vavasor tunc Regiæ Majestati et honorariis precipuis unæ, utraque parte ab omni alio contractu matrimoniali libera existente: Et quod dictus contractus matrimonialis inter dictas partes habitus fuit in Pallatio regio de Grenwich circa annum

Domini millesimum quingentesimum nonagesimum primum, sed non publice solemnizatus, saltem ad alterius ipsorum notitiam. In quorum fidem hoc presens scriptum, præmissa testificans manu mea subscripsi.

Datum Londini, tertia die Novembris Anno Domini 1592.

ED. BARKER.

Guillelmus Auberie legum doctor Almæ Curiæ Cant. de Arcubus London officialis principalis, universis et singulis, per presentes noticiam ducimus et testamur has literas testimoniales esse scriptas per Edwardum Barker Registrarium et Notarium probum fidelem et legalem, et adhiberi fidem. In cuius rei testimonium sigillum curiæ officialis de Arcubus apponi fecimus.

Datum Londini, 6 Die Novembris Anno Domini 1592.

III.

Correspondence between King James VI of Scotland and Queen Elizabeth: Super Destructione Armatæ (vocatæ Invincibilis) Hispanicæ.

Littera Jacobi Regis Scotorum ad Elizabetham Reginam gratulatoria.

Madame and derrest Sister.

In tymes of Strattis trewe Frendis are best tryit. Now meritis he thankes of you and your Countrey, who kithis himself a Freind to yor Countrey and Estate, and so this tyme must move me to utter my Zele to the Religion, and how neir a Kinsman and Neighbor I find myself to yow and yor Countrey — For this effect then have I sent yow this present heirby to offer unto yow my Forces, my Person, and all that I may comand, to be imployit against Strangers in whatsumever facion, and by quhatsumever meane as may best serve for the defence of your Countrey, wherein I promis to behave myself not as a stranger and forein Prince, bot as your naturall son, and Compatriot of yor Countrey in all respectis, now, Madame, to conclude as on the one part, I must hartlie thank yow for yor honorable begyning by yor Ambassadors in Offres for my satisfaction, so, on the other part, I pray yow to send present-lie down Commissioners for the perfyting of the same, quhilk I protest I desyre not for that I would have the Reward to preceid the Desertis, bot onlye that I with Honor, and all my guid Subjects with a fervent gud will, may imbrace this yor godlie and honest Cause, wharby yor Adversaries may have ado not with England but with the whole Ile of Britayne;

Thus praying yow to dispeche all your Matters with all possible speed, and wishing you a successe convenient to those that ar invadit by Goddis professed Enemies, I commit, Madame and dearest Sister, your person Estate and Countrey to the blessed Protection of the Almightye.

From Edinburgh the fourt of August 1588 your most loving and affectionat Brother and Cousing as tyme shall now trye

JAMES R.

Reginæ Responsio ad Literas prædictas.

Now may appeare, my deare Brother, how Malyce joyned with Might stryves to make a shamfull end to a vyllanus begyning. For, by Goddes singular Favour, having theyr Fleet weell beaten in our narrow Seas, and preparing with all Vyolence to atcheeve some Watering place to continew their pretended Invasions, the Windes have caried them to yor Costes, where I doubt not they shall receave small succour and lesse Welcom, unles those Lordes, that so traiterouslyke would burye theyr own Prince, and promeis an other Kyng Releef in yor name, be suffered to lyve at lybertye to dishonor youe — Peryll and advance some other (which God forbyd youe suffer them lyve to do) therefore I send you this gentleman, a rare Tongue Man and wyse, to declare unto you

my full opynion in this great Cause, as one that never wyll abuse
you to serve any own turn, nor wyll you do ought that myself
would not performe if I were in youre place; Yowe may assure your
self that, for my part, I doubt no whit but that all this tyrannicall
prowd and brainsyck Attempt will be the begyninge, though not
the end, of the Ruyn of that King, that most unkingly, even in
the midst of treating Peace begynnes this wrongfull Warr, he
hathe procured my greatest Glory that ment my sorist Wrack,
and hathe so dymmed the Light of his Sonneshyne, that who
hath a wyll to obtayne Shame, let them keepe his Forces Com-
panye;

But for all thys, for your best sake, let not the frendes of
Spayne be suffered to yeld them Force, for although I feare not
in the end the sequel, yet, if by having them unhelped you may
increase the English Hartes unto you, you shall not do the
worst Deede for your behalf; for if ought should be donne, your
excuse will playe the Boyteux if yow make not worke with the
lykely Men to do it, looke well unto it, I beseache yow, the
necessity of this matter makes my scrybleing the more speedy,
hoping yow will measure my good affection with the right bal-
lance of my actions, which to yow shall be ever suche as I have
professed, not doubting of the recyprocque of your behalf according as my last Messenger unto you hath at large sygnyfied,
for the which I render you a myllion of gratefull Thankes,
togither for the last general Prohybition to your Subjects not
to foster or ayde our generall Foes of which I doubt not the
Observations if the Ringleaders be safe in your handes, as
knoweth God, who ever have you in his blessed keeping, with
many happy yeares of

Yor most assured loving Sister and Coosin

ELIZABETH R.

Copied scrupulously by me from *Rymer Fœdera*, Tom. XVI, P. P.,
18 and 19. J. T. L.

22

IV.

Dudley imprisoned with the Earl of Essex 1602.

Da una lettera di Londra del Febbraio 1601 (ossia 1602 allo stile comune).

Di Londra con lettere delli 22 passato avvisano che in Londra et in Corte erano accadute alquante alienationi per conto del Milor d'Essex, il quale essendo stato alquanto tempo sequestrato per comandamento della Regina nella sua casa in Londra, et rimesso dipoi nella pristina libertà, haveva continuato verso la Regina a sollecitare di voler haver giustitia et ragione del Lord Cial, sopra l'ingiuria che pretendeva essergli fatta da detto Cial. Onde non movendosi la Regina a sue preghiere et sollicitationi, ma rimettendo il negotio alla decisione del Parlamento, il detto Conte d'Essex haveva intrapreso di farne vendetta per sè stesso et con l'aiuto de' suoi amici. Il che inteso dalla Regina, haveva espressamente et sotto pena fatto dire a detto Conte di non muoversi in punto alcuno, et di non ammetter nella sua compagnia passando cammino overo andando in Corte più de 80 gentilhuomini et servitori. Ma non ostante questo comandamento haveva detto Conte adunato insino a 1100 huomini, con i quali disegnava di ritrovarsi in Londra et in Corte. Onde la Regina avvertita di quella temerità, fece con quelli della sua guardia separar dette genti adunate, et fecero pregione il predetto Conte di Essex con li signori Dudley, Blount et alquanti altri che erano partigiani di detto Conte. Ma insin hora non s'è potuta sapere la causa di tale alteratione, et secondo l'ordinario delle genti è cosa nuovamente et straordinariamente avvenuta, parlandosi diversamente di questo fra alcuni con dirsi, che il romore fusse che detto Conte havesse qualche pratica col Re di Scotia, et altri, con altri disegni.

(*Omissis.*)

V.

Signor Lotti respecting Dudley's Lawsuit.

Dalla citata filza 4188, altro inserto del Lotti alla Segreteria.

Maggio 1607.

(Tutto in cifra.)

L'ultime mie lettere a V. A. sono state de' 9 col passato ordinario, et ragguagliavo l'Altezza Vostra, come quel tale Capitano
di nave a chi era indiritto un piego di lettere attenenti al Conte
di Varuic era partito per cotesta volta, et che per conto di quelle
provanze aspetterei il ritorno di lui, che degli affari qua del
Conte debba portare informazione migliore. Mi dicono i Burlamacchi et Calandrini mercanti in grandissima confidenza, che
trattano per il detto Conte di fare la compra di quella nave,
della quala mandava V. A. le noti (*sic*) attenenti a un cavalier
Femes, e si tratta ancora di fare certo partito de' beni di esso
Conte, con apparenza di cavar di qua 12 o 14 mila lire sterline
et condurle costà, ma in questi negozii vanno circonspettissimi,
et cosa veruna si avanza senza il ritorno di detto Capitano......
Quella informazione che ho potuto io destramente raccorre intorno alle cose del prefato Conte, quello ragguaglierò a V. A.
Et vien detto che al signor Ruberto Dudlei, et alla signora
Ceffilt sua madre, sia stato fatto gran torto, perchè effettiva-
mente vogliono che fra questo et il Conte di Lester fusse parola
di matrimonio, et che il signor Ruberto dovesse nascer legittimo.
Però il Conte di Lester dovette maritarsi poi con altra donna,
et chiamare anche nel suo testamento il signor Ruberto non legittimo, et tale comunemente è egli reputato in questo Regno,
et escluso però dalla Contea, maravigliandosi qua chiunque sente
che in Italia si facci egli chiamare Conte di Varuich. Poco avanti
la sua partenza vogliono che fusse fintione, ma chiamò il signor
Roberto prefato in giudizio un huomo di questo paese, e si que-
relò di lui che l'havesse chiamato bastardo, et per farlo con-

dennare, si messe con testimonii a voler provare il contrario, et
facilmente i suoi avversarii vista la conseguenza, che di sì fatta
pubblicatione et giuditio ne poteva nascere in danno loro per
quello che hebbero se il (*detto*) Ruberto fusse dichiarato legittimo, dovettero operare sì, che nella Corte medesima dove fu
intentata questa attione venissero condennati et multati detti
testimonii come subornati, et il procuratore della causa et il
signor Ruberto medesimo, il quale per questa cagione principalmente vogliono che partisse, et facilmente si procederà contro
i beni di lui per essecutione di quella sentenza. Ha detto signor
Roberto havuta una moglie figliuola d'uno cavaliere Candicci
(Cavendish), et di lei, figliuoli, ma tutti morti. Rimasto vedovo si
rimaritò con la figliuola d'un cavaliere, con la quale vive presentemente, et di lei ha figliuoli maschi et femmine, et s'intende
che detta signora sia stata chiamata avanti al supremo tribunale,
et che quivi sia stato provato et dichiarato per via di testimonii
di nobilissimo sangue *ad perpetuam rei memoriam* et senza ec-
cettione il matrimonio tra lei et il signor Ruberto, legittimo, et
i figliuoli legittimi et naturali, senza impedimento veruno alla
successione de'beni paterni. Quella Dama, che vive seco in Italia deve essere nipote del signor Ammiraglio d'Inghilterra, come
figliuola d'una sua figliuola; et la madre del signor Ruberto
debbe essere sorella del detto Ammiraglio, di maniera che è
certissimo che fra detta Dama et il signor Ruberto sarebbe
grado tale di parentela, che non ammetterebbe matrimonio senza
dispensa, et questo è il ragguaglio che io posso darne all'Altezza
Vostra, alla quale in quel modo che resti servita obbedirò io
con quella prontezza et fedeltà che debbo, perchè il piego di
lettere che si è detto di sopra era raccomandato, come per notitia della persona a chi era indiritto, a detti mercanti Burlamacchi et Calandrini. Per questa via la signora Ceffilta saputo
di dette lettere et pensando che ve ne potessero essere per lei
ha mostrato voglia di parlar meco, et essendosi tanto ralegrata
che il Conte di Varuich suo figliuolo, così chiamato da lei, habbia trovato così felice riscontro della protettione et gratia di
Vostra Altezza, offerse la sua possibilità, come già obbligata al
servizio di Vostra Altezza, et ricerco da me particolarmente
che io dovesse fare humilissimo baciamano in suo nome a Ma-

dama Serenissima, per rinfrescar la memoria della servitù che teneva con Sua Altezza in Francia per conto del matrimonio. Questa signora non ragionò punto, ma per terza persona ho bene inteso che ella riceva grandissimo dispiacere che il suo figliuolo dica d'essere ammogliato in Italia, ma nelle altre cose è amato da lei come l'anima propria.

(*Omissis.*)

VI.

The Patent for creating Alice Lady Dudley a Duchess of England.

See Dugdale's *Baronage,* vol. II, p. 225, and the Note in the margin, which says that he copied it from the original in the possession of Catharine Lady Levison, 1670.

Charles, by the grace of God, King of England, Scotland, France, and Ireland, Defender of the Faith, etc. To all Archbishops, Dukes, Marquesses, Earls, Viscounts, Bishops, Barons, Knights and all other our loving subjects, to whom these our Letters shall come, greeting. Whereas in or about the beginning of the Reign of our dear father King James, of famous memory, there was a sute commenced, in our high Court of Star Chamber, against Sir Robert Dudley, Knight, and others, for pretending himself to be lawfull heir to the honours and lands of the Earldoms of Warwick and Leicester, as son and heir of the body of Robert Late Earl of Leicester, lawfully begotten upon the Lady Douglasse his mother, wife to the late Earl of Leicester, and all proceedings stayed in the Ecclesiastical Courts, in which the said sute depended, for proof of his legitimation : yet nevertheless did the said Court vouchsafe liberty to the said Sir Robert, to examine witnesses in the said Court of Star Chamber, in order to the making good of his legitimacy ; divers witnesses were examined there accordingly. Whereupon,

by full testimony upon oath, partly made by the said Lady
Douglasse herself, and partly made by divers other persons of
quality and credit, who were present at the marriage with the
said late Earl of Leicester, by a lawfull Minister, according to
the form of Matrimony then by law established in the Church
of England; and the said Sir Robert and his mother were owned
by the said late Earl of Leicester as his lawfull wife and son,
as by many of the said depositions remaining upon record, in
our said Court, still appear, which we have caused to be perused,
for our better satisfation herein. But a special order being
made, that the said depositions should be seal'd up and no
copies thereof taken without leave, did cause him, the said Sir
Robert, to leave this our kingdom; whereof his adversaries taking
advantages procured a special Privy-seal to be sent unto him,
commanding his return into England; which he not obeying
(because his honour and lands were denied unto him), all his
lands were therefore seiz'd on to the King our father's use.

And not long afterwards, Prince Henry (our dear brother
deceas'd) made overture to the said Sir Robert, by special instruments, to obtain his title by purchase of and in Kenilworth
Castle, in our county of Warwick, and his mannors, parks, and
chases belonging to the same; which, upon a great undervalue,
amounted (as we are credibly informed) to about fifty thousand
pounds; but were bought by the Prince our brother in consideration of fourteen thousand five hundred pounds, and upon
his faithful engagement and promise of his princely favour unto
the said Sir Robert in the said cause, to restore him both in
honours and fortunes. And thereupon certain deeds were seal'd
in the ninth year of the reign of our said father, and fines also
were then levyed, setling the inheritance thereof in the said
Prince our brother, and his heirs.

But, the said Prince our brother departing this life, there
was not above three thousand pounds of the said sum of fourteen thousand five hundred pounds ever paid (if any at all) to
the said Sir Robert's hands; and we ourselves, as heir to the
said Prince our brother, came to the possession thereof.

And it appearing to our Council, that the said Alice Lady
Dudley, wife of the said Sir Robert, had an estate of inheritance

of and in the same descendable unto her posterity; in the nineteenth year of our said dear father's reign, an Act of Parliament was passed to enable the said Lady Alice, wife to the said Sir Robert, to alien her estate,[1] which she had by the said Sir Robert therein, from her children by the said Sir Robert, as if she had been a feme sole, which accordingly she did in the nineteenth year of our said father's reign, in consideration of four thousand pounds, and further payments yearly to be made by us to her, out of our Exchequer, and out of the said castles and lands; which have not been accordingly paid unto her by us for many years, to the damage of the said Lady Alice, and her children, to a very great extent.

Which Sir Robert settling himself in Italy, within the territories of the Great Duke of Tuscany (from whom he had extraordinary esteem), he was so much favoured by the Emperor Ferdinand the II, as that being a person, not only eminent for his great learning and blood, but for sundry rare endowments (as was best known), he had, by letters patents from his Imperial Majesty, the title of Duke given unto him; to be used by himself and his heirs for ever, throughout all the dominions of the sacred Empire. Which letters patents have been perused by our late Earl-Marshal and Heralds.

And whereas our dear father, not knowing the truth of the lawful birth of the said Sir Robert (as we piously believe), granted away the titles of the said Earldoms to others,[2] which we now hold not fit to call in question, nor ravel into our deceased father's actions; especially they having been so long enjoyed by these families, to whom the honours were granted (which we do not intend to alter). And yet, we having a very

---

[1] The wife of Sir Robert Dudley had her jointure settled and secured to her upon woods of Kenilworth, as at that time existing.

[2] To the son of Mary Dudley, sister of Ambrose Dudley, Earl of Warwick, and Robert Dudley, Earl of Leicester. This Mary married Sir Henry Sidney, K. G. of Penshurst, and Robert, their second son (the eldest Sir Philip having been killed at Zutphen), was created Baron Sidney in 1603, Viscount de L'Isle in 1605, and Earl of Leicester in 1618. The Title became extinct in this family in 1743. This first Earl of Leicester, of Penshurst, joined Letitia Dowager Countess of Leicester in prosecuting Sir Robert Dudley and the others before named for conspiracy.

deep sense of the great injuries done to the said Sir Robert
Dudley, and the Lady Alice Dudley, and their children; and
that we are of opinion, that in justice and equity these possessions
so taken from them do rightly belong unto them, or full satisfaction for the same; and holding ourselves in honour and
conscience obliged to make them reparation now, as far as our
present ability will enable us; and also taking into our consideration the said great estate, which she the said Lady Alice
Dudley had in Kenilworth, and sold at our desire to us at a
very great undervalue, and yet not perform'd or satisfied, to
many thousand pounds damage.

And we also casting our princely eye upon the faithful services done unto us by Sir Richard Leveson,[1] Knight of the Bath,
who hath married the Lady Katherine, one of the daughters of
the said Duke, by his said wife, the said Lady Alice Dudley;
and also the great services which Robert Holburne, Esq., hath
done to us, by his learned pen and otherwise (which said Robert
Holburne hath married the Lady Anne, one other of the daughters of the said Duke, by his said wife, the Lady Alice Dudley).

We have conceived ourselves bound in honour and conscience,
to give the said Lady Alice and her children such honour and
precedencies, as is, or are due to them in marriage or blood.
And therefore we do not only give and grant, unto the said
Lady Alice Dudley, the title of Duchess Dudley for her life, in
England and other our realms and dominions with such precedencies as she might have had, if she had lived in the dominions
of the sacred empire (as a mark of our favour unto her, and
out of our Prerogative Royal, which we will not have drawn
into dispute); but we do also further grant unto the said Lady
Katherine, and Lady Anne, her daughters, the places, titles, and
precedencies of the said Duke's daughters, as from that time
of their said father's creation, during their respective lives, not
only in England, but in all other our kingdoms and dominions,
as a testimony of our princely favour and grace unto them;
conceiving ourselves oblig'd to do much more for them, if it
were in our power, in these unhappy times of distraction.

---

[1] Of Trentham.

And we require all persons of honour, and other our loving subjects, especially our Earl Marshall, Heralds, and Officers at Arms, to take notice of this our princely pleasure, and to govern themselves accordingly; and to cause the said places and precedencies to be quietly enjoyed, according to this our gracious intention, as they do tender our displeasures, and will answer the contempt thereof at their perils. And we further command and require, that our said Heralds do make entry of this our pleasure and grant in their offices accordingly. In witness whereof we have caused these our Letters to be made Patent. Witness Ourself at Oxford, the three and twentieth day of May, in the twentieth year of our reign.

VII.

The Queen Consort[1] is angry with Dudley.

Dalla filza 4187 (nuova numerazione). Archivio Mediceo.

Inserto del Residente Lotti alla Segreteria.

Da Londra, de' 13 di Luglio 1605.

Le parole di corsivo sono in cifra nel dispaccio e qui spiegate.

(*Omissis.*)

La Regina si trovava alterata perchè un Cavaliere maritato Roberto Dudley, che dicono sia naturale del Conte di Lester la sera avanti haveva menato via una fanciulla Dama, della quale era innamorato, et si son subito dati grandi ordini, ma però non se ne sente nuova. *Questo gentilhuomo è di età di 35 anni in circa, di giusta statura et di barba bionda, et molto gentile in apparenza. Mi ha sollevato un grave scandalo con questo fatto. Doppo queste ragioni mi ha sollevato grave scandalo con questo fatto.*

Da altro inserto de' 20 di Luglio 1605 del medesimo Lotti.

(*Omissis.*)

---

[1] Anne of Denmark, wife of James Ist.

La Dama di Corte nipote del signor Grande Ammiraglio, che si diceva essersi fuggita con il Cavalier Ruberto Dudley bastardo del Conte di Lester, anch' egli nepote del prefato signor Ammiraglio, è stata fermata in Cales dal signor Governatore di quella piazza; essendochè le speditioni di qua v' arrivassero quasi in un tempo. Et perchè si scuopre che Ella facesse questa risolutione non per innamoramento, ma per rinchiudersi in un munistero, et servire a Dio nella vera religione, non si sa se i Franzesi permetteranno che Ella sia ricondotta qua forzatamente, anzi si pensa che quanto prima sien per lasciarla esequire la sua santa inspiratione.

(*Omissis.*)

VIII.

King James' wrath.

Dalla filza 4188 (nuova numerazione). Archivio Mediceo.

Lettera del Lotti Residente pel Granduca in Inghilterra al Segretario Cioli.

Londra, 1° Febbraio 1606 (stile comune).

(*Omissis.*)

Intendo che *il Re parla come disgustatissimo del Cavaliere Ruberto Dudley, et questo le sarebbe che Principe veruno lo ricevesse, et qua si è detto che Vostra Altezza fussi per servirsene. La principal cagione è che Sua Maestà non vorrebbe sudditi Cattolici et tanto meno quanto più valorosi et di merito.*

IX.

Letter from Antonio Standen, English spy, concerning Dudley's antecedents.

Dalla filza 933 (nuova numerazione). Archivio Mediceo, a pag. 494.

(Direzione). *Al molto Illustre sig. Belisario Vinta Cavaliere di San Stefano mio Signore Ossevv.**mo — Livorno.*

Molto Illustre Sig.' Mio Osserv.mo

Ho ricevuto quella amorevolissima di V.S., di che infinitamente ne la ringratio vedendo la memoria, che di me V.S. si degna tenere. Delle cose di questo mondo posso assicurare V. S. che ne tengo poco conto; pure ricordevole delle gratie et favori del mio già amorevolissimo Gran Duca Francesco, non posso ni devo, si no ingegnarmi a tutto potere servire et aggradire a quella Serenissima casa.

Questo, Signore mio caro, dico per conto di un caso accaduto qua, poco fa, ed è un matrimonio falso fra il Conte di Varuiche et una gentildonna fanciulla, figliuola lei di una figlia dell'Almiraglio d'Inghilterra, et a questo Cavaliere cugina in terzo grado. Hora questo Cavaliere ha moglie in Inghilterra, di casa nobilissima, et non men bella : sono stati insieme parecchi anni, et hanno tre figliuoli. Questa signora havendo inteso la partenza di questi; et presentendo che il marito havrà detto che prima di essersi congiunto con lei, havere conchiuso matrimonio con la già moglie del Cavaliere Tomaso Cierle poco fa venuto di Turchia; là onde pretende detto Conte essere libero per la morte della prima sciagurata, et senza pruova legitima di questo primo contratto, abandona la seconda, et piglia questa terza, con licenza di pigliarla per via di dispensa Papale, solo per conto della prossimità di sangue, non già sapendo il Papa li intrighi antecedenti. Là onde è seguito lo scandalo che a V. S. dirò. Il Re d'Inghilterra è stato informato del negotio, et l'Ambasciatore suo residente in Francia, s' è dolsuto in maniera sì sconcia col Cardinal Barberino, che ne son seguite male parole, sì del Pontefice, come della sedia Apostolica, come da Eretici non si può aspetar mai altro. Il Papa ha dichiarato la intention sua retta, et del tutto n' ha ampiamente informato il Cardinale; et se l'interessati non sono incaminati direttamente, a danno loro : et il fine ha di essere, che dove Sua Santità intenderà, che questa infelice coppia si fermeranno, di mandare al Vescovo di quel luogo una bella separatione, a tale che, et lui et lei sono ruinati ; maggiormente quella povera donna, perchè tutti li Ministri del Re l' hanno a tribulare dovunque capiteranno, sì per questa causa, come altresì per l'assunto del titolo di Conte di Varuic in persona sua, senza consenso di Sua Maestà, levando della Corona Reale 40,000 W. di intrata. Di che mi è parso il dovere darne a V. S. notitia, acciochè il Serenissimo nostro padrone sappia quel che passa, insieme Madama. Et quel che tanto commuove il Pontefice è che ha saputo che la vera moglie ha scritto al marito, che si contenta di rendersi Cattolica, et menare in qua i tre figliuoli con essa, et vivere seco, et veramente è caso di molta compassione. Il tutto sia detto in carità, perchè in quanto al Cavaliere io l' amo, et dico che il valor suo, et buone parte maggiormente nelle cose maritime meritano ogni preggio, et stima ; et volesse Iddio, che questa sciagura non li fusse intravenuta. Perdoni del fastidio, et il Signore Iddio sempre la guardi et conservi.

Di Roma, alli 27 di Gennaio 1607.

Di Vostra Sig.^{ria} Molto Illustre

S.^{re} Aff.^{mo}

ANT.° STANDEN.

X.

Dudley's letter offering himself for the Grand-Duke's service.

Segue nella citata filza 4185 anche l'appresso relazione.

(fuori) Conte di Varvick.

Discours concernant l'estat de la qualité de Seigneur Robert Dudley Comte de Warwick et Lescester. Au Grand Duc de Toscane. Reduit en trois chefs.

Le premier deduira sommairement ce qui est de sa qualité et de hault tige de sa Maison.

Le second fera veoir les raisons qui l'ont tire hors d'Angleterre et les pretensions qu'il y a a present.

Le troisieme descouvrira ses intentions fondees sur la faveur et protection qu'il requiert et espere de Vostre Altesse Serenissime, lorsqu'il aura droict sur ce que plus que justement il pretend en Angleterre.

Quant a ce qui est du premier poinct touchant sa qualité, il est tres notoire que Jehan Duc de Northumberland delaissa apres son deces deus infans masles. L'aisne avait nom Ambroise, qui fust Comte de Warwick, l'aultre puisnè s'appelloit Robert, au quel la Comtee de Lecester eschut en partage. Ce dict Robert fust tellement advance aulx faveurs et bonnes graces de la feu Rayne d'Angleterre, que son authorité fust quasi comme absolue, et avec ce fust esleve au grade de Grand Conestable, avec le quel il receust pareillement de la dicte Rayne tout sauverain pouvoir dans le Royaulme, come aussy sur tous les pais bas, sur les quelz il fust constitue generalissime, et confirme en icelle charge par la dicte Reyne, et par les estats des dicts pais bas.

Le susnomme Robert s'allia en mariage avec la Dame Duglas Haward issue de la tres illustre maison de Norfolcia, seur du grand Admiral a present d'Angleterre, pour lors vefve de-

laissee de feu Mylord Sheffild, de la quelle le dict Comte de
Lecester eust un filz dict Robert du nom de son pere, qu'est
ce Jeune Seigneur, dont est maintenant propos.

Quelques annees apres ce mariage le dict Comte de Lecester
fust espris nouvellement de l'amour de la vefve du Comte d'Essex, mere du dernier Comte d'Essex, que la feu Reine fist de-
coller, et appuyé sur sa grandeur en Angleterre, et sur la faveur
qu'il avoit aupres de l'oreille Royale la prist en famme, faisant
entendre que son premier mariage avoit esté nul. Toutesfois
nature ne peust oncques demantir la verité a l'endroict de son
dict filz, qu'il a tousiours cheri d'une affection tendre et pater-
nelle, et s'est comporté tousiours en son endroit, comme envers
son filz legitime et l'a confessé tel souvantes fois avant son depart de ceste vie, en presence de plusieurs Seigneurs, recognois-
sant aussy avec regret le tort irreparable qu'il avoit de la dicte
Dame Douglas Haward sa premiere et legitime famme, et le
preiudice et blasme ou son depart d'avec elle, faisoit tremper
sa reputation et l'honneur de son filz, qu'il aduouoit et decla-
roit estre son vray, unique et legitime filz, avec plusieurs et
grandes protestations, le constituant en sa derniere volunte uni-
versel heritier et successeur de tous ses biens terres domaines
et possessions.

Apres le decez du dicte Comte Ambroise Comte de Warwick
son dict frere rendist le mesme devoir a nature, et morust sans
lignée, ordonnant et establissant avant son trespas tous et un
chacun ses tiltres et possessions sur ce jeune Seigneur son ne-
pueu, comme filz unique et legitime de son frere, et pourtant
seul et vray successeur de ceste maison, et au quel par droict
de precession, doivent eschoir les tiltres unis et accoeuillis de
la Duchee de Northumberland, la Comtee de Warwick et celle
de Lecester.

Ses parents et proches allies, tant du coste paternel quant
par celuy de sa mere, ont poussé si avant leurs branches tant en
Angleterre qu'Irlande, qu'es deux Royaulmes se trovent soixante
deux, qui s'appellent Pairs qui luy appartiennent d'un fort proche
parentage, entre les quelz est son frere uterin du premier lict
de sa mere, qui gouverne la premiere et plus importante province du Royaulme. Son Oncle est aussi grand Admiral d'An-

gleterre. Et cecy servira pour declarer en blot la qualité de ce Seigneur et la tracer non au vif, ains a gros crayons, pour en faire concevoir a present quelque notice a Vostre Altesse.

Quant a ce qui concerne les raisons qui le tiennent absent de son pais, et ce qu'il y pretend, que nous avons mis pour second chef en ce discours, il plaira a Vostre Altesse l'entendre qu'apres la venue et establissement du Roy en la Coronne d'Angleterre, ce Jeune Seigneur, du commun advis et consentement de ses parents fist requeste a Sa Majesté, que droict luy fusse accordé, touchant les biens et tiltres, ou il estoit appellé par droict de succession, comme issu de legitime lict par le mariage contracte entre* le feu Comte de Lecester son pere et la susditte Dame Duglas Haward sa mere. Ce fust la premiere instance qu'il fict sur ce faict, car du vivant de la feu Reyne bien qu'il eust beaucoup d'assurance sur la faveur, il n'est jamais voulu entrer en dispute pour sa legitimation, pour ne controverser une chose de telle consequence, dont la dispute ne luy pouvoit susciter que soupcon et jalousie en son droict. Sa Majesté ne pouvant refuser une si juste demande luy accorde que justice luy soit faicte. Toutesfois, comme sa faveur n'inclinoit aucunement sur le droict de ce Seigneur, il tasche par secretes menees de detourner ailleurs la justice, mais s'estant en vain force a cest effect, et voyant Sa Majesté, que non obstant toutes les sollicitations faictes au contraire privement, justice balançoit du coste de ce Seigneur, et caressoit desia d'un œil favorable sa cause, il se declare ouvertement partie a ce Seigneur, tant en personne aux messieurs de son Conseil, que par lettres de menaces a ceux de la justice. Ceste borrasque du Roy obscurcist tellement le doux serain de justice, qu'on ne vit plus ses rayons, son cours fust arresté, et la cause est demeuree iusques a present indecise, par l'ostacle de Sa Majesté au grand tort et preiudice de ce Seigneur, mescontentement et regret de tous ses parents et amys et indignation des mieux avisés et moins passionés de la Court d'Angleterre. Le Malheur doncques s'estant tellement coniuré contre luy en son pais ou justice a les mains liees pour son droit, il a son dernier recours au Sainct Siege Apostolique, remettant sa cause plus que juste entre les mains de Sa Saincteté, commun pere de justice, pour avoir

audience en la Rota de Romme, ou, comme sur le public theatre du monde il veult decharger son droict et son honeur. Sa
requeste donc est a Sa Saincteté, que selon l'equité de sa cause
il soit iuge, et en demeurera tres satisfaict pour son particulier,
et obligé envers Sa Saincteté, pour luy rendre service et inter-
ceder la divine bonté pour Elle.

Quant a ce qui est du troisiesme chef, ayant avec la divine
assistence atteint le dessus de ses pretensions, tous ses desscins
sont fondez sur la faveur de Vostre Altesse Serenissime, soubs
l'auril de la quelle son intention est d'establir icy, desirant au
prealable d'entendre sur ce faict ce qui est du plaisir de Vostre
Altesse, la quelle, il ne doute poinct, comme un grand Prince,
luy appointera son humble et juste requeste, qui n'a autre but
apres le service de Dieu que celuy de Vostre Altesse Serenis-
rime, au quel Elle ne le trouvera inutile, si tant est que la
preuve Luy en soit aggreable. Et a ce faict i'ay eu charge de
Luy de vous faire entendre ce en quoy il pourroit estre digne-
ment et utilement employe par Vostre Altesse.

Premierement, sans deroger au merite d'aulcun, il n'est second a aucun Capitaine de mer, qui soit en Angleterre ce jour-
d'huy son experience admirable au faict de la navigation par
toutes les regions de l'univers, ne peust (si je l'ose dire sans
reproche) recevoir paragon.

En second lieu il s'est estudie particulierement a cest art
des le temps, que l'age l'a rendu capable d'y pouvoir vacquer;
les instruments a ce faicts, la plus part de son invention et
industrie luy montent en frais a la somme de 7000 scudi (*ecus*).

En troisieme lieu il a grande experience et practique aux
Indes, comme ayant este luy mesme, sur les lieux, dont il co-
gnoist tous les secrets et particularites, comme aussy par la
communication des avis iornalliers de ces quartiers la, dont la
feu Reyne, par sa faveur, et le grand Admiral son oncle luy
faisoient part avec tous leurs proiects et desseins la dessus.

4. Il est admirablement verse a la charpenterie d'une navire
de guerre, dont l'usage n'est quiere cognu ce jourd'huy avec
les perfections et secrets, qui la peuvent rendre tres absolue.

5. Il fera voir a Vostre Altesse par des raisons perenptoires
et assurees par quel moyen tres-facile et sans grands frais, elle

pourra obtenir le dessus, et se rendre bien tost seigneur absolu
sur la mer de Levant, malgre toutes les galeres Espagnoles,
infideles et aultres, qui voudroient entreprendre contre Vostre
Altesse Serenissime. Il pretend luy mesme d'avoir deux ou plus
de navires pour guerroier les infideles et trafficquer en telles
marchandises et regions du monde, que l'occasion et proffit luy
conseillera.

La reputation doncques de ce seigneur joincte a son scavoir
et merite, avec le hault tige de sa maison, attirera a soy tous
les meilleurs mariniers, pilotes, canoniers, maistre charpentiers
de navires, soldats et aultres galants hommes qui de toutes parts
aborderont a luy pour estre employes soubz son commendement.
Outre ce, ce sera un grand asyle et confort a ceux de sa nation, qui endurent si grande persequution pour leur foy, et auront
icy ou se consoler et rafreschir leur mesere, estans tous mis en
œuvre pour vostre service par le moyen de ce Seigneur: et Vostre Altesse obligera grandement toutte ceste nation Angloise,
la quelle tous jours ira exaltant son nom, et l'emploiera iusques
a la derniere estendue de ses forces, pour son service, et fera
chasque jour des vœux a Dieu pour sa santé, et des siens, et
pour l'accroissemet de sa grandeur.

Vostre Altesse Serenissime ayant pesé ce discours et rema-
sche avec sa prudence ordinaire la demande de ce Seigneur, qui
est autant advantageuse pour vostre estat, que l'appoinctement
luy en est desirable. J'espere disie qu'elle soubscrira librement
a sa requeste. La quelle si Vostre Altesse Serenissime a aggreable, il la supplie bien humblement de deigner luy en faire scavoir son desir par un mot de responce, luy octroyant et aux
siens la liberté du port de Lygorne avec telle protection et faveur qu'en tel cas seroit requis.

XI.

Letter of Grand-Duke Cosimo II
to the Earl of Northampton praising Dudley.

March 17, 1607.

Dalla citata filza 4186 a pag. 229.

Minuta del Granduca al Conte di Northampton de' 17 Marzo 1607
(stile comune).

Il Conte di Varuich come Vostra Signoria Illustrissima sa è
venuto a ricoverarsi in questi miei Stati per poter quietamente
vivere secondo la Religione, che egli fino a hora ha osservato: et
io oltre alla notizia che havevo del merito et valor suo, l'ho rac-
cettato anche tanto più volentieri, per sapere la parentela che
egli ha con Vostra Signoria Illustrissima, et haver inteso da lui
medesimo l'amore ch' Ella gli porta. Et avendo io in questo
poco tempo veduto ancora, che egli mostra una devotissima volontà verso il suo Re, et di conservarsi suo fedel vassallo et
servitore, mi è parso di doverne far fede a V. S. Illustrissima
con questa mia lettera, et pregarla, che sì come il detto signore
Conte tiene lei in luogo di padre, così ella lo favorisca come
figliuolo, mantenendolo nella buona grazia di Sua Maestà, et
ovviando principalmente che la Maestà Sua non porga orecchie
alle calunnie che le potessero sinistramente essere impresse nel-
l'animo da' nemici del sopradetto signore, il merito del quale
sarà cagione che anch' io ne rimarrò molto tenuto a Vostra Signoria Illustrissima, et dal Signore Iddio le desidero ogni pro-
sperità.

———

XII.

Sig. Lotti's letter about the ship-builder Matthew Baker going to Tuscany.

Dalla citata filza 4188. Inserto del Lotti alla Segreteria.—23 Maggio 1607.

(Tutto in cifra.)

Con l'ultime mie lettere de' 16 stante io davo conto a Vostra Altezza d'essere stato a Detfort, et di havere quivi sotto colore d'intendere qualche cosa intorno alla fabbricatione de' Navilij indotto Matteo Caccher a venire a starsi meco una mattina in Londra, et che all' hora pensavo d'intendere s' egli havesse accettato il partito di venirsene costà al servizio di Vostra Altezza. Et non ostante che egli mostri poco gusto di qua; et che per non si dilettare più i superiori del suo mestieri, venga poco adoperato, et dica per due anni non haver mai potuto risquotere un denaro delle sue provisioni, conoscendo anco il partito offertoli di reputatione per lui et d'utile, poichè gli accennavo che harebbe havuta una buona provvisione; in ogni modo con suo dispiacere ha ricusato di venire, solamente perchè l'età lo sgomenta, et veramente dice d'haver 77 anni et gli mostra ancora. Mi pregò bene che io volessi essere di nuovo a Detfort, dove mi ha fatto havere molti suoi modelli et strumenti di una maniera che par che dica, che se di qua almeno con questa sorte di cose egli potesse rendere a V. A. servizio communicherebbe tutto. Et domandatomi della salute del Cavalier Ruberto Dudley suo scolare, mostrava che volentieri si sarebbe messo ad insegnare la sua professione. Mi accennò che qui era un giovane fatto da lui, ma non conosciuto, perchè altrimenti non sarebbe lasciato uscire del Regno, et che voleva vedere, se questo harebbe accettato di venire a Vostra Altezza, quando pure Ella fusse restata servita. . . . .
. . . .
si aspetta.... il ritorno di quel Capitano di Nave che è venuto a

trovare il Cavalier Dudelei per inviar tutto (*cioè le armi che erano state comprate in Inghilterra per conto del Granduca*) sotto la carica di lui . . . . . (*omissis*). Quei Mercanti Burlamacchi et Calandrini . . . . . non affermano al certo che il Cavaliere suddetto compri la nave, e concludono che il padrone volendosene disfare, ad ogni modo cercherà ogni mezzo di lasciarla nelle mani di V. A.

(*Omissis.*)

XIII.

King James Ist recalls Dudley promising to make him Earl of Warwick.

Dalla citata filza 4188 (nuova numerazione). Archivio Mediceo.

Lettera del Lotti al Cav. Vinta.

Da Londra, 17 Ottobre 1607.

Qui vien detto da molti che la Maestà di questo Re faccia di nuovo richiamare il signor Cavalier Ruberto Dudely, con promessa di farlo Conte al suo ritorno, et Conte di Varuich. Quello che io so di più è che la madre di detto signore, havendomi più volte fatto domandar nuove di suo figliuolo, mi volse ultimamente raccomandare alcune lettere, et poi non me le ha mandate altrimenti, et il gentilhuomo suo servitore mi soggiunse: Habbiamo noi buone nuove di qua, et non disse più oltre.

(*Omissis.*)

XIV.

Autograph letter, in which Dudley negociates a marriage for Prince Henry, with a Princess of Tuscany.

Dalla filza 4190 (nuova numerazione). Archivio Mediceo.

Lettera autografa del Dudley diretta

Al Ser.ᵐⁱ Mad.ᵐᵃ Madre mia Signora
la Granducessa di Toscana.

Sereniss.ᵐᵃ Madama Mia Signora.

Havendo altri volti tractato con il Serenissimo Principe di Ingliterra per modo del S.ʳᵉ Cavalier Challiner suo governatore et confidentissimo, et occasione ancora di un suo servitore fidato mandato a me li raggioni mei di gran utile al Principe di parentarsi con S. A. S., che l' offerto poteva venire da parte del Principe per suo bene, come era proposto. et per questo et altri mei negotie con il Principi aveva una ciphera con il detto Cavallero. Ora fra altri risposti mi à scritto una lettera per mano di quel servitore fidato (per molte respecti), il quale essendo necessario per V. A. S. di vedere essendo mi pari scritto per ordine del Serenissimo Principe et suo bene particulare in quanto posso penetrare, tengo però mio obligo a V. A. S. come servitore di mandarlo la lettera stesso con il ciphero in Inglese, avendo redutto la parte importante nella lingua vulgare il meglio che poteva. Altramente non averebbe fatto tanto presumptione di scrivere a V. A. Serenissima in un negotio di tale consequentia, senza licentia o comandamenti suoi. Ma per la lettera credo

V. A. S. sarà satisfatto di esser mio debito a fare per suo serv:
(servizio?). Et così faccio reverentia bacciando umilmente la ve-
ste di V. A. S.

Livorno, il 13 di Maggio 1612.

Di V. A. S.

Fidele servitore

IL CONTE DI WARWICK ET LEICESTER.

— — — —

XV.

Dudley's house and possessions in 1614 A. D.

From the Register of the " Arroti " in the Archives of State.

Quartiere Santa Maria Novella, Leone Rosso.
Beni che furno di Orazio di Luigi Rucellai possiede
Signor Ruberto Dudleo Conte di Warwich et Leicester in
Inghilterra abitante in Firenze, Decima 1534 di nuovo.

Sustanze.

Una casa nel popolo di San Pancrazio sulla cantonata de' Tor-
naquinci, confina a primo, secondo e terzo Via, quarto Dionigi
Rucellai decimata con la stanza del Cocchio in fiorini 16. 16.
Per Arroto 1590, N° 64.
Due casette poste in detto popolo in via di San Sisto, con-
finate a primo Via, secondo Carlo di Andrea Rucellai, terzo
Filippo Del Sera decimate per Arroto 1579, N° 144 in fiorini 2, 10. 5
e ridotte poi per uso per partito 1583, N° 362.
E quali beni comprò detto signor Ruberto dal Reverendissimo
signore Lodovico Cherico di Camera, e Ferdinando fratelli e figli
di Orazio di Luigi Rucellai per scudi 4000 di lire 7 per scudo

a gabella del compratore per contratto rogato Ser Bernaba Baccelli sotti dì 5 di Aprile 1614, fede in filza N° 157.

E si hanno a levare dalla Decima del 1534, Gonfalone detto
a 167 da Orazio di Luigi di Cardinale Rucellai con detta Decima.

Acconcia con presenza del detto Ser Bernaba Baccelli suo
mandato questo dì 6 di Maggio 1614.

XVI.

Autograph letter from Dudley to Sig. Cioli about his ship the Cosimo.

Dalla filza 1375 (nuova numerazione). Archivio Mediceo.

Carteggio del Segretario Cioli.

(*Direzione*). Al Molto Ill.ᵣᵉ Sig.ʳ Mio Osserv.ᵐᵒ il
Sig.ʳ Cavalier Scioli Secretario di Stato a
S. A. R.
        In Corte.

31 Marzo 1618.

Molto Ill.ʳᵉ Sig.ʳ Mio.

Il Capitano Barry in una delle corsarie essendo con me l'altro diè, mi pregò a dire a V. S., che non mancherà venire a
Fiorenza. Quando venga, io piacendo a Dio, per reconoscere a
V. S. quelle favore che V. S. l'à ffatto con quel obgligo che li
deve et la l'ha prolongata a farlo con speranza che la Corte
et V. S. verebbe in queste parte, dove poteva adimplirlo.

Quelle nuove che io scrissi a V. S. delle gallere di Malta, io
haveva fra inteso, non essendo parlato de le gallere di Malta,
ma da altri vasseli arivato a Livorno dopoi. V. S. mi pardoni

per il briga ne ho dato con quelli mei lettere mandatolo. Et
così li bacie le mano di cuore.

Di Pisa, il 31 di Marzo 1618.

Di V. S. Molto Illustre

Affect.ᵐᵒ Servit.ʳᵉ
IL CONTE DI WARUICH.

Dopoi haver scritto ho recevuto la lettera di V. S. et non
dubito che scriveranno tanto et peggio della gallera nuova, perciochè so loro intentione: ma io dico che in loro presenza la
gallera regeva et caminava più del Cosimo, et così bisogniò che
la fa, si vogliono governarlo bene, et non metter tanta più pietra o savora dentro che nelle altri, et non credo che fanno per
ignoranza, essendo cosa troppo vulgare, che troppo pesa, met-
terà un vasselo troppo in fondo, et quelle qualità di regere et
caminare havendola una volta, non posso mai perdere, et però
è raggione che rendono conto di esso. Et di più replico: Sì bene
fusse vero che non regesse o andasse troppo in fondo, che cada
impedimento al caminare, io securo a S. A. S. che in due giorni
lo farò accommodare per un stratagemma mia, che non ha stato
mai penetrato. Et di questo stia securo. Quanto che Madama
parla del S.ᵗ Cosimo, veramente si non fusse di mia factura di-
rei che fusse bonissimo; et fa bene ordinare che suoi mastri
sequite quello: sì bene anche quello havendo emuli, stava due
anni indretto, inanzi che potevano chiarire il suo perfectione,
perciochè non volevano: et però bisogniò haver patienza in questa nuova a lassare un poco l'invidia sfogarsi, et che li gente
conoscono meglio la qualità del vasello; et io son securo che
conosco l'uno et l'altro, et ho visto provare, che se il S.ᵗ Cosimo
sia bono, questo non sarà mai male. Ben vero è che il S.ᵗ Cosimo
à questo avantaggio che importa assai, che in quello io era
presente insino che il corpo era fatto et passato periculo di
guastare, ma in questo ho dato solo il dissengnio et garbo, ma
non ho visto mai insino che era lesto a provare.

Questo altro passavolante mio varalo adesso. A questo anche
ho stato presente a finire il corpo et cose importante, et vide-

ranno per il successo quanto importa, ma con l'acquisto di due maladie grande et periculose.

V. S. anche piace ricordare Madama Serenissima che tanti difficultà et spaventi davano contro il molo di mio inventione: in ongni modo è riuscito bene: così faranno quelli si S. A. S. vole in dispetto delli emuli che riusce bene, conforma che l'è altramente hanno preso quasi tutti ministri preso un disdegnio tanto grande contra il vasello, che non è possibile che riuscisse si bene fusse perfectissimo. Et dico così, perciochè so alcuni puntilie prese in esso a causare questo disdengnio; dell quale uno è, perciochè alcuni periti scrivano confidentamente del governare del vassello, et che non poteva mai riuscire. Per la quale S. A. s. mi mandò per accomodarlo, come feci in pochi hore a loro gran disgusto, et il resentimento di quello resta ancora nell'animo, et causa che alcuni cercheranno querele, si possono, a lassare il vassello indreto a Messina: et per farlo per giustificatamente comminciano a devulgare questo rumore contra il vasselli, et causati da quelli come ho detto, che permettono e causavano che il vassello portava tanto più peso di pietra per savora delle altri.

XVII.

Letter from Dudley about his cause in Rome.

Dalla filza 1376 (nuova numerazione). Archivio Mediceo.

Carteggio col Segretario Cioli.

(*Direzione*). Al Molto Ill.ᵣᵉ Signore Mio Osserv.ᵐᵒ
Il Sig.ʳ Caval.ʳᵒ Andrea Sciolli Secretario Principale a S. A. S. Mio Signore
In Corte.

Molto Ill.ʳᵉ Sig.ʳ Mio Osserv.ᵐᵉ

In Pisa ne parlai a V. S. il favore a procurarmi quando ne haverebbe bisognia d'una lettera da S. A. S. mio signore in favore di mia causa et negotio a Roma, quale ne premio, et mi importa assai in mei negotio di consequenza, essendo lesto la causa per sentenza nella Camera Apostolica di Roma. Ora havendo notitia da mio Procuratore Cosimo Orlandini che ha procurato dal auditore della camera che della mia causa è deputato conformo al suo dessiderio al Mons.° Torello (fratello del Conte Torello Camerero di S. A. S.) per sententiarlo; però li prego V. S. procurarmi la lettera di S. A. S. proprio caldamente ad detto Monsignore Torello per favorire conforma a giustitia et con espeditione la mia causa, essendo deputato a lui per dare la sentenza difinitiva, et piacendo S. A. mostrare che li preme il bon successo della causa per mio bene, essendo suo servitore devotissimo et sotto la protectione suo etc., a me sarà una gratia singulare. V. S. mi farà gran favore in procurando questo lettera, et quanto primo, piacendo darlo al portatore di questo il sig.ʳ Giovan Babtista Terranuova, il quale ne ho ordinato mandarlo securo a mio Procuratore in Roma, per presentarlo, quando ella trova l'occasione opportuno. Et così ringratiandolo infinitamente per molti suoi favore, li bacce le mano di cuore.

Di Pisa, il 4 di Aprile 1618.

Di V. S. Molto Illustre

Affect.ᵐᵒ per servirlo
IL CONTE DI WARUICH, etc.

XVIII.

Dudley head of the arsenal at Leghorn.

Dalla citata filza 1376.

(*Direzione*). Al Molto Ill.ᵣᵉ Sig.ᵣ Mio Osserv.ᵐᵒ
il Sig.ᵣ Caval.ʳᵉ Sciolli Segretario Principale a S. A. S. Mio Signore
In Corte.

Molto Ill.ʳᵉ Sig.ʳ Mio Osserv.ᵐᵒ

Ne ho stato alcuni giorni qua più che pensai, perciochè li macestranza del Arsinale hanno stato impegati in altri servitic necessarie; et però non poteva avanzare cotesto vassello di mio inventione abastante per partirmi verso Fiorenza, come spero a fare indubitatamente fra otto o dieci giorni. V. S. posso dire a Sua Altezza Serenissima mio signore da parte mia, che il vassello sarà in mio opione (*sic*) conforma al mio pensiero per il servitio suo, et cosa buona. Ne ho anche pensato di una curiosità nelle reme per vogare con più facilità et forza, come spero che riuscerà havendo messo un remo di quella fogia supra la galliotta a Livorno per provarlo. Mi scrive che per adesso riusce bene conformo al intentione. Ma innanzi che io parli, ne anderò a Livorno per videre l'effetto, et ordinare quel che potrò per farlo riuscire, et anche videre la Sassaia et Petaccio nuovo ordinato da Sua Altezza Serenissima.

Ultimamente li ringratia S. A. S. mio signore infinitamente per la lettera sua scritto in favore di mio causa a Roma a Monsignore Torelli deputato giudice d'esso, il quale ha dato sentenza in favor mio, come dessiderato et mi importa assai, del quale, quando sarò a Fiorenza ne renderò conto a S. A. S. per mezzo di V.S., in che mi confido più che in huomo vivente, et posso commandarmi totalmente. Mi sono più dì allegrato per sapere della perfetta sanità di S. A. S., essendo il maggior consolatione questo mondo posso darmi. V. S. mi farà gratia a ricordarmi

humilissimo servitore a Madama Serenissima mia signora bacciando humilmente la vesta. Così di non fastigiarlo troppo li
bacce le mano di cuore a V. S. mia moglia, facciendo il medes-
simo alla signora sua consorta, ne fo fine.

Di Pisa, il 10 di Maggio 1618.

Di V. S. Molto Illustre

Affect.mo per servirlo

IL CONTE DI WARUICH, etc.

XIX.

Viscount Lisle is made Earl of Leicester.

Dalla filza 4193 (nuova numerazione). Archivio Mediceo.

*Da una lettera del Salvetti di Londra al Picchena
in data de' 6 di Settembre 1618.*

. . . . . . Dissi già a Vostra Signoria Illustrissima come il
Visconte di Lisle era stato fatto Conte di Leister a pregiuditio
di cotesto signor Conte di Waruuiche; adesso sento che il Barone Riche, che nel stesso fu fatto Conte di Clare; trovando
qualche scrupolo in quel titolo di Clare per appartenere già
alla Corona et suoi descendenti, supplica di cambiarlo, et che
sia su l'ottenerlo, per quello di Waruuiche, et che l'ordine sia
dato per rifare la patente in conformità, la qual cosa, se suc-
cede, sarà trovata molto strana, a chi tanto tocca.

(*Omissis.*)

Dalla citata filza 4193. Altra lettera de' 14 Settembre 1618.

Lettera del medesimo al medesimo.

(*Omissis.*)

...... Questo Barone Riche ha tre giorni sono hauto la nuova patente Regia che li permuta il nome di Conte di Clare in quello di Warwiche, di modo che cotesto signor Dudlie Conte del stesso nome, viene adesso a perdere la speranza di mai più rihavere qua nè questo titolo, nè l' altro di Leister di suo padre; et tutto questo è seguito per non havere hauto qua nessuno per lui, che si sia voluto mostrare, nè opporsi a cosa nessuna, che me ne dispiace infinitamente.

(*Omissis.*)

XX.

Patent of the Emp. Ferdinand creating Dudley Earl of Northumberland, 1620.

Ferdinandus 2.ᵘˢ divina favente clementia electus Romanorum Imperator semper Augustus, ac Germaniæ, Hungariæ, Bohemiæ, Dalmatiæ, Croatiæ, Sclavoniæ, etc. Rex, Archidux Austriæ, Dux Burgundiæ, Brabantiæ, Styriæ, Carinthiæ, Carniolæ, Marchio Moraviæ, Dux Lucemburgæ ac superioris et inferioris Silesiæ, Wirtembergæ et Teckæ, Princeps Sveviæ, Comes Habspurgi, Tirolis, Feretiskyburgi et Goritiæ, Ladtgravius Alsatiæ Marchiæ, Sacri Romani Imperii, Burgoviæ, ac superioris et inferioris Lusatiæ, Dominus Marchiæ Sclavoniæ Portus Naonis et Salinarum etc. Illustri sincere Nobis dilecto Roberto Dudleo, Duci Northumbriæ, Comiti de Warwich, gratiam nostram Cæsaream et omne bonum, Majestatis Imperialis ad cujus excelsum fastigium, divina providentia, sumus erecti, Preheminentia, atque dignitas si alia in re ulla consistit, eo certe in studio cum primis se se extollit, quod justitiæ et æquabilitati qua nimirum unicuique suum tribuitur tuendæ et conservandæ impendit, cogitationes suas in id convertens, ut eum depravati perditorum hominum mores, legum severitate coerceantur, vice autem versa, qui cæteris natalium splendore, vitæ integritate, fide inconcussa,

aliisque virtutibus antecellunt, uberiorum quoque honorum præ-
miis condecorentur. Tum vero potissima illorum hateatur ratio,
qui prosapiæ suæ vetustate conspicui, eamdem tam ipsi, quam
eorum majores non modo præclaris actionibus in secundæ fortunæ splendore, illustriorem reddere satagunt, verum etiam
laudatissimi Animi moderatione atque virili constantia, sortem
quoque adversam, uti rerum humanarum sunt vicissitudines,
fortiter excipiunt, et quemadmodum idem solis gressus est, sive
cœlo sereno sive nubilo, sic hi memores generosæ propaginis,
unde sanguinem traxerunt, ad varios instabilis fortunæ aspectus
nec vultum nec animum mutant, sed unam, eamque præcipuam
curam habent, ut Fidei, Deo, Religioni, et Reipublicæ debitam
nulla indigna actione contaminent, sed quacumque etiam via
vel ratione possint, in afflictæ patriæ solatium, vel supremorum
orbis principum beneficium, studia atque consiglia sua utiliter
conferant, adeoque non sibi tantum et suis, verum reipublicæ
majori ex parte se natos, vivis rerum exemplis profiteantur. Cum
igitur fide digno testimonio, ac diversis autenticis literarum do-
cumentis compertum habeamus ex ea vos familia in Angliæ
regno originem ducere, quæ viros complures a singulari pruden-
tia et auctoritate in primariis Regni functionibus cum dignitate
sustinendis, exercitatos, et proinde domi forisque cælebres et
belli pacisque artibus claros produxerit, unde per varios honorum gradus, quod historiæ, aliaque passim monumenta testifi-
centur, Regum benignitate in Regno sint provecti, atque inter
cæteros Avus olim vester paternus Joannes Dudleus Comes de
Warwich postquam observantium suam erga Regem, amorem
in Patria multis argumentibus et occasionibus non minus gloriæ
quam periculi plenis abunde comprobasset, Suprema Ducalis
dignitatis prærogativæ libere, et inconfiscabiliter insigniri, et
pro se ac hæredibus suis masculis, Dux Northumbriæ dici atque
ad Nomen, Titulum, Statum, Gradum, Locum, Sedem, Prehemi-
nentiam, Honorem, Auctoritatem, et Dignitatem Ducis Northumbriæ legitime promoveri et de iis omnibus realiter investiri me-
ruerit. Temporis vero successu, cum intestinis omnia dissidiis
in dicto Angliæ Regno fluctuarent et novarum opinionum fervor
antiquæ Religionis Cultores profligasset, Vos quidem resolutione
generosa tempestatem illam prudenter declinando, voluntariam

e patria secessionem fecisse, variisque cristiani orbis regionibus cum fructu peragratis, fortunarum vestrarum jacturam magno excelsoque animo in lucro reputasse. Interim in tot ærumnis, atque molestiis diuturnis a præclaris majorum vestrorum vestigiis ne levi quidem motu deflectere, sed ex quo tempore Florentiæ (donec melioris fortunæ spes adfulget) sedem fixistis, ob singularem vitæ morumque integritatem, prudentiam, rerum usum, raras et ingeniosas inventiones, non modo Magno Hetruriæ Duci affini et Principi nostro carissimo propius innotuisse, verum etiam nominis vestri famam ad Serenissimi Principis D. Philippi 3. Hispaniarum, utriusque Siciliæ, Hierusalem etc. Regis Catholici Archeducis Austriæ, Ducis Burgundiæ affinis et fratris nostri carissimi notitiam pervenisse. Quorsum accedat peculiare quoddam observantiæ studium quod in nostra, sacrique Imperii et Inclitæ Domus Nostræ Austriæ obsequia prolixe nobis reverenterque per litteras aliquoties obtulistis, in quo laudabili instituto nequaquam ambigimus, quin deinceps quoque firmiter atque constanter sitis perserveraturi, Hisce aliisque de causis animum nostrum merito moventibus haud omittendum duximus quin familiæ vestræ preheminentiæ, decus et ornamentum, simulque nostram erga Vos, vestrosque benigni propensique Animi affectionem, non tam ad ampliandam, quam ejusdem honorem et dignitatem avitam conservandam (In quo quidem Cæsarei nostri muneris ac ipsius equitatis ratio versari videtur) nostro testimonio comprobatam relinqueremus, quo sic posteritas vestra hujusmodi gloriæ stimulis incitata, ad eadem virtutis studia tanto alacrius, ferventiusque contendat; Qua Propter ex certa nostra scientia, animoque bene deliberato, sano et maturo accedente consilio, et ex potestatis Nostræ Imperialis plenitudine, vigore præsentis Nostri Diplomatis, Declaramus supranominatum Illustrem Robertum Dudleum, Comitem a Warwich, tanquam descendentem ab Avo suo paterno Joanne Comite a Warwich libere et inconfiscabiliter creato Duce Northumbriæ, et successive filium illius primo genitum Ill.ᵐᵐ D.ⁿ Cosimum, et aliᴖs ordine primogenituræ semper observato ex legittimo ipsius matrimonii fœdere æterna serie procreandos per universum Sacrum Romanum Imperium, et Regna, ditionesqne nostras hæreditarias, Ducem Northumbriæ vocari, scribi, nominari, honorari, atque reputari, eoque titulo tam in judicio quam extra, tam scripto, quam viva voce, nec non in rebus spiritualibus et temporalibus, ecclesiasticis et profanis, aliisque negotiis et actionibus quibuscumque uti, et ab aliis decorari posse et debere. Quam tamen declarationem nostram non alio sensu intelligi volumus, atque decernimus, quam ut unicuique suum tribuatur, et debita honorum ornamenta Principi exuli, etiam in Sacro Romano Imperio, aliisque terris ac provinciis nostris, sarta tecta conserventur ; *Mandamus* proinde universis et singulis Electoribus, aliisque Principibus Ecclesiasticis et Sæcularibus, Archiepiscopis, Episcopis, Ducibus, Marchionibus, Comitibus, Baronibus, Militibus, Nobilibus, Clientibus, Capitaneis Vice dominis, Præfectis, Castellanis, Locum tenentibus, Officialibus, Heroaldis, Caduceatoribus, Burgi Magistris, Judicibus, Consulibus, Civibus, et generaliter omnibus et singulis nostris, ac Sacri Romani Imperii, Regnorumque, et Provinciarum nostrarum hæreditariarum, subditis atque fidelibus dilectis cujuscumque dignitatis, gradus, ordinis, et conditionis existant, Ut Vos Robertum Dudleum Comitem a Warwich, vestrosque successive hæredes masculos, Duces Northumbriæ agnoscant, eoque titulo nominent, compellent, reputent, Et tam scripto quam nuncupatione verbali honorent, et ne quid per alios in contrarium attentetur viribus prohibeant, atque avertant. Et enim hæc seria mens atque voluntas Nostra Cæsarea, cui omnes prompte obtemperaturos clementer confidimus, quatenus indignationem nostram gravissimam, aliasque pœnas arbitrarias evitare voluerint, Quod literis hisce patentibus manu nostra subscriptis, et Aureæ nostræ Imperialis Bullæ typario firmatis palam facere voluimus.—Datum in Civitate Nostra Viennæ, Die nona Mensis Martii Anno Domini 1620. Regnorum Nostrorum Rom.^{ni} primo, Hungarici 2°, Bohemici 3°, etc.

C.* FERDINANDUS.

Locus Bullæ Aureæ Imperialis Pendentis.

Vice R.^{mi} D.^{mi} Jo. Swicardi Archicancellarii et Elect. Mog. V. L. Volm. — Ad mandatum Sacræ Majestatis proprium.

C.* HERMANUS QUESTENBERGH.

Et quia suprascriptas Literas Patentes ex earum proprio originali exaratas cum ipso earum originali penes prædictum Ill.^{mum} et Ecc.^{mum} D. D.° Robertum Dudleum Northumbriæ Ducem servato, diligenti habita collatione, ad verbum rescontrare et concordare reperui, Ideoque In fidem Ego Robertus Roffius q.^m Tiburtii f., Magna Ducali Auth.° Jud. Ordinarius Notariusque p.^{ns} Florentiæ hic me subscripsi, meoque solito signo signavi. Hac die 18 Aprilis 1637. — Laus Deo.

XXI.

Letter from Amerigo Salvetti
about Dudley appointing him his agent in London.

Dalla filza 4194 (nuova numerazione). Archivio Mediceo.

Da una lettera di Amerigo Salvetti al Picchena in data di Londra
3 Settembre 1620.

(*Omissis.*)

Ho riceuto una lettera da cotesto sig.° Conte di Waruich, nella quale mi prega di pigliármi, insieme con un Inglese l'assunto di tutti li suoi affari in questo Regno, havendomene a questo effetto mandato procura autentica. Ma perchè V. Sig.^{ria} Illma non me nè dice cosa alcuna, non mi risolvo, senza comandamento espresso del Serenissimo Padrone d'ingerirmi in affari d'altri, massime questi, che sono di tal qualità, che bisogna giornalmente trattarli con persone di Stato, che senza autorità di costà non ardirei, nè potrei sperare di fare mai in suo servizio cosa buona. Et se bene il sig.° Conte nella sua procura si è compiaciuto di nominarmi Agente di Sua Altezza Serenissima, non solo non me ne servirò, ma nè anche la mostrerò, come non

26

mi sono mai fin qui mostrato per tale a nessuno. Supplico V. S. Illma ad accennarmi la volontà del Serenissimo Padrone, che tanto osserverò.

(*Omissis.*)

XXII.

Dudley asks leave to make reprisals on the English ships, and promises Cioli a present.

Dalla filza 1447.

(*Direzione*). Al Molto Ill.^{re} Sig.^e il Sig.^e Caval.^{ro} Sciolli mio Osserv.^{mo} Secret.^{rio} Principale a S. A. S. in mano propria
          In Corte.

Molto Ill.^{re} Sig.^e Mio Osserv.^{mo}

Adesso non videndo più speranza d'Ingleterra in quel mei negotie S. A. S. per gratia suo ha tanti volte raccomandato a S. M.^{ià} però bisongnio venire ali ultima remedia per giustitia quale S. A. S. posso concedermi et nega a nessuno. In quale V. S. sta bene informato, et anche sarà meglio per questo maniera di supplica qua incluso con li consideratione che seguita : per la quale V. S. viderà, che io non voleva communicare l'intentione del negotio a sig.^e Doctore Chelese (Cellesi ?), et havevo io raggione, perciochè non haveva lui autorità in scritto da S. A. anzi non me voleva elargarmi troppo, perciochè sono molto obgligato alla casa di Zozifante, con quale li Celese non hanno tropo intrinsicetza. L'intentione delle supplica sono differente assai, però li prego remandarmi il primo et seguitare questo meglio foundata contra tutti obgectione, come ne ho considerato in esso a risponderlo, et anzi a dare S. A. S. mio signore molti boni et giusti protesti a farlo, nel quale mi elargerò quando sarà di bisonio. Intanto prego V. S. negotiarlo ingeniosamente per riuscire, et V. S. sarà più di securo del quatuor milla ducat promesso per condurlo e bon fine: et ansi di più; subito che S. A. S. ha concesso a la restitutione domandata, mia moglia manderà un presente sua alla sig.ʳᵃ sua consorte di qualche consideratione.

Il negotio bisongnio passare pochi mani, però ho scritto la supplica con mio mano proprio, perciochè essendo devulgato, sì bene fusse concesso di S. A. S., non riuscerebbe come doveva. Però V. S. piace opperare che sia referto solo al signor Fiscale, quale cognosco per intelligente et huomo da bene et amico di V. S., et farà il giusto senza passione o per compiacere, et si bisongnio per forza entrare un altro (come non credo) mi pare che il signor Giunio meglio approposito, si V. S. non ha interesse securo a qualche altro, al quale mi remitto. Et quanto a sottoscrivere l' ordine per informatione, li ultime 4 linie della suplica dichari benisime, resta solo si S. A. piace meglio haver sodisfactione (della giustitia domandato per informatione) o per sentenza, dove va la concienza.

— ⸚

XXIII.

Endorsement of the Sentence of the Curia Apostolica [1]

Dall' Archivio Diplomatico.
Pergamena proveniente dal R. Archivio del Bigallo.

(*Estratto.*)

1627, 17 Novembre, Ind. X.

Lettere di Gregorio Naro Auditore Generale della Camera Apostolica, comandando per questa, sotto pena di mille Ducati d' oro al Granduca Ferdinando, ed a tutti gli altri Ministri di

---

[1] The Sentence itself is too lengthy a document to be quoted entire.

Giustizia che sequestrino, vendino tutti i beni del Parlamento e Parlamentari d'Inghilterra e di tutti li Inghilesi *in solidum* eccettuati i Cattolici professi per dare e pagare a Ruberto figlio d'altro Ruberto Dudleo Duca di Nottumbria, a Cosimo Dudleo Duca di Varuich suo figlio e ad Elisabetta Sathuella moglie del suddetto Roberto ed a tutti gli altri figli che nasceranno dai sopradetti Coniugi otto milioni di lire sterline et altre dugentomila per i frutti a cagione dell'indebita occupazione e confiscazione fatta del suddetto ducato, e ciò a tenore della sentenza promulgata da Pietro Niccolini Vicario Generale dell'Arcivescovo di Firenze e confermata dal suddetto Naro.

XXIV.

Salvetti's letter to Sig.ʳ Dimurgo Lambardi about the Sentence of the Curia Apostolica.

Dalla filza 4196 (nuova numerazione). Archivio Mediceo.

Da una lettera del Salvetti al signor Dimurgo Lambardi in data di Londra 2 Ottobre 1626, così truscriviamo.

(*Omissis.*)

Qui si va sussurrando di non so che sentenza che cotesto signor Roberto Dudlie o Duca, come si fa chiamare, habbia procurato dal foro ecclesiastico di farsi dichiarare creditore di questo Regno di 200 mila lire sterline. Non vorrei già che fusse vero, per non dare gelosia a questi mercanti del fare scala a Livorno con le lor nave et effetti; et perciò io ne li dico un motto, acciò che in caso ci fusse tal cosa possino Loro Altesse rimediarvi, come faccio io da questa banda, col dire non potere essere tal cosa; et che essendo, sia un suo capriccio particolare, et non punto da sconcertare il lor traffico di Livorno, dove non possono aspettare che ogni sorte di rispetto et cortesia.

(*Omissis.*)

XXV.

The Duchess of Northumberland asks Sig. Salvetti to negociate the Dudley cause.

Dalla citata filza 4197 (nuova numerazione). Archivio Mediceo.

Lettera del Salvetti al Cioli.

28 Giugno 1630.

Dalle lettere di Vostra Signoria Illustrissima de' 17 et 23 del passato con la giunta di sua mano de' 25 sotto dell'ultima ho inteso quanto mi ha per parte del Serenissimo Granduca nostro signore comandato intorno a quello che io fussi richiesto dalla signora Duchessa di Northumbria di affaticarmi in suo servizio in questa Corte. Io ho riceuto da Sua Eccellenza ampla informatione della qualità del suo negozio, et non ostante che quando io la ricevetti io fussi in procinto di uscire di questa città, volsi nondimeno fermarmi fino a lunedì prossimo per trattare con alcuni signori, per sentire che speranza si poteva havere di consolare cotesta signora. Ma perchè si tratta di cavare denari di mano del Re per pretensioni di debito, fin quando viveva il Principe Henrico suo fratello, et la somma di dodicimila ducati, in congiuntura di tanta strettezza, essendo considerabile, ritraggo sarà cosa dificilissima, almeno per un pezzo, di venirne a quella conclusione che sarebbe necessaria alle presenti occasioni di Sua Eccellenza. Et se bene il signor Majordomo di Sua Maestà gli haveva scritto d'haverne hauto promessa per il pagamento, et che infra tanto egli l'haverebbe sovvenuta presentemente della

sua propria borsa (come io sono certissimo che l'haverebbe
fatto) la sua morte ha omninamente alterato tutto, perchè quelli
che promettono hora di parlarne al Re con la prima buona
occasione, non havendo verso della signora Duchessa quei ri-
spetti di affetto che gli haveva il signor Majordomo, vuole dire
che s'haverà da loro sempre buone parole, che per il resto io
ne dubito.

Con l'inclusa do parte a Sua Eccellenza di tutto, et come,
per quello che potrà dependere da me, di assigurarsi, che io
non mi straccherò mai di fare quanto sarà mai possibile in suo
servizio, dispiacendomi molto che sia per riuscire impiego di
molto poco gusto, per trattarsi di cavare denari dall'erario Regio in questi tempi tanto penuriosi. Finito la vacanza, et che
la peste me lo permetta, io ritornerò a Londra subito. Intanto
daremo tempo a quei signori, che hanno promesso di parlarne
al Re, quando la congiuntura li serva. Ai quali, se li riuscirà
di ritrarre da Sua Maestà promessa et riconoscimento del debito, sarà tanto meglio, tutto che bisognasse dipoi aspettare che
ci fusse denari per il pagamento. Insomma il negozio mi sarà
a cuore, ma la salute propria molto più; massime hora che
l'infezione della peste essendo arrivata vicina a casa mia sono
forzato d'andarmene.

(*Omissis.*)

XXVI.

Death of the Duchess of Northumberland.

Dalla citata filza.

Lettera del medesimo al medesimo.

Londra, 31 Ottobre 1631.

Al mio ritorno a Londra ho riceuto due lettere di Vostra
Signoria Illustrissima de' 13 et 20 di Settembre, la prima delle
quali portandomi la nuova della morte della signora Duchessa

di Northumbria, non ho potuto leggere, senza compatire grandemente il signor Duca di così gran perdita. Il Signore Iddio lo consoli, come per questo suo interesse di qua io cerco di consolarlo, con speranza che fusse per riuscirmi, mentre il signor Duca potesse giustificare il contratto accennato a Vostra Signoria Illustrissima con altra.

(*Omissis.*)

XXVII.

The Grand-Duke is interested in Dudley's obtaining restitution.

Dalla citata filza 4208.

Minuta di lettera del Granduca al Salvetti.

.... Settembre 1632.

Noi habbiamo sentito volentieri che da voi sia stato incaminato il negozio del signor Duca di Nortumbria in modo che speriate di conseguire ben presto il denaro che deve servire per nostro rimborso, et succèdendo, come ci promettiamo dalla vostra diligenza lo conserverete appresso di voi per seguirne la nostra volontà, secondo che vi scriverà il Balì Cioli nostro primo segretario di Stato, e Dio vi prosperi, etc.

XXVIII.

Sig.^r Salvetti sends Dudley 8000 scudi, restitution from the Crown of England.

Dalla citata filza 4198.

Altra lettera del medesimo al medesimo.

26 Agosto 1633.

(*Omissis.*)

Al signor Duca di Northumbria sarà pagato dai signori Guadagni scudi ottomila, che così gli ho questo giorno ordinato di
fare, et che ne piglino riceuta per mia discarica, godendo molto
di essere così bene uscito da un tanto intrigato negozio, et d'havere
servito Sua Eccellenza.

(*Omissis.*)

XXIX.

The young Earl of Pembroke dies in Dudley's house.

Dalla citata filza 4208.

*Lettera del Poltri (Lorenzo) al Salvetti in data 8 Gennaio 1635
ab Incarnatione (1636).*

In cinque soli giorni di malattia si è morto in questa città
il signor Conte di Pembroke, senza che gli habbia giovato rimedio alcuno. Il male è stato creduto di vaiolo, ma è più tosto
stato di petecchie. Il signor Duca di Nortumbria ha fatto tutto
quello che è stato possibile, ma finalmente era venuta la sua

hora. Sua Altezza l'ha fatto visitare più volte, et ha sentito con dispiacer grande questo grave accidente, compatendo al dolore, che di questo cattivo avviso sentirà il signor suo padre, con chi passerà V. S. quegli offitii di condoglianza che le parranno opportuni, mostrando il dispiacere che ha Sua Altezza, come ella sappia fare meglio, che io prescrivernele il modo.

Il cadavere si manda a Olivola in Lunigiana luogo del signor Marchese Spinetta Malaspina, genero del signor Duca di Nortumbria, et è stato condotto dal signor Carlo Cotorel et da un altro del paese, essendosi accompagnato con passaporti per tutto quello che possa succeder per viaggio. Mi dispiace di dover dare a V. S. questo avviso, ma conviene accomodarsi a quello che occorse, et le bacio, ec.

XXX.

Dudley asks a Commenda for his son Don Antonio.

Dalla citata filza 1411 (nuova numerazione). Archivio Mediceo.

(*Direzione*). All' Ill.ᵐᵒ et Clariss.ᵐᵒ Sig.ᵉ Mio Osserv.ᵐᵒ
il Sig.ᵉ Ballì Cioli primo Secretario di Stato e Consellere Secreto di S. A. S. etc.

In sua mano.

Ill.ᵐᵒ e Clariss.ᵐᵒ Sig.ᵉ Mio Osserv.ᵐᵒ

Alcune mese fa V. S. Ill.ᵐᵃ mi scrisse delle beningnia mente di S. A. mio signore di tirare inanzi Don Antonio mio figlio e Cavaliere per navigare, e di favorirlo per questo fine con la prossima commenda di grazia che cascasse. Intendo per la morte del cavalier Carlo Picchelomeni è cascata una commenda: supligo V. S. Ill.ᵐᵃ di favorire il mio detto figliolo apresso di S. A., e lei, per grazia sua, mi haveva promesso di fare, e non son

27

abile ancora d'alzarmi in letto per scrivere a S. A. e anco con fastigio scrivo questo. Baccio le mani di V. S. Illma di vero servitore.

Di Villa, le 9 di Luglio 1638.

Di V. S. Illma

Circa il vestito di Don Carlo ho già dato ordine e denare al signor Dottore Grazia che sia fatto bene con espeditione, ma dubito che il giovane ha qualche intrigo per la testa. Piaccia a Dio, e una volta osserva la parola come deve con suoi patroni.

Affect.^{mo} e obglig.^{mo} Serr.^{re}

IL DUCA DI NORTHUMBRIA, etc.

XXXI.

Don Antonio elected Knight of St. Stephen.

A dì 21 di Gennaio 1636.

Gl'Ill.^{mi} Sig.ⁱ Dodici Cavalieri del Consiglio deliberorno:

Che per vedere le Provanze, che di sua Nobiltà vorrà fare il sig. Dr Antonio del sig. D.ª Roberto Dudleo Duca di Northumbria, supplicante l'Habito di Cav. Milite per Giustizia: Et per referire quanto le parrà di potersi a S. A. S. rappresentare, s'intendino et s'habbino per eletti, e deputati in Commissari li Sigg.ⁱ Cavalieri Banderuoli et Cap.° Paccheroni.

C.^a FRAN.^{co} ANSALDI, V. Cancell.

Fu spedito dal Consiglio li 5 Maggio 1637.

XXXII.

Dudley announces to Sig. Cioli his son Antonio's death.

Dalla citata filza 1411.

Illmo e Clariss.^mo Sig.^e Mio Osserv.^mo

So quanto sono obgligato alla cortesia e favore di V. S. Illma e con quanto disgosto mi manda l'aviso della morte del Cavaliere Don Antonio mio ben amato figliolo, e realmente era buono e obediente a me; basta è obgligo della creatura di ubedire voluntiere la voluntà del Creatore: E così fo io per grazia di Dio: altramente ne stimo assai il perdito di un figliolo sì ubediente. Mi consolo, che è morto in servizio della Religione, del quale era Cavaliere e di S. A. S. nostro Patrono. Piacerà V. S. Illma farmi favore di mandare l'inclusa con la prima occasione al sig.^e Generale delle gallere; e veramente ne resto molto obgligato alla sua cortesia a detto mio figliolo, faccendo per lui quanto fu possibile da fare dal principio del viagio sin alla fine di sua vita, e suplico V. S. Illma, come il più confidente amico e patrono, che ho, e della casa mia di ringraziarlo ancora con dua parole in scritto, e per fine baccio le mani di V. S. Illma, come vero servitore.

Di Villa, le 19 di Novembre 1638.

Di V. S. Illma e Clariss.^ma

Ne resto con infinito obgligo a S. A. mio signore, che ha piaciuto per grazia sua di sentire dispiacere del perdito di detto mio figliolo etc. e compatiri a me del perdito.

Affect.^mo e Obgligatiss.^mo Serv.^re
IL DUCA DI NORTHUMBRIA.

XXXIII.

Dudley's letters to Sig. Cioli about Don Carlo robbing his house.

1.

Illmo et Clariss.^{mo} Sig.^e Mio Osserv.

Hoggie scrissi a V. S. Illma per rendere conto a S. A. S. mio signore come Don Carlo è entrata in casa (mentre ch'era alla messa) con parechi bocchi di fuoco, et a portata via l'argenteria che hebbe fuora per valsuta di Ducati 300 in circa, e S. A. sa che io ne dubitava già di questo suo mal intentione, et d'altro peggiore. Se non si fa qualche resentimento grande per un delitto sì grave fatto contra il Padre in Pallazio di S. A. con mancamento di più della parola dato a S. A. tanti volti, come V. S. Illma sa et è ben informato, et ne ha avertito già per lettere a questo Giovane della Potentia de S. A.; pare che questo è fatto in spreggio del Principe, del Padre et del consiglio datoli da Vostra Signoria Illma. È venuto, per quanto posso congetturare da Lucca, et forza la si ritornerà con la buttina. Pertanto mi rimetta totalmente alla prudenzia di Sua Altezza, di fare quello che giudicherà più espediente di prevenire maggior male: come apparisce già per l'inditie che ho detto a S. A., et per la maniera del procedere ha cattiva intentione, et è stato mal consigliato da quello cha una volta l'accennai a lei per le sue lettere, et veramente merita d'essere castigato, in modo di confessare qualche cosa d'avantagio di quel che sapiamo, et da lui ne hebbe già umbra di quel che in parte è seguito.

Credo che Sua Altezza mi darà licenzia, et anco commandamento di non dare più provisione a Don Carlo, sin che sono rimborsato della valsuta del argenteria che ha presa; ma se lui si rimetterà in potere della clemenzia di S. A., o che S. A. per la sua potentia la può haverlo per mortificarlo ben bene in una fortezza, li darò per suo vitto quel tanto che sarò commandato da nostro Signore et Principe. Et questo è quanto ho pensato d'agiugnere all'altra mia lettera a V. S. Ill.ᵐᵃ, et per fine li baccio affettionatamente le mani con mio humilissimo riverenzia a S. A.

Di Villa, le 24 di Gennaio al tardo 1638.

Di V. S. Ill.ᵐᵃ et Clariss.ᵐᵃ

Aff.ᵐᵒ et Obgligatis.ᵐᵒ Serv.ʳᵉ
IL DUCA DI NORTHUMBRIA.

2.

Dalla citata filza.

Altra lettera del medesimo al medesimo.

Ill.ᵐᵒ et Clariss.ᵐᵒ Sig.ᵉ Mio Osserv.ᵐᵒ

Ho riceuuto le due lettere di V. S. Ill.ᵐᵃ in risposto delle mie circa Don Carlo, et se bene molti sperava bene di lui, non sentendose più parlare, io ne aspettava aloro più cattività di lui, quando stava quieto, et la mia famiglia può giustificare che l'aspettava; et quando andai alla messa dominica passata, non havendo in quell tempo più di un servitore in casa di andare meco, lassai espresse ordine con la donna vecchia di casa di serare le porte, così non poteva entrare senza un petardo. Ma trovo adesso che questa donna lasciava l'uscie operte a posta che entrasse, et era lui nascosto in un fosso vicino, et hebbe subito notitia della mia partenza a Boldrone per sentire messa essendo il dì domenica. Et così entrava concertatamente con questa dona, come a suo tempo si troverà tutto. Io stimava più per male l'insolenzia sua contra Sua Altezza di fare questo celeratagine in Palatia sua, et con mancare la parola data, che per la valsuta et per suo cativo animo verso di me; ne sono certe, et è gran grazia di Dio che mi ha dato questo avertimento senza esser in casa, che se io fusse stato, morì lui o io; et così riescirà forza un'altra volta, et ne sto lesto aspettandolò, perchè non havuto quello che aspettava, et egli sa che di questo io posso valermi in pochi mese di ritinere la sua provisione; sì bene importa il spoglio per 40 libri et più d'argenteria. È vero quell che V. S. Ill.ᵐᵃ mi accenna, che ha bisongnio di più effi-caci rimedie; ma non sono in mio potere, sono nella potentia solo di S. A. S. mio signore di danare a chi ha mancato già cinque volte la parola di Cavaliero in scritto. È detto che è ritornato a Luca o dove sarà, se bene forzi non renderanno la sua persona in mano di Sua Altezza Serenissima, crederei non di meno ad instantia d'un Principe sì potente, si terebbe lui là in prigione a domare, considerando l'escessi che ha fatto, et ne ho visto tenuto a Fiorenza un Gentilhuomo Genoese molti anni ad instanza del padre in Genoa, come adesso è ancora qui il figliolo del Marchese Obise; et però crederia, che per mezzo di S. A. si farebbono l'istesso a lui o a Luca o in altra città per prevenire che non va vagabondando per il mondo, et dishonorare la casa sua, et forze in fine capitare male nell'as-sociare con banditi, perchè lui qui hebbi con suo servitore nove pistolle et terserolle fra lor due, et è sicuro. Et per fine bacio le mani di V. S. Ill.ᵐᵃ

Di Villa, le 30 di Gennaio 1638.

Di V. S. Ill.ᵐᵃ et Clariss.ᵐᵃ

Affet.ᵐᵒ et Obgligatiss.ᵐᵒ Servitore
IL DUCA DI NORTHUMBRIA.

XXXIV.

Don Carlo a rebel.

Dalla citata filza 1411.

Lettera del Duca al Cioli.

Ill.ᵐᵒ et Clariss.ᵐᵒ Sig.ᵉ Mio Osserv.ᵐᵒ

Questo disgraziato figliolo Don Carlo è venuto un'altra volta a Castello, et è qui in cheasa (*sic*) se starà. Mi pare una mezza ribellione contra sua Principe e il padre di mancare la parola con S. A. tanti volti. Crederei che qualche imbasata asperissima, come merita, o qualche bando severo li farebbe stare meglio in cervello et aviarsi alla guerra. Lui finge così, e d'aspettare da S. A. qualche lettera di servire alla guerra il Serenissimo Principe. Non mi pare la strada di procurar grazia con il mancamento di parola quasi ogni dì a S. A. S. mio signore, et a me stimo (per tal mancamento) che mi dasse tante punelati; rimittendo ogni cosa alla prudenza di S. A. A me pare un escesso grande: e per fine baccio le mani di V. S. Ill.ᵐᵃ, come vero servitore.

Di Villa, lo 7 di Marzo 1638.

Di V. S. Ill.ᵐᵃ et Clar.ᵐᵃ

Affet.ᵐᵒ e Obgligatiss.ᵐᵒ Servit.ʳᵉ
IL DUCA DI NORTHUMBRIA.

XXXV.

Don Carlo seeks a refuge in Church.

Dalla citata filza 1411 (nuova numerazione). Archivio Mediceo.

Lettera del medesimo al medesimo.

Ill.ᵐᵒ et Clariss.ᵐᵒ Sig.ᵉ Mio Osserv.ᵐᵒ

Don Carlo si trova per ancora alla chiesa di Castello con suo servitore bandito: hanno dua arcabusi e otto pistolli, dicono con le spade di campania sono armati come il Capitano spagniolo della Comedia. Il capitano del Bargello di Firenze è stato dilligente, e mandato della familia di pigliarlo, ma non potevano, per essere dentro il simiterio della chiesa; offrirono un altro prova, e non volsi io, essendo sicuro che lui tirarebbe a loro, et è ragionevole in tal caso, che loro tiravano a lui. Dubito che qualche amico suo in Corte li dà di risposte di speranza, come fusse da Sua Altezza, e questo sarebbe suo ruina, e li farà insolente come è, conosco ben suo umore: bisogno a quello cer-

vello risponderli asperamente, come fece V. S. Ill.ᵐᵃ con gran
prudenza, con dirli che la potentia di Sua Altezza li troverebbe,
se andassi a Constantinopili, e accompagnarlo con qualche commandamento severo, che sotto pena della teste ucisse fuora dello
Stato infra 30 hore, e che non entra senza licentia di Sua Altezza
sotto l'istessa pena, et a chi li riceve in casa, perchè lue è stato
assai in villa d'amici appresso a Pisa e qui. V. S. Ill.ᵐᵃ viderà,
che con speranza e cortesia lui sarà il più insolente corpo si
può trovare: ma con asperetza e di ordine severe e rescentiti
verrà d'essere umile, et serà quel S. A. commanderà; e questo
è mio parere, salvo etc. E per fine baccio le mani di V. S. Ill.ᵐᵃ

>   Di Villa, le 9 di Marzo 1638.

>   Di V. S. Ill.ᵐᵃ

Ho scritto a S. A. mio signore dell'insolentia di Don Carlo,
et prego che questa lettera non sia visto, se non da lei; di fare
quel che la sua prudenza pare meglio; a chi mi rimetto e
confido.

>   Obg.ᵐᵒ et Affet.ᵐᵒ Servit.ʳᵉ
>   IL DUCA DI NORTHUMBRIA.

XXXVI.

Don Carlo capitulates.

Dalla citata filza 1411.

(*Direzione*). All'Ill.ᵐᵒ et Clariss.ᵐᵒ Sig.ᵉ Mio Osserv.ᵐᵒ
il Sig.ᵉ Balì Cioli, primo Secretario di Stato e Cons.ʳᵉ
secreto di S. A.
In Pisa o a Livorno.

Ill.ᵐᵒ e Clariss.ᵐᵒ Sig.ᵉ Mio Osserv.ᵐᵒ

Mando a V. S. Ill.ᵐᵃ per Sua Altezza Serenissima mio signore
la capitolatione di Don Carlo con suo Principe e con il padre,

di mano proprio ; pregandolo di rimandarmi doppo l'originale,
e servare la copia se li piace. Pare a me troppo gran presun-
tione d'offrirlo ad un Principe sì potente et in suo proprio stato,
essendo cascato in delitto della testa di entrare lo Stato con
arme, et con mancamento di parola al Principe tanti volte, et
di spogliare il padre dell'argenteria in Palazio proprio di S. A. etc.
Però per quanto depende da me, non farò altro, se non tratta,
in una fortezza, remittendosi alla clemenzia di suo Principe, o
che sia fuora dello Stato ; altramente dirà che io tratta seco
per paura di suoi arcabusi e tersaroli e brave, ma si viderà da
me ben ingannato e delle suoi debiti non mescolerò mai : ne
ho abastanti de'mei. Mostra anco d'haver poco voglia di videre
la guerra per la sua scrittura, sì bene ha detto publicamente
che andarebbe, se avesse 200 scudi, ma non li credo, parlava
fintamente per scusa, et nella scrittura scuopre l'animo ; e quando
lui haverà sodisfatto a Sua Altezza mio signore per il mancamento ha fatto, poi li darò mio risposto di quel che può sperare
da me : ma sempre osservarò quel che ho scritto a V. S. Illma
di darli 200^v più dell'argenteria per servire alla guerra il
Serenissimo Principe Don Matias, et il solito provisione quando
sarà là ; anzi per servizio del Principe li darò 35 scudi il mese ;
et è tutto quanto son abile a fare a non lasciare l'altri morire
di fame o patire troppo per amor suo. E però V. S. Illma vede
(come al più confidente amico che ho nel mondo) che fo quanto
posso non capita male. Il dubio a pensare è che piglerà il denaro e poi non anderà, o fingerà qualche scusa della sanità, o
che è stato valigiato per la via, o simil fintione ; perchè della
parola non si può più fidare. Di questo confido nella prudenza
di V. S. Illma di pigliare qualche ripiego, con qualche commandamento da Sua Altezza, sotto grave pene, di pigliare il partito,
o di non entrare più nello Stato senza espresa licenzia di S. A.
e partirsi ; perchè se non è astretto severamente, con il buono
farà nulla, se non di consumare et impegnare quanto ho con
ozio in Fiorenza. Però in questo supplico S. A. humilmente di
pigliare rimedio con severità, come ha meritato, altramente si
burlerà di tutti, e ne ha di cattivi consellieri e si presume
troppo di qualche uno potente, altramente non sarà possibile
che havesse l'ardire che mostra in spregio del suo Principe e

28

del Padre, per le suoi capitolationi, e per fine baccio le mani
di V. S. Illma da cuore.

Di Villa, le 17 di Marzo 1638.

Di V. S. Illma et Clariss.^{ma}

Affet.^{mo} e obglig.^{mo} Servitore

IL DUCA DI NORTHUMBRIA etc.

Segue nella citata filza l'appresso documento.

(*A tergo, di mano del Duca, sta scritto :*)

La capitolatione di Don Carlo con S. A. S.
      per mancamento di parola, e con il pa-
   dre l'argenterie preso in palazio di S. A.

Il Conte Don Carlo di Varuich per obbedire, come deve a S. A. S.
et al signor Duca suo padre, si contenta di andar volontaria-
mente in forteza, con che non possa sotto qualsivoglia pretesto
esser ritenuto in essa più di quatro mesi, et che possa andar
liberamente per tutta la forteza come li piacerà, et che deva
tener i sua servitori, et che detti possino andar fuori et tornare,
et che passato che saranno i quatro mesi possa esser libero di
sè, et di poter andar et star per tutto il Stato di S. A. S. senza
poterlo astringere di andar nè alla guerra, nè fuori senza il suo
consenso et gusto. Et che anco doppo i detti quatro mesi il signor Duca suo padre li deva paghare i sua debiti, et li dia una
giusta provisione; et tutto acciò si levi ogni occasione di mai
più poterli dar minimo disgusto; perchè non si agiustando i
mei debiti, quali sono stati cagione di ogni romore, non si po-
trebbe chiamar ben agiustato il negozio.

XXXVII.

Don Carlo in the Fortezza.

Dalla citata filza 1411.

Lettera del Duca al Cioli.

Illmo et Clariss.^{mo} Sig.^e Mio Osser.^{mo}

Mi duole il cuore della mala creanza d'infastidire V. S. Illma con più lettere circa il Conte Don Carlo, ma il negotio è tanto intricato e scabroso, che si vole la prudenza sua di digerrirlo, a tal fine che nè il Conte, nè altro intercessore per lui può lamentarsi più di crudeltà. Ho pensato però questa notte di 3 capi per risposta :

Il primo è se lui pretende la giustitia in favor suo, bisogno che si rimetti al solito in carcere, di defendersi e recevere la sentenza dei Giudice e patirlo, ma questo non li consiglio, sarebbe mal per lui.

Il 2.do se lui si humiglia alla clemenza del Principe come delinquente, conviene che senza capitolazione si rimette in una fortezza, dove et in tal modo S. A. mio signore li commanderà ; poi suplicherò io humilmente alla benignità di S. A. S. che sia mandato quanto primo alla guerra per servire il Serenissimo Principe Don Matias : li perdonorò la valsuta dell' argenteria ch' à presa, e li darò 200^w di più per condurlo al campo (se bona fide vol andare) e là haverà da me ben pagato la provisione di 35^w il mese (e passa la paga di Capitano) suplicherà S. A. ancora, per grazia sua di raccommandarlo al S.^{re} Principe che sia trattato apresso di sè, come fa ad altri signori di qualità, o vero che degnerà d'accettarlo per camerero suo, come è stato qui appresso il Serenissimo Principe Giovan Carlo, che quando sarà abile di ricevere qualche carica honorata alla guerra, degnerà d' impiegarlo.

Il 3.ro se Don Carlo non accetta nè giustitia nè clemenza, nè di tirarsi inanzi alla guerra, non può lamentarsi più se non di sè stesso etc., e merita per castigo d'essere confinato a Porto Feraio a beneplacito di S. A. e sotto pena del fondo di torre se non vadi subito, o esce senza licentia di S. A., e haverà da me per il suo vivere quel che S. A. mi commanderà. Il Governatore è suo amico, la cere è buono, e il luogo è commodo: e sarà bene di farlo quanto primo, perchè non manchino di quelli da Fiorenze li danno consiglio del demonio, e lui precipeterà dell'altri suoi fratelli con l'istesso, e non si può rimediarlo; vanno secretamente quando è sì vicino non ostante il commandamento di Sua Altezza per la lettera di V. S. Ill.ᵐᵃ e mio, in contrario. Se il Conte non ubedisce S. A. di quanto ho accennato qui, per suo bene merita ogni rigore, a non meno di quello che ho supplicato a Sua Altezza per la mia supplica in mano del signor auditore Staccoli. Però se li piacerà la può conferire con lui (come Dottore del Consulto) di quanto ho pensato qui di mettere in consideratione apresso di S. A. S. et se non ubedisse questi, n'è necessario il rigore supplicato. E per fine baccio le mani affetionatamente di V. S. Ill.ᵐᵃ

Di Villa, le 19 di Marzo 1637 ab Incarnatione (cioè 1638).

Di V. S. Ill.ᵐᵃ e Clariss.ᵐᵃ

Affet.ᵐᵒ e Obglig.ᵐᵒ Servitore
IL DUCA DI NORTHUMBRIA etc.

XXXVIII.

Ambrogio is told to write to Carlo.

Dalla citata filza 1411.

Lettera del Duca a suo figlio Ambrogio.

Don Ambrogio ditte a vostro fratello con mandarlo questa per risposta del succorso di denare lei chede per lui, che tengo per una fintione sua al solito e per pretesto; perchè scontando per tre mese adesso della sua provisione resta debitore a me

ancora per 107 scudi delle 200 lui confessa d'haver riceuto per
l'argenteria mia doppo le 24 di Gennaio passata, benchè ¹/₄ più etc.;
perchè, se questo non fusse, essendo lui a' Capuccini in contumacia con S. A. S. per la testa, sicome il Ill.ᵐᵒ sig.ᵉ Ballì Ciolli
l'ha ben avertito per ordine espresso di Sua Altezza, e anco
sta là con l'arme in mano d'arcabusi, cascarei io nella medes-
sima contumacia e meritatamente di succorrerlo, se non per
salvare la vita di fama, senza espreso ordine di S. A. mio signore, e tanto più che può rimettersi se vole alla clementia
di Sua Altezza in una fortezza, come l'istesso signor Ballì l'ha
accennato etc., et là non mancherà le cose necessarie, nè d'in-
tercessione per suo bene.

A' dì 28 di Marzo 1638.

IL DUCA DI NORTHUMBRIA.

───────

XXXIX.

Don Carlo's letter to his brother.

La risposta di Don Carlo a suo fratello si manda con questa copia,
e pare risposta poco a proposito a questa lettera.

(*Segue la detta risposta.*)

(*Direzione*). All'Ecc.ᵐᵒ Sig.ᵉ D. Ambrogio Dudleo
                              Sua mano.

(*Di mano del Duca*). Copia della lettera di Don Carlo
  a suo fratello.

Ill.ᵐᵒ et Ecc.ᵐᵒ Sig.ᵉ Fratello Amatiss.ᵐᵒ

Ho inteso l'intenzione del signor Padre, et li devo dire che
la azione non è buona, perchè doverebbe cavarsi il boccone di
bocca per soccorso del figlio, et l'ordine che dice havere da S. A.
prima son burlati da me et non veduti; il che dà *del tiranno*

al suo Principe, il che non è, et s'inganna se mi ha per ignorante, et *se pensa assediarmi et forzarmi d' andare in fortezza
s'inganna* assaissimo, et incorrerebbe *nella scomunica* se m'im-
pedissi il vitto, sì ancho chi lo consiglia; *però guardi quello che
fa.* Però la sua prudenza doverà conoscere per un grande affetto
del figlio in contentarsi l'entrare in una fortezza per ricattare
l'honore del signor Padre, che per non l'haver conosciuto a
tempo stimo certo che sarà impossibile che più acconsenta; il
sig.ʳ Padre l'amerò, honorerò sempre per padre, ma mi dorà
di lui in eterno!, perchè è et sarà la mia rovina et disreputa-
zione, et li dica che il trattare all'Inglese in Italia è impru-
denza, et la rovina di sua figli, se bene non lo crede, et tanto
basti. Però amiamoci noi, acciò Iddio faccia riconoscere i grandi
errori ai più prudenti huomini del mondo, e le baccio le mani.

> Di V. E.

Li 29 di Marzo 1638.

Obb. fratello et Se.ʳᵉ che l'amo

D. CARLO CONTE DI VARUICHE.

XL.

Don Carlo in the Convent.

1.

Dalla citata filza 1411.

(*Direzione*). All'Ill.ᵐᵒ e Clariss.ᵐᵒ Sig.ᵉ mio Osserv.ᵐᵒ
   il Sig.ᵉ Balì Cioli, primo Secretario di Stato, e
   Concelliere secreto di Sua Altezza Serenissima

In Pisa.

Ill.ᵐᵒ et Clariss.ᵐᵒ Sig.ᵉ Mio Osserv.ᵐᵒ

Piacerà S. V. Ill.ᵐᵃ di dire da parte mia humilmente a Sua
Altezza mio signore come hoggie venne dua Padre Capuccini

per avisarmi in carità d'alcuni cose non li piacevano punto circa Don Carlo, e che mi guardasse bene. Ne fo reflessione dell'avvertimento di Padre sì santi in dua parole, imaginando che erano mandati dal soperiore per buono fine de prevenire qualche male come credo, e che haveva lui bisognio d'una gran mortificatione per li cattivi consigli datoli, perchè così dicevano loro. Mi rimetto primo a Dio, e poi alla prudenza di S. A., e dubito che non è più tempo di sperare ben di lui per adesso, e però si vole qualche risolutione in fatto per la potentia di S. A. Il Padre Guardiano non li lascia uscire del convento per qualche rispetto non mi volevano dire coteste Padre chiaramente. Dicevano di più che havevano parlato con Monsignore Nuncio, e non darebbe lui licenzia che fusse forzato d'uscire del convento, senza l'instanza particolare di Sua Altezza, che all'ora lo farebbe. Delle bone avertimente non ha mancato da V. S. Ill.ma, et una volta fu persuaso da dette Padre di rendersi in fortezza, ma subito fu divertito d'un cattivo spirito, che in voce dirò a V. S. Ill.ma, e merita castigo. Però non ci è più speranza che vol ubedire l'ordine di V. S. Ill.ma da parte di S. A. S. e per fine baccio le mani di V. S. Ill.ma come partialissimo servitore.

Di Villa, le 11 di Aprile 1638.

Di V. S. Ill.ma

Se io ho raggione di fare reflessione dell'avvertimento caritativo pochi paroli di detti buoni Padri V. S. Ill.ma può videre per la copia incluso. S. A. havuto già l'originale. In carità spero bene, ma in prudenza non voglio fidare più, perchè tocca a me e a nissuno altro etc. Perchè in parte è seguito circa l'argenteria e dello arcabusi e tersaroli portati qui dua volti seco per inditio della lettera et dell'avertimento e le tiene al presente; e senza tradimento, in casa lo stimo poco.

Aff.mo e Obgligatiss.mo Serv.re

IL DUCA DI NORTHUMBRIA.

2.

(*Direzione*). All'Ill.ᵐᵒ e Clariss.ᵐᵒ Sig.ᵉ Mio Osserv.ᵐᵒ
il Sig.ᵉ Bali Cioli primo Secretario di Stato e
Cancelliero secreto di S. A. S.
In Pisa.

Ill.ᵐᵒ e Clariss.ᵐᵒ Sig.ᵉ Mio.

Il signor Dottore Grazia advocato mio amico confidente ha
presso la fatiga con spesso andare a Don Carlo di persuaderlo
di entrare in una fortezza per ubedienza a S. A. S. mio signore,
dove piacerà S. A. di commandare, se continuo firmo nel proposito bono di farlo a persuatione del detto signore Dottore. Ne
ma a V. S. Ill.ᵐᵃ la lettera stessa il sig.ᵉ Dottore mi scrive: chi
piacerà a lei per sua grazia di mandare l'ordine dove deve andare; che non sia mutato, come altri volti da cattivo consiglio;
et io non mancherò la parola già dato a V. S. Ill.ᵐᵃ a suo tempo
per l'andare in Germania al servire il Serenissimo Principe Mathias; e per fine baccio le mani di vero servire a V. S. Ill.ᵐᵃ

Di Villa, le 15 d'Aprile 1638.

Di V. S. Ill.ᵐᵃ

Spero che Don Carlo lo faccia senza capitolazione.

Aff.ᵐᵒ e Obglig.ᵐᵒ Servitore
IL DUCA DI NORTHUMBRIA.

3.

(*Direzione*). All'Ill.ᵐᵒ e Clariss.ᵐᵒ Mio Sig.ᵉ Osserv.ᵐᵒ
il Sig.ᵉ Bali Cioli primo Secretario di Stato e
Conseliere secreto di S. A. S.
In Corte a Livorno o Pisa.

Ill.ᵐᵒ e Clariss.ᵐᵒ Sig.ᵉ Mio Osserv.ᵐᵒ

Mando a V. S. Ill.ᵐᵃ la lettera, che mi scrive il Padre Vicario di Capucini, dove è Don Carlo in chiesa; ne li ho avertito

spesse volte per mezzo di amici d'ubedire l'ordine di S. A. S. mio signore, almeno di non affrontare più l'autorità di Sua Altezza con uscire fuora di convento: per magiore spregio l'à fatto più d'una volta inanzi che li padre volse fare come scrivino. Mi confesso ignorante nel rispondere a quell che il Padre chiede per lui. Supplico V. S. Ill.ᵐᵃ d'avisarmi per ordine di S. A. quel che devo fare, et per fine baccio le mani di V. S. Ill.ᵐᵃ come vero servitore.

Di Villa, le 23 di Aprile 1638.

Di V. S. Ill.ᵐᵃ

Affet.ᵐᵒ e obgligatiss.ᵐᵒ Serv.ʳᵉ

IL DUCA DI NORTHUMBRIA.

4.

Dalla citata filza 1411.

Lettera del medesimo al medesimo.

Ill.ᵐᵒ e Clariss.ᵐᵒ Sig.ᵉ Mio Osserv.ᵐᵒ

In risposta della lettera di V. S. Ill.ᵐᵃ Don Carlo il giorno seguente li scrisse, entrò nel convento per violenzia, sì come il Vicario del convento mi fece sapere, et essendo adesso nelle stanzie dove era, e non esce più fuora, credo che lasceranno stare sinchè S. A. ritorni. Pertanto li ho mandato la lettera di V. S. Ill.ᵐᵃ, ma adesso è tanto in necessità, et ha pregiato li buoni consiglie sin adesso, che bisognia entra per forza in Fortezza, o perire. Non si può dire più che la fa spontaniamente o per ubedire, perchè tiène di presente, et ha sempre qui tenuto un servitore Bergamasco bandito, contra la parola sua data a S. A., essendo da me prohibito di continuo. Però per queque, che (*sic*) depende da me, faccia che vole, non li fiderò più, nè mescolerò con il fatto suo, come ultimamente ne scrissi a V. S. Ill.ᵐᵃ, e ne so troppo del suo cattivo intentione, e per fine baccio le mani di V. S. Ill.ᵐᵃ, come vero servitore.

Di Villa, le 27 d'Aprile 1638.

Di V. S. Ill.ᵐᵃ e Clariss.ᵐᵃ

Affet.ᵐᵒ et obgligatiss.ᵐᵒ Servit.ʳᵉ

IL DUCA DI NORTHUMBRIA etc.

XLI.

Don Ambrogio goes to Rome with the Cardinal as his page.

Dalla citata filza 1411 (nuova numerazione). Archivio Mediceo.

Lettera diretta al Cioli.

(*Direzione*). All' Illmo et Clariss.^{mo} Sig.^e Mio Osserv.^{mo} il Signor Balli Cioli, primo Segretario
di Stato di S. A. S. etc.
In sua mano.

Illmo et Clariss.^{mo} Sig.^e Mio Osserv.^{mo}

In risposto della lettera di V. S. Illma circa Don Ambrogio
mi protesto che non ho saputo mai dell' andare a Roma del
Serenissimo signor Cardinale, nè ho cercato mai che Don Ambrogio andasse ; anzi haverei supplicato il contrario a S. A.,
come lo supplico per questa volta, massime che Dona Teresia
mia figlia in Monasterio mostra intensione di farsi monaca ; et
non so, se tutto quello che ho del mio è abile di farlo con me-
diocro decoro. Bisognio che qualche uno ha trattato questo negotio di sua testa senza il mio sapere. Io non soglio offrire cose
passano le mei forze. La mia provisione per grazia et bontà
di S. A. S. mio signore è 157 scudi il mese incirca. Passano
scudi 50, che pago adesso ogni mese per Don Carlo mio figlio,
et se io do 40^w il mese per Don Ambrogio et 17^w per uno a
governarlo, considera V. S. Illma quel che resterà, ciò 50^w per
mantenere un Duca di Northumbria con tre figlij maschie et di
più una figlia femina a far monaca. Ci è di più il vestire Don
Ambrogio di corte et mutare l'habito si vole centinai di scudi per
servire un Principe sì grande in luogo sì iminente. Poi si vole
la spesa grande d'una persona di governo seco, altramente come
giovano inesperto, si spenderà in un dì quell chi l'appertiene
per un mese, altramente non essendo abile di supplirlo, nasce-

rebbe di vergonia, perchè non ho nè podere nè entrati del mio,
nè denare scarsamente di monaccare la detta figlia; et di questo ne do parola al Serenissimo Cardinale et a V. S. Ill.ᵐᵃ di
quell che sono. Però mi rimetto alla bontà del Serenissimo signore Cardinale, non mancando in me la bona voluntà di fare
quel che posso per suo servitio. Et con quello ossequio che li
devo, et per fine baccio le mani di V. S. Ill.ᵐᵃ

Di Villa, le 9 di Giugno 1637.

Di V. S. Ill.ᵐᵃ et Clarissima.

Affet.ᵐᵒ et obgligatiss.ᵐᵒ Servitore

IL DUCA DI NORTHUMBRIA.

XLII.

Dudley offers his services to Prince Giovan Carlo de' Medici, High Admiral.

Dalla citata filza 1411.

Lettera del medesimo al medesimo.

Ill.ᵐᵒ e Clariss.ᵐᵒ Sig.ʳ Mio Osserv.ᵐᵒ

Qui si dice volgarmente che il signor Principe Giovan Carlo
mio signore è fatto Generalissimo dell mare per il Re Catolico.
Ne ho sentito con grandissima consolatione, essendo carigo me-
ritevole per Sua Altezza, e mi duole dell'animo, che non posso
caminare senza groce per ancora, di poter venire a farli rive-
renza e darli il bon pro di sì gran honore, pregando a V. S.
Ill.ᵐᵃ in questo caso di necessità di farlo per, e offrire all detto
Serenissimo Principe, mio umilissimo ossequio, e che se l'esperienza che havuto io di molti anni nelle cose dell mare, meritano di servire S. A., che mi commanda, et anco in persona,
ben che sono vecchio, sarò sempre pronto per suo servizio e
d'ubedire le suoi commandamenti, come umilissimo servitore,
e per fine baccio le mani di V. S. Ill.ᵐᵃ

Di Villa, le 5 di Settembre 1638.

Di V. S. Ill.ᵐᵃ

Affet.ᵐᵒ e obglig.ᵐᵒ Ser.ʳᵉ

IL DUCA DI NORTHUMBRIA etc.

XLIII.

Henry Dudley's letter respecting his Lawsuit with Carlo his brother.

Dalla filza 5535 dell'Archivio Mediceo (nuova numerazione) a pag. 518.

Carteggio del Cardinale Leopoldo dei Medici.

Serenissimo Signore.

Se bene io habbia altre volte presso la clemenza e bontà di Vostra Altezza interposti li miei ossequientissimi offitij per impetrarli gratie, non posso ragionevolmente astenermi di ricorrere alla solita benignità e generosità di V. A. S. supplicandola con ogni zelo maggiore a degnarsi di ordinare che fu relassato l'ordine che V. A. si compiacque sospendere quattro anni sono per l'essecutione di un mio credito liquido, contro li effetti del Duca mio fratello in giuditio, incaminato nel magistrato della mercantia, havendo già a tale effetto pagato tutte le tasse delle spese. Resta solo che V. A. si compiaccia di revocar l'ordine che fu fatta la giustitia; poichè l'impedimento e sospensione di questa esecutione rende a me danno notabilissimo. Perciò la supplico a concedermi questa gratia, che con questo atto di giustitia verrà sempre più obligata la mia somma devotione. E rassegnando a V. A. la mia osservanza, profondamente l'inchino.

Di V. A. Ser.ᵐᵃ

Genova, 7 Maggio 1662.

Hum.ᵐᵒ Dev.ᵐᵒ Ser.ʳᵉ Oblg.ᵐᵒ

D. HENRICO DUDLEY.

XLIV.

Don Carlo Dudley asks the Grand-Duke to be sponsor to his daughter Carlotta Luisa.

Dalla filza 1006 (nuova numerazione). Archivio Mediceo.

Ser.ᵐᵒ Mio Signore.

Lo sgravamento della Duchessa mia in una figlia acresce a V. A. S. una humilissima serva, et dà occasione a me di ricevere li honori et le grazie, che si è V. A. degnata di farmi sperare col tenerla al sacro fonte insieme con Madama Reale, alla quale, col prossimo ordinario ne darò avviso per concertare il tempo che alle Altezze Loro più parrà. Io che son nato sotto la protezione di V. A. devo in ogni occasione confermarle l'humilissima mia prontezza in servirla et obbedirla; perciò la supplico di gradire questo mio dovuto ossequio et humilmente a V. A. bacio le vesti.

Fiorenza, li 20 Decembre 1650.

Di V. A. Sereniss.ᵐᵃ

Humiliss.ᵐᵒ Obbedientiss.ᵐᵒ et Fedeliss.ᵐᵒ Servitore

IL DUCA DI NORTHUMBRIA.

THE END.

TABLE OF CONTENTS.

DOCUMENTS.

ILLUSTRATIONS.

www.ingramcontent.com/pod-product-compliance
Lightning Source LLC
Chambersburg PA
CBHW020100030726
47498CB00006B/1879